The Courtesan and Mr. Hyde

Mad Scientists Society

Book 1

ISBN: 978-1-949862-41-6

Book cover and interior design by E. McAuley:
www.emcauley.com

To all the Mad Scientists out there.
Keep dreaming big.

For notes on content please visit

catsteinbooks.com/content-notes

The Courtesan and Mr. Hyde

"Perhaps a small subset of your services?
I have two dollars and forty-seven cents."

Prologue

Detroit, Michigan
June, 1890

Steaming liquid streamed from the spout of the autokettle, splashing over the rim of the delicate porcelain cup to pool in the saucer below. Hal lifted the cup with a sigh. At least the tea was properly steeped this time. Someday, when their experiments had changed the world and brought them wealth and fame, perhaps the Society wouldn't have to meet at a second-rate club with poorly-calibrated mechanical devices.

No, that was unfair. This club was full of progressive, scientifically-minded people—who were only occasionally raucous—and housed this lovely alcove where he and his friends could sit around the fireplace, share their work, and ignore the torrential rain outside. Only the machines were second-rate. And maybe the tea.

"Don't know why you insist on drinking that swill." Nemo sprawled in a faded armchair and took a swig of something from a polished flask. Probably whiskey.

Hal shrugged. "I suppose I could ask the kitchen to try that masala chai recipe of yours."

Nemo arched a single dark eyebrow. "I meant alcohol, but that would be an improvement, yes."

"Ol' Harry's contemplating joining a temperance union, dontcha know?" Victor lazily waved his glass of wine as he strode into the alcove. As usual, his sandy hair was slicked perfectly into place and his clothes were the height of fashion. Yet somehow he managed to exude an air of rakish insouciance.

"You know very well I am not," Hal shot back. "And don't call me that." He adjusted his spectacles. He didn't strictly need them, but the electrophoto lenses darkened in bright light and provided enhanced low-light vision. Also, Hal thought he looked quite sporty in a pair of spectacles. "Besides, once my elixir is perfected, we won't need temperance unions anymore. We'll be able to separate out and control our baser urges, restricting them to certain times and places, or even eliminating them altogether."

Victor lowered himself into the last available chair, shaking his head in disbelief.

"This is why we named ourselves the 'Mad Scientists,'" Nemo said with a chuckle.

Hal bristled. "As if your submarine is any less outlandish than my experiments, 'Captain'?"

"The Narwhal will be fully functional within the next year or two and it will revolutionize transportation and exploration as we know it."

Victor made a sniffing noise that could almost be termed a snort, if Victor had been a snorting sort of man.

Nemo replied with a mocking smile. "And how are your electrical experiments, Dr. Franklin?"

"Coming along quite well, thank you."

Which meant no progress at all.

"I'll be making a breakthrough any day now," Victor insisted, probably more to convince himself than his friends.

The trio lapsed into silence, commiserating in their lack of anything notable to contribute to the scientific community.

"We all will," Hal said at last, setting down his teacup.

He held out his right hand, palm downward. “In Scientific Solidarity.”

Nemo’s palm came down atop his, then Victor’s.

“Solidarity,” they intoned together.

Talk turned to the latest science journals and the viability of a new micro steam engine, but Hal’s own work continued to nag at him. Maybe the ideas he and his friends were pursuing really were mad. But they were meant for the good of society. Done in the name of progress and in hope for a brighter future. Tease though they might, they’d pledged one another loyalty and support.

They *would* succeed. It was only a matter of time.

Chapter 1
Uninhibited

Two months later

Hal dropped a bit of food into the habitat of his long-suffering pet. The rat crawled out from beneath a worn bit of flannel and sniffed cautiously at the morsel.

"Nothing strange in there," Hal assured him. "I'm sorry for feeding you peculiar things in the past, but that's all over now. You've been a great friend and a true contributor to the advancements of science. Today, it's time for human trials."

It was ridiculous, wasn't it, to be apologizing to a rat? This is what scientists did. Rats were sacrificed all the time in the name of progress, as were stray dogs. Sometimes scientists pulled orphans off the streets to test their new therapies.

Hal fought back a shudder. He was a doctor. He'd pledged to help people, not use them as experimental test subjects. He'd had a hard enough time giving drops to his poor rat. The rat he'd sworn not to name in an attempt to remain emotionally unattached.

Hal reached for the flask of elixir. He could recruit others to test the formula eventually, but he wasn't subjecting anyone else to it until he was certain it was safe. Not when he was already plagued with guilt for experimenting on Eddie the rat—who, in a surprise to no one, did indeed have a name. Hal was intimately acquainted with failure. Such was the nature of science.

He lifted the flask to Eddie in a toast. "To you, my trusty assistant. And for science." Hal gulped down the syrupy liquid before he could change his mind.

The potion didn't have a strong taste—only the hint of an apple that had been left sitting too long and had just begun to ferment. It oozed down the back of Hal's throat, settling heavily in his stomach, and he quickly washed it down with a cup of room-temperature tea he'd forgotten about until that moment.

He sat down at his desk, tidying up the pens and papers, and stashing things in drawers until the desktop was as spotless as it had been since he'd first purchased it.

"Well, it doesn't seem to be poisonous," he observed.

Nor did it seem to have any noticeable effect. He felt exactly as he'd felt before drinking the concoction. No change in energy level, heart rate, breathing. No unusual sensations.

He removed his spectacles and rubbed the bridge of his nose. "Damn," he muttered.

Hal reeled. He didn't swear. Not out loud. He was careful and particular about what he said, only relaxing—slightly—around his friends. Society had certain rules, after all, and he'd always been reluctant to break them. He'd been the boy who was teased for being a Little Goody Two-Shoes.

"To hell with those bullies," Hal declared.

Well. He stood up, grinning. It seemed the elixir worked after all. He didn't feel at all bad about his uncouth language. In fact, he felt rather exhilarated. That nagging voice that always cautioned him to mind his manners and obey the rules hadn't gone away, precisely. It was simply… subdued. Easy to dismiss.

"All right, Eddie. Time to put this drug to the test! I'm ready to tear up the town. Carouse with the best of them."

The rat gnawed on his food, uninterested.

"No more nights of talking to a rodent. I'm off to seek some human companionship. Drinking to excess and making noise in the streets. Consorting with loose women."

Ooh. That did sound particularly appealing. Unfortunately, Dr. Henry Jekyll, the prude, didn't know where one found loose women. He would have to seek out some habitually debauched fellow and pry the information out of him.

Hal locked up the laboratory and started out into the night, his special spectacles allowing him to see easily in the dim light of the gaslamps. His brisk strides carried him quickly from his middle-class lodgings to an upper class area, dotted with the lavish stone mansions of shipping magnates and lumber barons. Here, the gas lighting gave way to electricity, and the latest steam carriages lined the cobblestone roads.

One particular mansion, a red-brick Second Empire edifice with enormous dormer windows punctuating its mansard roof, boasted so many cars in front of it that Hal had to cross the street entirely to get around them.

He paused, taking in the bright lights behind every window and the noises of merriment seeping from inside the walls.

A party. One of those lavish, hedonistic affairs so many of his wealthy classmates at medical school had bragged about. Hal had never been invited, of course. Hell, he hadn't even been invited to the less fancy parties. Tonight, he was going to discover what he'd been missing.

He walked back across the street, meandering through the carriages to peer at the entrance. A man stood at the door, greeting finely-dressed visitors and checking invitations. Not that way, then.

Hal circled around the house, looking for an unguarded servants' entrance, or a window he could climb through. That do-gooder voice in his head told him this was absolutely not acceptable, under any circumstances; but with the potion running through his veins, he found he had no difficulty ignoring it. He grabbed hold of the ledge of a window that stood slightly ajar, and hauled himself up. The room beyond was some sort of parlor or sitting room, and a few people stood at one end of the room, chatting and looking up at a ridiculously large painting of what Hal guessed to be the owner's dog.

Hal pushed the window fully open, swung himself through, and darted out of the room behind the backs of the other guests. Once safely in the hall, he wandered for a bit, following the noise into a large and heavily occupied ballroom. Guests decked out in upscale garb covered nearly every foot of space, and he could hardly hear anything above the din of music and voices. In a crowd of this size, no one even looked at him. He was nothing but another face. Perfect.

He picked up a drink from a tray, scanning the room to assess the situation. Not far away, a woman in a shockingly revealing red dress clung to a man's arm, laughing and batting her eyelashes. Hal grinned. Loose women. Perfect! Tonight he could experience all the wild indulgences he never allowed himself.

He took a sip of his drink and his mouth puckered. It was an appalling concoction. He couldn't tell if the alcohol in the cocktail was gin, whiskey, or something else entirely, but there was certainly a lot of it.

Starting on a circuit of the room, Hal attempted to sip at the drink, hoping he'd become accustomed to it. His eyes sought colorful gowns, considering the potential for flirtation. Maybe tonight, with his loosened tongue, he could actually attempt such a thing. Or maybe he'd get right to the point.

Hello, gorgeous. Care for a fuck?

"Fuck," he said aloud, for the first time in his entire life. "Damnation. Cocksucking bas—"

"Are you swearing at someone in particular?" inquired the most melodious voice he'd ever heard. "Or merely for your own edification?" Sweet and low, with just a touch of laughter, the voice burrowed beneath his skin and set his blood ablaze.

Hal whirled around to discover a woman in a figure-hugging dark blue dress, holding a glass of champagne and smiling at him. She was pale-skinned, with a dusting of freckles across her cheeks, light brown hair that had been curled into ringlets, and intense gray eyes. She gave him a suggestive lift of her eyebrows, and his heart began to hammer in his chest.

This was the woman. He could do this. Ask her to slip away with him for a night of debauchery. What was going to stop him?

He took a generous swig of his cocktail.

And choked.

Chapter 2
A Sheep in Wolf's Clothing

Callie gave the peculiar young man two sharp slaps on the back. The coughing subsided, and he straightened up, his face red and his eyes watery.

"S-sorry," he wheezed. "Strong stuff."

She didn't doubt he spoke the truth. Most of the drinks at these parties were highly potent, which was why she stuck to champagne. What was odd was that this man didn't seem accustomed to drinking hard liquor.

"Not your usual libation, I gather?"

He coughed once more. "How could you tell?"

Callie laughed. He was cute, in a scholarly sort of way. His hair, so black it almost gleamed blue, was untamed by oils or pomades, and an unusual pair of glasses with pale-green lenses disguised the color of his eyes. His suit, while of good quality, looked entirely out of place among the dinner jackets and white bowties of the other male guests. He had crashed in, she suspected.

"Is this your first time at one of Mr. Ackner's parties?"

The man glanced around, as if checking to see whether anyone else was watching them. No one was, of course. Most of the guests were half-drunk already, and those who weren't were too preoccupied with their own business. This was the native habitat of the self-absorbed rich.

"Mr. Ackner," the man repeated. "The stove manufacturer?"

"Correct."

"Huh." He shrugged. "I considered one of his stoves for heating my laboratory, but I wasn't impressed with the quality. Went with a competitor." His eyes went wide for a split second, as if he were startled by his own words.

"I can't speak for the quality of his stoves," Callie replied, "but he does hold grand and extremely well-attended parties."

Which was why she was here. To mingle with the richest men in the entire Detroit area. To find herself a new protector. The goal she'd set herself a decade ago was within reach. Six more months as a glamorous mistress and she'd have the funds to put her plan into action.

She needed to get back to work. Nothing could come of wasting her time flirting with this mysterious party-crasher. No matter how intriguing he was.

"It *is* quite the extravagant affair," the man said. His gaze fixed on Callie, sweeping up and down her body. "I'm glad I came. Mr. Ackner's stoves may be second-rate, but his guests certainly are not." Again, his face twitched a bit. Callie had the impression he wasn't accustomed to speaking so boldly. Perhaps the alcohol had loosened his tongue.

She tried to quash her curiosity. It was time to move on. She glanced around, seeking potential wealthy lovers. That bastard Hinsberg caught her eye and gave her a wink. Callie quickly turned her gaze away. She could overlook the fact that he was twice her age, but he was cold and cruel, and that was entirely unacceptable.

She took hold of the party-crasher's arm and steered him toward the exit, telling Hinsberg without words she was otherwise occupied. The young man flinched at her touch but didn't try to pull away, allowing her to lead him out into the hall.

"Are we headed to a private chamber for amorous purposes?" he asked, a hopeful note in his voice. He thrust a hand into a pocket. "I brought coins. How much do your services cost?"

Callie shook her head, trying not to laugh at his bizarre naivety. "More than you have."

"Oh." His shoulders slumped.

Callie tossed back the remainder of her champagne and set the empty glass on a decorative table in the middle of the corridor. Ackner could pay for new furniture if it left rings. Her companion looked down at his own half-finished drink, then shrugged and discarded it.

"Perhaps a small subset of your services?" he offered. "I have…" He made a quick check. "Two dollars and forty-seven cents."

Callie wouldn't so much as touch someone for anything less than twenty dollars. "Let's just talk," she suggested. She pushed open the door to what appeared to be a small study. She flicked on the light, pulled the man inside, and shut the door behind them. "Why don't you start by telling me your name."

"My name?" That startled look came over him again, but this time it didn't subside. "Um. Well." He rubbed his temple. "Harry. Harry… Hyde."

Callie couldn't suppress a snort of laughter. "Harry Hyde? Really? You can't come up with a better pseudonym than that?"

He only shrugged, his cheeks reddening.

Callie extended a hand, not wanting to embarrass him further. "A pleasure to meet you, Mr. Harry Hyde. I am Miss Calliope Finch."

He shook her hand, his head tipping slightly to one side to regard her with a studious gaze. "Calliope?"

"My parents are in the theater. They thought it quite natural to name their daughter after a Greek muse."

"Could have been worse. You could have been a Terpsichore." His teasing grin was wonderfully tempting, and Callie had to again remind herself of her purpose here. She could only spare him a few more minutes.

She smiled back at him. "True."

"What name do you go by, Miss Calliope Finch? Opie? Lio?"

"Callie."

He bowed, an extremely polite and formal gesture. "A pleasure to meet you, Callie."

"Thank you." She curtsied, matching his formality. "I'm afraid I have business to conduct this evening, so I haven't a great deal of time to spare. I do want to thank you, however, for providing me a distraction from an odious acquaintance."

"Is your business of the sensual sort?" Hyde inquired. "Because I spied some decorative armaments hanging on the walls of the ballroom. I will duel the other fellow for the opportunity for your company."

Thank God Callie no longer had a drink in hand, because she was certain she would have spewed it at this pronouncement. She wanted to laugh uproariously at the thought of this bookish man dueling over a courtesan in one of the fanciest ballrooms in the city. She was sorely tempted to let him try it, simply for the entertainment.

Instead she focused on her goals for the evening. "You certainly have sex on your mind tonight," she said, keeping her voice casual.

"Oh, I have it on my mind every night," he replied with no hesitation. "It's only that I never allow myself to indulge, you see, and I was rather hoping that tonight I might find a beautiful woman, and since you are the most beautiful woman at this party…" He trailed off, blinking. "I'm sorry. I'm terribly bad at flirting. And I haven't much time, so I suppose I ought to let you be on your way and seek out a different woman."

The disappointment in his tone was keen. And he sounded particularly unenthusiastic about the prospect of a 'different woman.' A bit of warmth seeped into Callie's cheeks. It wasn't often she received truly sincere compliments.

"I have to go," she told him, allowing some of her own disappointment to show. "But I hope you enjoy the party. Take care to be inconspicuous, because it's clear you don't fit in at all."

He sighed. "Yes, well, the elixir doesn't appear to help with that."

Elixir? Another odd piece to the puzzle. If this Mr. Hyde had appeared to possess wealth enough to fund her project, she would have whisked him off to bed and spent all night trying to unravel his mystery.

Sadly, his two dollars and forty-seven cents suggested otherwise.

"Goodnight, Mr. Hyde." She stepped forward and pressed a long, gentle kiss to his mouth, her hand delving into his pocket as she did so. When she stepped back, his eyes were wide with shock, his mouth agape. "It was truly a pleasure to meet you." Callie flashed the penny she'd filched from him. "Special discount because you're cute."

And with that, she whirled from the room. Six months. Maybe as few as four if she could find someone especially generous. Then she could start her library and indulge with whatever eccentric men caught her fancy.

Chapter 3
Meet and Greet

Hal gulped his tea, trying to hide the embarrassment his confession had elicited. Outside the alcove, men—and the occasional woman—wandered by, drinks and cigarettes in hand, chatting about mundane, non-scientific things. He hoped to God none of them were listening in.

Victor scooted his chair closer, bringing the three friends almost into whispering range. "I'm sorry, I must have misheard that. You did *what*?"

Hal took a deep breath and tried again, speaking more slowly this time. "I snuck into a party at Mr. Ackner's mansion, drank some appalling alcoholic concoction, and flirted with a woman who may have been a lady of the night."

Victor and Nemo exchanged a worried look.

"I was disastrously inept at the whole thing." Lord, what a fool he'd made of himself. He'd woken that morning with a throbbing head and a sense of mortification so deep he'd seriously contemplated staying in bed and claiming illness.

But Dr. Jekyll didn't do such things, and this was all in the name of science, so here he was, up and properly dressed, attending the weekly meeting of the Mad Scientists Society, and spilling the whole story.

"The elixir didn't change me in any outward way," Hal explained. "I looked the same, and I gained no abilities. All it did was negate my sense of propriety, letting the bad parts of me loose."

Victor rubbed his temple. "Hal, your 'bad parts' are almost saintly compared to the average man. Honestly, you say you let them loose, and all you did was go to a party and get drunk?"

"I wasn't even drunk. The cocktails were so strong I could barely swallow them." The lingering headache was an aftereffect of the elixir, he suspected. It was a dull, pulsating pressure encircling his head, different than the sharper pain he remembered from the one or two times he'd drunk to excess back in his college days. "But I was certainly free with my tongue. I vow I said every ridiculous thing that sprang to mind, without a thought. It was no wonder the lovely courtesan I encountered wanted nothing to do with me. I must have seemed completely inane."

Except she had kissed him. Kissed him! And left with a smile, calling him "cute." That didn't seem like the behavior of someone who thought him inane.

"At least I gave her a false name," he sighed. "I was feeling free of my usual self and, frankly, wanted nothing to do with him. But when she asked I needed to say something. I panicked and made up an absurd name. I even called myself Harry." Hal cringed.

"But does the potion work properly?" Nemo asked. "That's what matters, isn't it? Did it do what you expected?"

"No, not quite," Hal admitted. "This version of the elixir allowed my bad traits to run free for a time, but a night of freedom doesn't appear to have diminished them at all. My intent is to fully separate the good and evil halves of a person. To draw out the evil bits and then use a therapeutic treatment to reduce their influence."

Nemo's brow furrowed. "Therapeutic treatment like… carousing?"

"I…" Hal shifted in his chair and stared down into his tea. "That part of the plan is somewhat… nebulous. Perhaps a safe location where a patient can misbehave until the baser urges are gone."

Victor barked a laugh. "Dr. Jekyll's Resort and Spa. Fulfill all your most hedonistic wishes with the latest miracle cure. People will flock to it. You'll make a fortune."

"If it helps with the betterment of society, let them come." Hal's shoulders hunched as his exact words penetrated his consciousness. "Er… no pun intended, apropos though it may be." He ran a hand through his hair. "As you can see, I am still plagued by my own baser urges and will need to continue to experiment."

Nemo glanced heavenward. "You do realize that *everyone* has 'baser urges' and they're not nearly so awful as you think they are?"

"That's irrelevant. The point is that I may still need to tweak the formula. Today I intend to make an antidote that can restore the good side if the evil is in control. Once I can use the two potions to isolate the good and the evil, I can begin the task of eliminating, or at least suppressing, the evil half."

"As usual, you're an idealist, Dr. Jekyll," Victor replied. "I don't think the world is as straightforward as you make it out to be." He lifted his drink. "But all the same, good luck to you. I have no intention of giving up drink or sex, but I see how your scheme could be used to help those who cannot indulge in moderation. Now, let me tell you what I observed during that lightning storm two days ago."

Hal only comprehended about half of Victor's chatter about currents and charges, but he admired his friend's enthusiasm for the subject. With new electrical devices popping up daily, Victor was poised to make himself a prominent name in the scientific world if any of his experiments proved useful.

As always, their meeting flew by, the chiming of the mantel clock to mark the hour startling them all out of their conversation.

"I ought to go," Hal apologized, rising from his seat. He would have liked to stay and chat longer, but if he wanted to make that antidote tonight, he needed to stop in at the apothecary before it closed. "Work calls."

"And beautiful courtesans?" Nemo teased.

"I'm not trying the elixir again tonight," Hal replied, ignoring the slight churning in his gut that suggested he might be lying to himself. "It's probably not a good idea until I have the antidote ready."

Yes, the antidote. Mixing it should be relatively simple now that he had the elixir working. Perhaps if he sampled the antidote in his usual state of mind it would even enhance his good side and suppress those frustrating, improper impulses.

Even just easing his lust a bit would be helpful. After last night's kiss, he'd endured a full night's worth of lurid dreams, all featuring Miss Calliope Finch.

Outside the club, a steam trolley huffed by, and Hal raced to hop aboard, trying not to think about the newspaper article about runaway trains he'd read the other day.

It's perfectly safe. Think about something else. Anything else.

He dropped a penny in the collection tin.

"One fare. Thank you," the automated voice intoned.

One kiss, please. Hal fingered the coins remaining in his pocket. Blast. Thinking of Calliope was no better than thinking of train accidents. Both could send him careening over a cliff.

He badly needed those ingredients from the apothecary. If he didn't find some way to occupy his mind, he was going to go mad.

Several blocks further, he hopped down from the trolley. Still in one piece, thank God. The carefully-shined windows of the apothecary greeted him with neatly-painted words advertising, "Drugs, Herbs, Tisanes, and Remedies." Ordinary medicines, most of them, but they were both the foundation and inspiration for all Hal's experiments.

Inside, Mr. Robert—a tall, stocky Black man with bushy gray mutton chops—occupied his usual place behind the counter, carefully wrapping a small parcel for a woman in an emerald-green dress.

"Here you are, Miss Finch," the apothecary said, handing over the package with a smile. "That should last you another three months."

Hal nearly jumped out of his skin. The woman turned toward the door. Her wide-brimmed straw hat was tilted back just enough to reveal a pretty, heart-shaped face, dotted with a small spattering of light-brown freckles. Miss Calliope Finch.

Surprise flashed across her face for a second, giving way quickly to a bright smile. "We meet again," she said.

What are you doing here? Hal wanted to blurt. Last night, he would have. He took a moment to consider what to say, but only managed to come up with, "Yes."

Miss Finch eyed him curiously for a moment. "Is that all you have to say, Mr. Hyde? You were far more talkative last night."

Mr. Robert's eyebrows lifted at the false name.

"Yes. Well." Hal groped for an explanation. "I was in, er, somewhat of a different state of mind last night."

"I see," Miss Finch replied. "I hope your visit here isn't an indication that you're suffering some lingering effect?"

Hal winced. She thought he'd drunk himself silly. Or perhaps she'd rightly guessed he'd been drugged. But she couldn't know it had been an experiment in the name of science.

"Not at all. I'm quite well. Merely picking up ingredients for work."

"Ah. How interesting." Her cloud-gray eyes gleamed with curiosity. "What is it that you do, Mr. Hyde?"

"Chemistry. Research," Hal answered, pleased to have thought up a truthful answer that told her very little.

"A scholar? I should have guessed from the unusual glasses and the tweed suits." Her mouth hitched up in one corner in a smile that might have been flirtatious. The respectable part of Hal hoped it wasn't. The majority of him hoped it was.

Miss Finch bobbed her head politely. "I'll let you get on with your shopping. Good day, Mr. Hyde."

Hal nodded back. "Good day, Miss Finch." He watched her walk out the door before turning to Mr. Robert.

"'Mr. Hyde,' eh?" Robert inquired. "What are you doing giving false names, young Jekyll? And how do you know a notorious woman like Miss Finch?"

"She's notorious?" Gossip was unseemly, but Hal's interest was piqued nonetheless.

"You honestly don't know? Miss Finch was Gerald Ackner's mistress this past… oh, year, I suppose? Up until about a month ago, when he decided he needed to marry and began courting some Chicago socialite. Before that she was with some other wealthy fellow. She's said to be glamorous, but unconventional. Lots of men hoping to be next, so they say."

Ackner's mistress? Good grief. That explained why she'd been at the party. Clearly she remained on good terms with her former paramour. And Hal had propositioned her. With his two dollars and forty-seven cents. How had she managed not to laugh in his face?

"You look a little stunned, son," Robert remarked. "Don't be. She's a good girl, even if her profession is a bit… salacious."

"Y-yes, she is very kind from what I know of her." She hadn't mocked him, though he'd given her every reason to.

"Indeed. Kind, smart, responsible. Much like yourself, my boy. Now, what can I get for you today?"

A lengthy discussion about the exact ingredients and a long walk back to his house did nothing to push Miss Finch from Hal's mind. After hanging his hat and coat, he hurried through the connecting passageway to the laboratory next door, laying out his ingredients on his worktable. The bottle of his experimental elixir taunted him.

You broke into Ackner's house and propositioned his former mistress. You! Dr. Prude. Think what else you could do if you just took a few more sips?

Hal deliberately picked up the bottle and measured out only what he needed to create the antidote. He wasn't giving in tonight. This was for science.

Nothing could come of an acquaintance with a high-society courtesan. Tomorrow, when he tested the elixir again, he would take himself to an entirely different part of town. He would never see Miss Finch again, and in time he would forget all about her.

Hal stirred his potion slowly. Hopefully it would help

him isolate his good qualities. Because right now he feared he had a terrible habit of lying.

* * *

Callie hadn't anticipated walking any distance when she'd set out for the apothecary to pick up her contraceptive draught. The cute green ankle boots looked wonderful with her dress, but she could now safely say they were insufficient for extended wear. She leaned against a wrought-iron fence, just to take a bit of weight off her feet.

Why on earth had Mr. Hyde walked all the way home when there was a perfectly serviceable steam trolley with a stop just up the street? It cost only a penny, and judging by this neighborhood and the quality of his clothing, he wasn't lacking for money. He didn't move in elite circles, certainly, but this was a well-kept, upper-middle-class area. He could afford a trolley.

Hyde had chosen to walk, however, so Callie had tromped after him in her inappropriate footwear. He'd seemed agitated and distracted the entire walk, which had made it easy to follow him unobserved.

Callie studied his house as the setting sun cast a warm yellow glow over it. Mid-century construction, she guessed, with a neatly manicured yard, a low, wrought-iron fence much like the one she now leaned on, and pale curtains obscuring most of the windows. It appeared well-built and well-maintained, which suited him. She couldn't imagine him in an untidy house, and she suspected the inside to be as neat as the outside.

A small corridor set with tiny windows ran from the western side of the house to connect it to the nearly-identical house next door. The iron fence continued on to encircle both structures, with no gates or other dividers between. The two yards merged seamlessly.

Interesting. Did Mr. Hyde own both properties? There didn't seem to be much activity to suggest he lived with many other people.

Callie crossed the street, walking toward the westernmost house. Mr. Hyde had entered the other building, but no lights illuminated the windows, despite the fading sunlight. In this second house, however, light now shone from several ground-floor windows.

As Callie approached, she spied the shadow of a man moving about. The figure was the correct size to be her Mr. Hyde, and he appeared to be standing in one location and working, except when he went to fetch something.

His laboratory. Likely he lived in the one house and worked in the other. Which meant he'd been telling the truth about his visit to the chemist. But why lie about his name? To hide the fact that he'd crashed in on a party? Why go to the party at all?

Callie wanted to take notes. People fascinated her, with all their quirks and foibles. And she'd never met anyone like Mr. Hyde before.

Abandoning her surveillance of his laboratory, she made her way through the open front gate and up to the front porch of his other house. A narrow brass plaque above the mail slot read, "Dr. H. Jekyll, M.D."

"Jekyll," she murmured, turning and heading back to the street. She'd catch the trolley home. No more walking in these boots. "Much better than Hyde, honestly."

Before she departed, she cast one final glance back at the shadow behind the laboratory curtains. "It's nice to finally meet you properly, Doctor."

Chapter 4
One Down

The gentle breeze and the bright blue sky above Belle Isle Park made a picture-perfect setting for the first Detroit Yacht Club regatta of the season. Callie tilted her parasol behind one shoulder, allowing her to sidle flirtatiously close to Mr. Cabot McKensie. She'd narrowed her list of potential lovers to three promising candidates, but she didn't know any of them particularly well. As a result, she had a full week of social events scheduled, in the hopes of befriending the men and making the best possible choice.

Cabot McKensie was young and handsome, with no money of his own, but a sizable allowance from his father. He spent freely, but rarely gambled, and had no history of serious trouble. Callie had interacted with him a few times during her stint as Ackner's mistress, and he'd always been good-natured and charming. He was also, Callie had learned, extremely fond of boats.

"This yacht here," he said, pointing at the boat cruising by on the river and paying very little attention to the fact that Callie was close enough to wrap an arm around. "The Sally Mae II. She's a great deal sleeker than Sally Mae I. Took two races last year, and this year she's got a new crew. She's expected to be a top contender."

"She's a lovely craft," Callie replied, because she wasn't certain whether it was insulting to use the term "boat."

"Isn't she, though? But wait until I get out there with Miss Dash. This year I'll only be competing in a few small races, but once I've got her in tip-top shape and the crew and I have a bit more experience, we'll be out there with the best of them."

"Sounds delightful."

"Doesn't it though? We're currently trimming her out with all new sails and rigging. Sparing no expense."

Callie nodded, but took a step to the side to put a bit more distance between herself and Mr. McKensie. Again, he didn't seem to notice. His attention was fixed on the boats, and he rattled on about all his grand plans for his yacht.

Callie might have paid closer attention and tried to learn something, but for her frustration that her first outing had proved a disappointment. McKensie would be spending a large sum of money on his yacht, making him unlikely to have a great deal left over to splurge on a mistress.

And she'd arrived at this event with such high hopes. Not only was he handsome and charming, but he was rumored to be a good lover as well. Maybe she could still talk him into a few nights of fun. Every little bit helped, after all.

As Calle debated whether to continue her attempts to flirt or to simply give up and search out the next man on her list, an eager voice called out, "Miss Finch, I'm so happy to see you!"

She spun around, and even Mr. McKensie turned, startled out of his monologue by the unexpected intrusion.

"D—" she stopped herself just shy of calling him by his real name. "Mr. Hyde. A pleasure." She gave him a small nod.

He wore another tweed suit today, a dark brown herringbone that looked smart on him. His strange spectacles were dark in the bright sun.

"I heard this was the place to be today," he rambled, "and I hoped that meant you would be here, and here you are!" His gaze flicked over Mr. McKensie and his expression stiffened. "Is this a friend of yours?"

"Cabot McKensie," the young boating enthusiast introduced himself, thrusting out a hand. "Are you interested in sailing, Mr. Hyde?"

"No, not at all."

McKensie's brow furrowed. "Oh."

The two men shook hands, regarding one another with suspicion.

"You're here to mingle, then," McKensie said, sounding as scandalized as if Hyde had declared himself here to dance a polka naked.

"That's right."

"Hmm. I'm afraid I can't spend time on socializing today. I need to keep my eye on the yachts. They'll be my competition, you know."

Hyde grinned. "Well. I thought you were competing with me, but you seem to have other interests. Wonderful!"

McKensie frowned in confusion, then shrugged. "Have a nice day, Mr. Hyde."

"I hope to. Thank you." He offered his arm to Callie. "Would you like to go for a stroll, Miss Finch?"

"I suppose we may as well." She closed her parasol, looped her arm through his, and they began to wander past the crowd watching the race. "No sense in wasting all day on a lost cause."

Hyde beamed at her. "Honestly, I thought it would be far more difficult to lure you away from your companion."

"I'd been preparing to take my leave of him when you arrived," Callie admitted.

"Ah." His smile faded. "There goes my hope that you simply liked me."

"If I didn't like you, I would have remained where I was and waited for a different opportunity to leave."

"Oh." He cocked his head to the side, regarding her with a bemused expression. At the apothecary, he'd appeared to be holding himself back. Here, he seemed genuinely speechless.

She tugged on his arm and steered him into the crowd. "Come, let's watch the boats. That's what we're here for, ostensibly."

He broke out of his stupor. "I love that you use words like 'ostensibly.' Do you whisper erudite terminology to your lovers in bed to arouse them?"

Callie laughed. "No. But now I know the secret of what to do with you. Here." She pulled Hyde with her into a vacant spot at the water's edge. "This is a good view."

They watched silently for a few minutes until he said, "I honestly have no idea what's happening."

"The yachts race around the course for a certain number of laps," Calle explained. "The finish will happen just over there, which is why this is the prime viewing location."

He edged closer to her. "It's quite boring, isn't it?"

"If you'd placed a bet on one of the yachts, you'd be more excited."

"Ah! Good thinking. I haven't gambled yet. That's another vice I need to try."

Calle did her best not to frown. Drinking, whoring, gambling. All things he was clearly unfamiliar with, yet seemed interested in. Was he on some sort of experimental anti-purity crusade? She'd known all sorts of unusual people, but had never in her life heard of such a thing. Maybe if she learned more about Dr. H. Jekyll, she could decipher his peculiar behavior.

"Ah, Miss Finch," an unwelcome voice called. Hinsberg sauntered up to her. "My offer still stands, you know."

"And my answer is still no." Callie stepped away, pressing herself against Hyde, who wrapped a possessive arm around her waist.

Or was it protective?

Hinsberg chuckled. "You'll come around eventually. Until then, Miss Finch." He swatted her across the backside before turning away.

Callie lifted her parasol, thinking to jab him with it, but Hyde was already moving. He released Callie, grabbed Hinsberg by the back of the coat, and flung him into the river.

Hinsberg hit the water with a resounding smack, spraying fat droplets across a number of nearby spectators, and drawing the attention of dozens of others. He spluttered and coughed as Hyde gazed down upon him, arms folded across his chest and wearing a smug smile.

"Next time, keep your goddamned hands to yourself."

One of the women who had been splashed during the commotion gasped at the swearing, slapping the back of her hand to her forehead. "Arnold! Where are my smelling salts!"

A man—Arnold, presumably—caught her as she swooned theatrically.

Hyde made a huffing noise. "That's what she gets for tightlacing. Not healthy."

Arnold glared at him. "You scoundrel!" he snarled. "Insulting a woman, using vulgar language in a public space, and assaulting an upstanding citizen? How dare you. Someone summon a constable."

Hyde's eyes widened in alarm. He thrust a hand into his pocket, pulling out a small vial of a greenish liquid. He gulped it down, shivered, then blinked rapidly for several seconds.

"M-miss Finch," he said, taking a few steps away from Callie. "I'm sorry for the disturbance." He glanced toward Hinsberg, who was stumbling onto shore, water streaming from his clothing. "But I'm not sorry about that." He nodded once, then spun and ran.

Chapter 5
Invitations

The formal dining room of the Pike household could have been a lovely place for the evening meal, with its elegant furnishings and wood-paneled walls. The pleasant glow of an electric chandelier spread across an array of quality china and tasty foodstuffs. If only the atmosphere weren't disturbed by the constant noise of a host of electrical servants.

"Do. You. Want. Some. More?"

Hal tried to wave away the skeletal frame of the tea-pouring servant that had wheeled up to him. "No, thank you."

It ignored him and refilled his cup. At the same time, a small sweeping device rammed the leg of his chair, trying to capture any crumbs he may have dropped during the meal. He tried his best not to grimace. Why did machines always seem to have it in for him?

"I'm so pleased you were able to join us on such short notice, Dr. Jekyll," Mrs. Pike gushed. "Poor Mr. Stromberg came down with a cold, you know, and it would have been such a shame to let all the lovely food Cook prepared go to waste."

"Yes," chuckled one of the other guests, a Mr. Clark. He patted his rotund belly. "And much as I enjoy the food here, even I can't make up an entire missing person."

Hal nodded, sipping at the tea he hadn't wanted. Honestly, he hadn't eaten much. He'd been too preoccupied with the memories of what had happened earlier in the day, or else distracted by the buzzing and hovering of the mechanical servants.

"But, of course, the main reason you're all here," Mr. Pike declared. "The temperance union. We're looking to increase our membership, and would like to invite all of you to join us on this important crusade for social betterance."

"Hear, hear!" agreed Clark, raising his glass of tonic water. His wife, seated unfashionably beside him, patted his arm fondly.

Mrs. Pike beamed at them. "Oh, I knew we could count on you and Betty! She was telling me all about how she'd convinced you the other day."

"Very persuasive, you know," Clark agreed.

"And the rest of you?" Mr. Pike inquired, glancing around the table. "Becher, of course, has business as well as personal reasons to support our cause."

The tall man with the long red sideburns and a curling moustache hoisted his own glass in salute. "I would love to see my tonic water gracing tables across the world, naturally. But more importantly, I wish to contribute to the spread of health and sobriety."

Pike and Becher clinked glasses.

"Such a blessing, to have a cause rooted in scientific fact," Pike declared. "Jekyll. What have you to say, as a medical man of wholesome habits?"

Wholesome habits such as flirting with courtesans and throwing men into the river? Hal could only imagine what his companions would say if they knew.

"I'm afraid I don't champion the prohibition of alcohol," he replied truthfully.

The room fell dead silent, but for the hum of the machinery. Several mouths hung open.

"I have a number of friends who enjoy alcoholic beverages in a rational and moderate manner," Hal continued. "I see no reason such a practice ought to be outlawed, regardless of whether I personally wish to indulge."

"But certainly they would be willing to give it up for the good of society," Mrs. Pike argued.

"They would sacrifice needlessly," Hal disagreed. "What do people who live in dry counties do? They go elsewhere for their spirits. If the entire nation went dry, half of Detroit would be popping across the river into Canada to get their fix. Smuggling would become rampant, I imagine. No. A ban on spirits isn't the answer. Better to work on the problem: helping people to better themselves by eliminating or mitigating the bad elements of their personalities that lead them to overindulge or participate in other inappropriate behaviors."

The entire table stared at him as if he'd suddenly turned the green color of his elixir. In truth, he thought he'd been rather restrained in his argument. If he'd been in his Hyde persona, he would have gone on at length about enabling organized crime, the perils of tempting law-abiding citizens to illegal behavior, and the fact that, dammit, sometimes a man deserved a bit of a drink at the end of a long day. Hal certainly wanted one now.

He pushed up out of his seat. "Please excuse me. I can see that your organization and I are not suited. I'll take my leave and let you get on with business. Thank you for the excellent meal, and a very good night to you all."

He nodded farewell and hurried for the exit, tripping over the carpet sweeper and stumbling into the hall as if he were a drunkard himself. What a day. He snatched up his coat and hat and rushed home in an attempt to soothe his frustrations with exercise.

Even at a brisk walk, a restlessness spread through his limbs. He itched with lack of fulfillment. He'd wanted to rant at the Pikes and their teetotaling friends. Still wanted to, if he were honest. He'd been bottling up his thoughts and emotions for so damned long.

Ugh. And curse words that he didn't say kept dancing through his mind. Hal tugged at his necktie, as if looser clothing could relieve the constant sensation of being stifled.

I'm such a fool.

Why hadn't he thought through the ramifications of testing the elixir on himself before drinking it? He ought to have prepared himself. But he'd let that impulsive side win. The Hyde side. And now that he'd had a taste of letting his guard down, he wanted more.

Wanted it badly enough that he'd allowed himself to test the formula during the day. And look what had happened. He'd assaulted a man—who did deserve it, at least—and fled a potential altercation with the authorities.

Hal pushed up his glasses and rubbed the bridge of his nose. "I'm not even sure how effective the elixir is," he lamented. When that man had threatened to summon the police, his ordinary, sensible side had broken through, taking charge and gulping down the antidote to prevent himself doing anything else wild. And then he'd bolted to avoid any sort of explanation. He still wasn't certain which part of himself was responsible for that.

He plodded up his front steps and opened the door, pausing when he spied a note on the floor. It must have been shoved through the mail slot while he was out. He bent and scooped it up, unfolding it to reveal a pleasant, curvy handwriting.

Special sale! One long, luxurious kiss for the bargain price of one explanation!

-CF

Below was written an address. Hal stood gaping at it until a gust of wind banged the door closed behind him.

"No, no. Absolutely not. I can't go see her." Maybe if he said the words aloud firmly enough he'd be able to convince himself.

"Actually, it might be for the best," he argued. "If I go now, as I am, with no elixir in my veins, I can speak to her in an entirely rational manner."

The rational manner of a man who habitually talks to himself.

"I can give her the explanation she deserves and then inform her that I will no longer be seeking her out."

Better than sitting around his empty house moping. Wasn't it?

Hal scurried to his laboratory and drank another dose of antidote, to be certain he was in his right mind. Feeling both calmed and fortified against foolishness, he checked the address once again, tucked the note into the pocket of his vest, and headed out.

Miss Finch's residence was far enough that he took the trolley—clinging white-knuckled to the handholds the entire time. Fortunately, the ride was smooth and soon he was walking the last few blocks to an unassuming two-story building. It was made of brick, with simple architectural details and a few vines growing up the walls. Well-maintained, but not flashy. He rapped on the door.

It swung open immediately, and a large, bald-headed man waved Hal inside.

"Evening." The man picked up what looked like a ledger book from a small table and flipped it open. "Name?"

"I, uh, um…" Hal stammered.

"John Smith. Gotcha." The man made a note. "Which of the ladies are you here to see?"

Hal's eyes darted back and forth, taking in the well-lit entryway. To either side were sturdy, exterior-style doors labeled with numbers. Apartments, it appeared. A staircase with a polished wooden banister led up to two more similar doors. What was this place? Some sort of combination boarding house and brothel? Why would Miss Finch live here? With as much money as Mr. Ackner possessed, surely he would have provided his mistress with her own private residence.

"Uh…" Hal tried to compose himself. "Miss Calliope Finch."

"Upstairs, on the left. She expecting you?"

Hal stuck a hand in his pocket, fingering the note. "Yes."

The man nodded and made another mark in the book. "Have a nice night." He closed the book and took a seat in a large armchair near the foot of the stairs, picking up a newspaper.

I should have stayed home, Hal lamented. He'd been telling himself the same thing since leaving his house. Still, his feet carried him up the stairs to her door, where he knocked once again.

A few seconds passed before the door opened. Miss Finch stood in the entryway, attired in a silk dressing gown, her hair unbound. Hal's jaw dropped open. Never in his life had he seen a woman in such a state.

He snapped his mouth closed and cleared his throat. "I, uh, received your note."

Her gray eyes gleamed, and she gave him a radiant smile. "I can see that. Please, come in."

He stepped across the threshold, once again questioning his decision. Maybe he should have taken a dose of elixir instead of antidote. At least then the constant internal debating might cease.

Hal took three steps into the room and froze. It looked to be a sort of parlor or sitting room, where one might relax and entertain guests. A plush carpet covered the ground, and the room was furnished with a sofa, several chairs, and a few small tables. Unlike in a standard parlor, however, every wall was lined floor-to ceiling with bookcases. And every bookcase was completely full.

Hundreds of books, in this one room. Perhaps as many as a thousand. Miss Finch owned more books than *he* did. And he was an avid reader as well as a scientist. Good Lord, who was this woman?

"So, Dr. Jekyll, have you come to spill all your secrets?"

Hal only barely heard her words over the questions rattling around his brain. *Why this place? Why these books? Why me?*

"I've come to offer you…" His head tipped to one side as he frowned at her. "I'm sorry, what did you call me?"

"You *are* Dr. H. Jekyll, are you not? Or do you prefer to retain the cover of Mr. Hyde?"

"I… yes. I'm Dr. Jekyll." No sense in prevaricating. She knew where he lived. Of course she'd discovered who he was.

Miss Finch raised her eyebrows flirtatiously. "Or shall I call you Harry?"

Hal cringed. "No, thank you. I am not fond of that particular nickname."

"Henry, then?"

"Hal."

Her smile was a thing of beauty. "Nice to properly meet you, Hal. Now, you said you have something to offer me? I do hope it's a full explanation of our previous encounters." She walked toward him until he could feel the warm caress of her breath. "Because I very much want to give you that kiss."

Burning desire surged through every inch of Hal's body. The desire to kiss her. Pull her close. Lay her down on that sofa and bury himself deep inside her.

Yes, yes, yes.

He took a step backward. "No. Thank you."

Chapter 6
Resistance

What had just happened? In a logical world, Callie would have a warm pair of lips pressed against hers right now. Smooth silk would be sliding against wool as their bodies came together and their limbs entangled. Instead, chill air hung between them. Empty space.

She tugged the dressing gown more tightly around her. The room hadn't grown any colder, but his unexpected rejection made her shiver nonetheless.

Jekyll took another step away from her. "Perhaps we should, er, sit?" he suggested, waving a hand at her furnishings.

Callie's brow furrowed. His gaze was every bit as intense as it had been when she'd approached him. His fingers flexed at his sides. Was he intentionally restraining himself? Why? He'd always been completely open about his interest in her.

She settled onto her sofa, not wanting to pass up the opportunity for a possible explanation for his peculiar behavior. Maybe that was why he'd pulled away. He seemed the sort of man who might not want to accept a kiss until he'd upheld his part of the bargain.

Jekyll took a seat in one of her chairs, holding himself stiffly rather than relaxing back into the cushions. His gaze swept her up and down, lingering on the place where the bottom of her robe gaped open to reveal a portion of bare leg.

He flinched and lifted his eyes to meet hers, stubbornly refusing to look elsewhere.

"Is my state of undress bothering you?"

"No." He paused a long moment, then added, "No more than your party attire did." The corner of his mouth quirked upward, for a fraction of a second. That was more like the man she knew.

Callie folded her hands in her lap. "Well, then. What was it you wished to tell me?"

He took a deep breath. "I owe you an apology and an explanation for my erratic behavior these past few days."

An apology? Callie couldn't think of anything he needed to apologize for. He'd been odd, certainly, but gentlemanly.

"You know my real name, so you must know at least a small bit about me," he continued. "I am a scientist. A physician and a chemist. I have made it my life's work to develop a formula to free humanity from the evil aspects of our nature."

Callie's brows rose, but she managed not to snicker at the outlandish statement. "You honestly believe that's possible?"

"I hope it is. I've done a great deal of research on the matter, and have had a measure of success with my current project."

"You've shed your own evil nature?" Could that be his issue? Had he drunk some potion that had him shying away from her advances?

"Oh, no. I've let it loose."

"Excuse me?" Callie leaned toward him, studying him in puzzlement. "I'm sorry to be skeptical, but you seem about the least evil person I've ever met."

Jekyll closed his eyes briefly, then shook his head. "No,

no." He pushed himself up from his seat and began to pace. "Not tonight. I haven't drunk any of the elixir since this morning."

Callie rose as well, matching his stride as he circled the room. "You weren't evil this morning, either. You were quite charming and gallant, in fact."

"I was wild. Interrupting, flirting, using foul language. Making plans to drink and to gamble."

Callie burst out laughing. Jekyll stopped pacing and turned to stare at her, but she couldn't control the mirth rolling inside her. She clutched her stomach until the laughter subsided.

"I don't see what's so funny." His frown was part disapproval, part confusion.

"I'm sorry. Your definition of 'evil' is hilariously tame. Flirting and drinking? Really? What about real evils? Violence. Oppression. Malevolence."

His head cocked to one side. It was a habit of his, whenever he was looking at her and thinking.

"You do like to use big words," he remarked. "Is it because you read a great deal? You have an enormous collection of books."

"Yes, it's quite the prodigious assortment," Callie replied. "My parents are thespians. I started reading theater scripts at a very young age, and I'm afraid it grew into something of a literary obsession."

He turned to peruse the volumes on the nearest shelf. "Poetry. Lovely. Byron, of course. Rossetti, Brontë, Eliot. And a few I'm not familiar with." His gaze drifted to the next shelf over. "What else do you have here? And what books do you most prefer? Science? Philosophy? Novels?"

"Yes. All of those. And illegal erotic publications."

Jekyll's head swiveled around and he gaped at her, his cheeks reddening.

Callie gave him a broad smile. "Just trying to steer the conversation back to the topic of evils."

"Evils. Yes, of course." He looked away from her once again. "I know we are all flawed, but I would hope that even my bad parts would not be as terrible as all that. I wouldn't dare give the elixir to a criminal, or someone known to have done violence or harm to others. The consequences could be dire. Regardless, I am not yet ready to experiment on another human subject. Not until I have a better grasp of the effects and consequences of the formula. I must make further notes and observations first."

Fascinating. So he was testing his drug on himself because he didn't want to harm anyone else. That certainly fit with what she knew of him. Though she didn't see much difference between the Jekyll of this evening and the "Hyde" of this morning, other than his reluctance to flirt and a hesitancy before he spoke. As far as Callie could tell, he was the same man, only now he was holding himself back.

She laid a hand on his arm. "Thank you for explaining. Would you like that kiss now?"

The pause before he drew back was brief, but palpable. "No, thank you." He cleared his throat. "I, uh, I'd best return home. You understand now why I made advances toward you. I think it advisable that we not see one another in the future. I will cease interfering in your affairs." His nose wrinkled and he rubbed his temple. "I'm sorry. I meant that figuratively."

Callie laughed. "I've enjoyed your interference thus far." It was a pity he wasn't wealthy enough to suit her purposes. She'd never had an affair with a scientist before. Or with any man who'd shown genuine interest in her books. It would be nice to get to know him better. "Please, don't feel you need to keep your distance on my account."

"Yes, well, thank you." He shifted his weight nervously from one foot to the other. "You are very kind. But I'm afraid I must be going."

Callie once again closed the space between them. "Then I suppose it will be a goodnight kiss."

His body swayed slightly toward hers, his lips parting, but once again he reluctantly withdrew. "No, Miss Finch, you owe me nothing. I came here because you deserved an explanation, not because I hold you to any sort of obligation. I will not claim your kiss nor expect anything of you in the future, if, indeed, we ever do chance to meet again." He stepped toward the door. "Goodnight, Miss Finch, and best of luck in all your future endeavors."

"Wait!" Callie called as he reached for the doorknob.

He froze.

"One moment." She dashed into her bedroom, grabbing a penny from atop her chest of drawers—the same penny she'd pinched from his pocket the other night. She hurried back into the front room and walked up to Jekyll, holding out the coin.

He turned up his palm, accepting it. "What's this for?"

"It's the penny you paid for our first kiss." She pressed his fingers closed around it, then stepped back. "Now *you* owe *me* a kiss."

Chapter 7
Strike Two

Mr. Jules Stevenson wasn't the most interesting man in the world, but he was friendly and had a pleasant French-Canadian accent. Callie enjoyed listening to the sound of his voice, even if he did talk mostly about his shipping business. Regrettably, he also preferred to confine his social activities to his home and the homes of his friends. After several days of failed attempts, Callie had finally managed to talk him into accompanying her on a night out. If it went well, she might be able to end her search and make him a long-term offer. If not… she'd keep looking. She'd go stir-crazy with a man who never wanted to take her anywhere. She'd grown up in theaters and opera houses, among crowds and noise and color. While she loved and valued her quiet hours at home with her books, time spent out in the world was the other half of her soul.

"I'm afraid it's a bit rowdy here tonight," Stevenson sighed, steering her through the large room teeming with gamblers and merrymakers.

Callie nodded rather than contradict him. She'd been to this particular club plenty of times, and while it was more crowded than usual, and therefore somewhat louder, it wasn't anything extraordinary.

"There's a popular card tournament tonight," Stevenson

continued, weaving around a table toward the bar. "I only found out while I was lunching with Gerald, or I would have made other plans."

"Not to worry. I'm quite content with the atmosphere here tonight," Callie replied. "It looks festive. I'd be happy to play a few hands of cards myself, if there are tables allowing women to play."

There would be. This club had always been happy to take anyone's money, no matter who they were.

Most of the women here tonight were courtesans and mistresses, conducting the same business Callie was. But she'd also spotted one daring widow known for her ruthless card play and another woman near Callie's age wearing trousers and drinking whiskey at the bar.

Callie allowed Stevenson to buy her a glass of champagne before leading him into the heart of the excitement, where onlookers had gathered around several tables of card players.

"Again?" an agitated man cried. "That's not possible. You must be cheating."

"He's not," said a burly man in a tidy uniform—a member of the club staff tasked with watching for cheaters and keeping peace between winners and losers. He would also physically escort out any troublemakers. "He just wagers better than you do."

"It's all a matter of skill," replied a surprisingly familiar voice.

Callie released Stevenson's arm and squeezed past a few other people for a better look. Probably not the smartest business move, but her curiosity was too strong to ignore.

There, just on the other side of the club bouncer, sat Dr. Hal Jekyll, in his usual tweed, his black hair gleaming in the electric lamplight. He'd tucked his glasses into a pocket of his vest, giving her a good look at his eyes for the first time. They were a light golden-brown color, warm and friendly.

"Also, you've been over-imbibing," Jekyll said to the man he'd bested. "It's why I chose to play against you rather than against a more sober foe."

The defeated man rose from his seat and departed, grumbling to himself. The chair sat there, empty. Inviting.

No, Calliope. You have business. You have a library to think about. A plan for the betterment of humanity.

She needed to be flirting with Stevenson, not with a man who, one, didn't have money, and, two, had already rejected her.

Another man came striding toward the empty place. Callie zipped into the seat before he could reach it. She grinned across the table at Jekyll. "Deal me in," she said.

"Calliope!" His eyes lit up.

She nodded politely. "Hal. Good to see you."

"Yes, it is! It's been much too long."

Much too long since you all but ran from my apartment, refusing to kiss me?

After not seeing him for several days, she'd assumed he was maintaining his resolve to stay away from her. Tonight he must have once again imbibed his experimental elixir.

Jekyll slid his fingers into a small pocket, withdrawing a coin. A penny. He rolled it around in his fingers for a few seconds, then carefully returned it to the pocket. Callie's shoulders tensed.

"I-I cannot, Miss Finch. I'm sorry. Goodnight."

He hadn't looked back at her after those stammered words, but he'd taken the coin with him. And it seemed he'd been carrying it on his person ever since.

The dealer shuffled and handed out cards to everyone at the table, beginning the new round of play. Callie was no cardsharp, but she played well enough for casual entertainment. She rarely played for money, however, not willing to risk her savings on a bit of fun.

Stevenson came to stand behind her shoulder, handing her some coins to pay her way into the game. Jekyll eyed him, frowning. He turned his attention to his cards, but stuck one finger into the pocket where the penny rested.

Damn. Why couldn't the man she ought to be kissing and the man she wanted to kiss be one and the same? She shoved the thought to the back of her mind and concentrated on the cards.

Ten minutes in, she could see why Jekyll was winning. His demeanor was one of calculating concentration, though he made his wagers with a cool detachment. Whether he won or lost any given hand seemed irrelevant. He simply continued on, his head cocked in his thinking manner, as if viewing the entire game as a mathematical curiosity. Which perhaps it was, to him. All part of his experiment.

"You play well, Mr. Hyde," Callie remarked, as yet another man abandoned his seat. She could run experiments of her own, starting with confirming his current temperament and his reasons for being here. "It is Mr. Hyde, isn't it?"

"Er… yes," he replied. His gaze darted to Stevenson once again, before settling on Callie. "You also play well, Miss Finch."

"I try." She wasn't gambling her own money tonight. Her wagering was better when she had no emotional involvement in the game. "I'm not up to your skill, though. Will you be joining the tournament?"

He gathered up his winnings. "I don't think so. I was considering getting drunk, and if I play that way, I'll lose all my money, like the other fellows."

Odd. Callie sifted through her mental notes. He was out

gambling, and not flustered by her presence—both indications that he was under the influence of his elixir. But his logical play and disinclination for mixing gaming and drink suggested he hadn't simply thrown caution to the wind.

She gulped down the last of her champagne. "I could use another drink myself. Shall we swing by the bar?"

"Yes. Let's." He hopped up from his seat, to the obvious relief of a couple of other players. Callie rose as well, and eager gamblers swiftly took their places.

Callie waved a hand at Stevenson, who'd been watching in silence this entire time. She couldn't forget her purpose here.

"Allow me to introduce my friend Mr. Jules Stevenson," she said to Hal. "He owns a local shipping company, and I'm sure you've benefited from his services." She smiled at Stevenson, who nodded politely. "Jules, this is Mr. Henry Hyde. Mr. Hyde is a scientist with an interest in human behavior. Are you here for research purposes tonight, Mr. Hyde?"

"Er…" He fidgeted for a few seconds, pulling out his spectacles and carefully adjusting them on his nose. "Yes. Tonight was gambling night. And drinking."

Hal hurried for the bar, and Callie almost had to jog to keep up.

"Your friend is… unusual," Stevenson whispered. He didn't seem at all jealous or even bothered by the fact that her attention had strayed from him.

"Yes. I'm still trying to puzzle him out."

Stevenson nodded. "I'd heard you had scholarly tendencies. Perhaps you and he ought to collaborate."

Well, *that* was an innuendo if ever Callie had heard one. She looked sharply up at Stevenson.

"I suspect you and Hyde suit better than you and I," he

said. "I admit I don't know him, but you both seem to have a sort of eager curiosity about the world. I'd rather stay at home and do sums and shuffle papers."

Callie nodded. Two down. Damnation.

"But I would be happy to buy you another drink."

"Thank you."

They continued on to the bar. Hal leaned on the wooden counter, grinning across at the bartender. "Whiskey, please."

"Hal?" The trouser-wearing woman spun to gape at him, pushing her long black hair out of her face. Her skin was a warm medium-brown, her eyes dark and expressive. "What the devil are you doing here?"

Hal's eyes went wide. "N—" He broke off, his gaze darting here and there. "Nisha?"

Nisha turned to the bartender. "Forget the whiskey. My friend here would like a gin and tonic." When Hal opened his mouth to object, she cut him off. "Trust me. You'll prefer a cocktail to anything neat, and it's bitter, like that over-steeped tea you like to drink."

"Okay."

"Care to explain what you're up to?"

"Um." Hal's eyes darted to Callie, for just an instant, but Nisha caught the look.

"Ah." She chuckled. "Have a nice evening." She saluted him with her drink and wandered off into the crowd.

"I think it's time I retired for the evening as well," Stevenson remarked, placing a few coins on the bar to cover the cost of Callie's champagne, plus a generous tip. "Goodnight, Miss Finch. Mr. Hyde."

Callie suppressed a sigh as she watched him depart. Why was this so difficult? She'd never had trouble finding a new paramour in the past. Maybe she'd been too specific in her requirements. If her third candidate didn't pan out, she'd have to reevaluate everything.

"Is he leaving because of me?" Hal asked.

"At least partly, yes."

"Oh. Sorry about that." He accepted his drink from the bartender and took a sip. "Actually, that's dishonest. I'm not really sorry at all." His gaze drifted to the exit. Faint music from the ballroom down the hall penetrated the hum of voices. "Would you like to dance, Calliope?"

Callie picked up her own drink and nodded in that direction. "Might as well."

Chapter 8
Under the Influence

Hal swayed in Callie's arms. Or maybe that was the room swaying because he'd had one more gin and tonic than was prudent. No matter. They were dancing. She was smiling. Nothing could quash his good spirits. Not even drinking too many spirits.

The pun made him laugh. Some might even have called it a giggle.

Callie's grip on him tightened. "You don't hold your liquor very well do you?"

"Nope!"

"But you are charmingly honest."

A bit of confusion intruded on Hal's euphoria. "I would have expected the elixir to cause me to lie more. Peculiar. I will add that to my observations."

He misstepped and stumbled, managing to keep his feet only because Callie held onto him. She guided him away from the cluster of other dancers to an unoccupied sofa along the wall.

"Let's sit."

The sofa creaked as Hal sank down onto the cushions. Callie sat beside him, her thigh pressing into his, her hand still firmly gripping his arm.

"So you did take that elixir of yours tonight?" she asked.

"I thought so. Tell me about your observations. I assume you make notes after every experiment?"

"Oh, yes. When I arrive home I write down what I remember. Then I write down more the next morning, after the elixir has worn off, or after I have taken the antidote." He fished a small vial of the green liquid from a pocket. "I have it with me, but I'm not going to drink it. I'm having fun here with you, and my usual self is so terribly boring and proper."

"But tonight you're not." Her brows arched, her smile full of amusement.

"No. I'm wicked." Hal let his eyes rove up and down Callie's figure, lingering on the low neckline that displayed her breasts to great advantage. "I've been having dreams about you at night." Warmth spread through his cheeks, but he pressed on, determined to seize every opportunity to flirt with her. "Shall I tell you about them? They're *extremely* wicked."

Callie leaned into him, bringing her lips within kissing distance. "I would love to hear all about them. I'm dying to know exactly what your definition of 'extremely wicked' is." She straightened abruptly. "But perhaps not tonight. You are thoroughly intoxicated."

"True. It feels rather nice. Shall we dance?"

She laughed. "No. You can hardly walk."

"Cards?"

"I thought you said you didn't want to lose any more money."

Hal blinked, remembering the less-than-stellar card game before his most recent drink. Inebriation had a decidedly negative effect on his ability to count the cards and calculate the mathematical probabilities. "Ah. Yes. I have a specific amount of money set aside for the experiments. Don't want to go over, you know." He yawned and shifted to lay his head on Callie's shoulder. "Well. Suppose I'll just stay here."

She chuckled. "And this is your wicked side."

Hal peered down into the valley between her breasts. He'd be having lovely dreams again tonight. "Oh, yes. Very wicked."

She slid an arm around him. The movement gave him an even better look. Someday, he'd take that dress off her and see everything.

"I think if you're going to be properly scientific about this experiment you need more data," Callie mused.

Experiment one: how many buttons must I undo to make Calliope's dress fall off. Experiment two: repeat experiment one.

"I'd like to help, if I may," she offered.

Help? He probably did need help with her buttons. It had been much too long since he'd even attempted such a thing.

Hal shook himself out of his daydream. No, she was talking about something else. His *real* experiments. "You… want to help me?"

"Yes, I'd love to. I've always been fond of science, and I find your elixir fascinating. I'm not sure it's working the way you think it is, or the way you intended it to, but perhaps with both your inside and my outside perspectives, we can gather a clearer picture of its effects and effectiveness."

Hal looked up into her eyes, no longer caring—or at least not caring much—about what lay beneath her dress. Miss Calliope Finch used big words, kept an apartment full of books, and wanted to assist him in noble scientific pursuits. She was glorious.

He tilted his mouth toward hers, while his fingers dug into his pocket to feel the imprinted metal of the penny she had taken and then returned.

"I owe you a kiss, Calliope," he breathed. "I think I'd like to give it to you now."

He moved in closer, his lips skimming over hers, his entire body tingling in anticipation.

She pulled away.

* * *

Callie's body took exception to the loss of Hal's warmth, but her good sense held firm. Not tonight. Not like this.

Take him home, urged the inner voice that had grown slightly tipsy on champagne. *He can even pay you. You know exactly how much money he has left.*

She rose from her seat, needing the extra space between them to fuel her resolve.

"Callie?" He pushed himself up off the sofa, weaving a little. "What's wrong? Don't you want to kiss me?" He glanced around. "Is it because we're in public?"

Callie had to laugh at that. This crowd of drunkards, whores, and gamblers wouldn't even notice anything as tame as a kiss, much less object to it. "No." She took his arm. "It's getting late. Let me walk you home."

Hal yawned. "I am getting tired. Maybe a kiss after we reach my house?"

"Not that either." Callie steered him toward the exit, moving at a sedate pace to prevent any stumbling. "It wouldn't be right to kiss you tonight. You're much too drunk."

His face fell. "Oh. Sorry."

"You don't have to be sorry. This was a fun evening, and I'm glad to have had the opportunity to spend it with you."

She'd had more fun than she'd had in months, in fact, in large part because *he* was having so much fun. His genuine happiness was infectious, and his scientific excitement about anything and everything enthralled her.

They fetched their outerwear from the cloakroom and stepped out into the Detroit night, the cobblestones shining in the glow of the soaring electric light towers.

"Let's hail an autocab," Callie suggested, leading Hal toward the corner where the steam-powered vehicles picked up passengers.

"Oh, no, that's not a good idea," he replied. "Machines don't like me. Even the trolleys make me uncomfortable, but I can ride them, since they're stuck on the tracks. One of those things…" He waved a hand at an approaching cab, accidentally hailing it. "It will probably veer off and drive into a house if I'm in it."

The cab pulled to a halt in front of them. "Evening, sir, miss." The driver tipped his hat. "Where to?"

"Oh, no, th—" Hal started, but Callie climbed up into the cab. Too much the gentleman to abandon her, he followed. Callie gave the address, dropped a coin into the fare box, and the vehicle started off.

Hal sat rigidly in the very center of the seat, hands clenched. She patted his thigh in reassurance.

"We won't crash. These cabs are quite safe."

"Machines don't like me," he repeated. He placed a hand atop hers, pinning her hand to his leg.

Their eyes met. Heat snaked through Callie's body. She wanted him. She could have him. Tonight she had no other obligations. Nothing to stop her.

Nothing but herself.

"Isn't it odd for a scientist not to like machines?" she asked, trying to distract herself with conversation.

"Yes. My friends love machines. Victor builds all sorts of strange electrical devices, and Nemo has designed some sort of submersible." He shuddered. "I'm never riding in it. But I don't like machines. They always malfunction for me. I prefer to stick to chemistry."

"Like your elixir."

"Yes." He leaned toward her, his fingers tightening on hers. "Did you mean what you said? About helping me?"

"Absolutely. I already intend to write up my observations from tonight. I'll deliver them to you tomorrow. Maybe we can discuss plans for other opportunities to experiment."

Excuses, Callie. You're just making excuses to spend time with him.

And so what if she was? She had every right to spend time with whomever she liked. All she needed to do was take care that it didn't interfere with the business of setting up her library. A few outings for scientific research now and then wouldn't hurt anything.

The autocab reached Hal's residence without incident, despite his fears, though he did tumble drunkenly to the ground when he tried to climb out. Callie helped him to his feet as the cab trundled off, and walked him to his door.

"Goodnight," she said. "And thank you for a lovely evening."

"Thank *you*," he replied. "Would you like your kiss now?"

Yes.

"I'm afraid not. You're still very drunk, and worse, you're under the influence of your elixir. That's not how I want this. I want you to kiss me because you want to. Not because some potion tells you to."

Hal swayed toward her. "My good side wants you too. I dream the same dreams with or without the potion. Very wicked, remember?"

Callie gave him a quick peck on the cheek. She couldn't

allow anything more tonight. "I remember. You can tell me all about it tomorrow, when I bring you my notes. And if you still want it then, we'll have that kiss."

"Oh, I'll want it," he vowed.

She didn't doubt that. Whether he'd permit himself to indulge was another matter.

Chapter 9
Bottle-Ache

Cheerful sunlight streamed through the window to fall across Hal's bed. Somewhere outside, a rousing chorus of voices joined together in a chant he couldn't quite decipher. He winced and turned away from the window. The pounding in his head didn't relent.

"Leave me the hell alone," he grumbled. Neither the people nor the sun paid him any heed.

He yanked the coverlet up over his head, squeezing his eyes closed and trying to will himself back to sleep. The pleasure of his dream had all but slipped away, the wild heat of Callie's kiss and the warmth of her skin no more than a haze. Hal groped for the memory, trying to sink back into the embrace of slumber.

A sharp rap on the door drove spikes of pain through his sensitive skull. He didn't answer. Whatever it was couldn't be that urgent, and his household staff knew he sometimes worked late and slept in.

The knock came again, louder. Hal groaned.

"What is it?" he called, more gruffly than usual.

The door opened. He jerked upright. What was happening? No one intruded on him in his bedroom. The movement caused additional throbbing in his head and he let out an involuntary grunt of pain.

"Overindulged a bit last night, eh?" Victor asked. He leaned against the doorjamb, arms crossed casually over his expensive suit, the very picture of the idle rake. He probably had a dozen remedies to avoid feeling like this after a night out.

"What are you doing here?" Hal threw off the blankets. Might as well get up. He needed to get to work, and feeling sorry for himself wasn't going to help anything.

"Heard a rumor you were painting the town red last night. Drinking and gambling in the company of a woman of questionable virtue."

"That's a nasty phrase. She's a lovely woman."

Victor smirked. "So it's true then?"

"I'm testing the elixir. You know that." Hal stepped over to the window, squinting from the bright sunlight. "What's that racket?"

"Temperance march. Taking up the whole street. Bunch of nuts, if you ask me."

"I didn't." Hal turned away from the window and reached for his eyeglasses. Even a small reduction in the glare of the light would help his head. "They tried to recruit me the other day. I told them no."

Victor straightened up. "So then you went out and got sloshed? What for? To spite them?"

"No. I told you, I was testing the elixir. The results haven't been exactly what I expected. I need to write down my observations from last night and compare with previous notes." Hal waved a hand at his friend. "Now get out so I can dress."

Victor's smile turned seductive. "You don't want me to watch? How disappointing."

Hal's head hurt too much for banter. "Didn't we establish years ago that I wasn't interested in you that way?"

"I'm still pining," Victor joked.

"Also, you know I don't know how to flirt."

"I think you *could* if you ever bothered to let yourself relax." He shook his head. "Get dressed. I'll be in the dining room. Your housekeeper told me your cook would have a nice hot breakfast ready any minute. I might leave some for you."

Hal scowled. "You're a terrible friend."

"I'm a wonderful friend and you love me," Victor retorted, and spun away.

Half an hour later, washed, dressed, shaved, and feeling he might possibly survive if he drank an entire pot of strong tea, Hal stepped through the ornately carved archway into his dining room. His stomach churned a bit at the scent of the eggs and toast that awaited him. A pair of empty plates sat on the table beside his. He reached for the steaming pot of tea, wrinkling his nose at the extra plate. Victor hadn't eaten that much, had he?

"This is the third I've heard of this week," the dulcet tones of a woman's voice floated from the parlor.

Hal jerked. Callie? Here? Already? He poured his tea and hurried into the next room, trying his best not to slosh the drink in his haste. Callie knelt on the cushioned bench beneath his bay window, peering out at the street beyond. The skirts of her pale blue gown bunched up beneath her bustle, exposing her low boots and stocking-clad ankles. Victor stood improperly close, peering over her shoulder.

"Yes," Victor agreed. "It's peculiar. They seem to have become unusually outspoken of late. Not sure it'll do much good in a city packed with clubs and saloons."

"I also heard Whitney's Opera House is showing one of those temperance dramas." Her shoulders lifted in a shudder. "Ick. Moralistic claptrap."

"Indeed." Victor angled himself for a better look out the window, putting himself so close to Callie that Hal's entire body tensed in response. "I'm all for the betterment of society, but people also ought to be free to enjoy the pleasures of life without censure." Victor's voice was husky, and Hal had the sudden urge to dump his piping hot cup of tea down the back of his friend's pristine suit coat.

"Miss Finch," Hal said, making his voice both loud and prim. "What a surprise to see you here so early."

Callie hopped down from the bench and greeted him with a smile. "Hal. How are you this morning?"

"Fine." *Aside from the aching head and inappropriate surges of jealousy.* "You have brought me your observations, I assume?"

"Yes." Her hand slipped into a well-disguised pocket in the seam of her skirt and withdrew several pieces of paper. "I'm excited to see your laboratory."

Hal's eyes widened in surprise. He forced a neutral expression back onto his face, but couldn't stop the quickening of his pulse. Had he agreed to show her the laboratory? That cursed elixir made him so foolish, but if he'd made her a promise he couldn't go back on his word.

"A science enthusiast, are you?" Victor asked, giving Callie the roguish grin that had been charming men and women alike for as long as Hal had known him. "Wonderful! Always nice to see a lady putting her mind to good use. No sense being just another pretty face, eh?"

Hal sipped at his tea to quash the still-simmering urge to douse Victor with it. How could anyone be so smooth? Victor had mastered easy flirtation and cool confidence. No stammers. No clipped words. Not even a slight pause while he weighed possible responses in his head. Hal was awkward even after imbibing the elixir and multiple alcoholic drinks.

Memories of the night before ran through his mind. At least he hadn't drunk so much that he'd forgotten everything. He'd been plenty flirtatious, but in a babbling, restless way. Embarrassing, really, how he'd grinned at Calliope all night and clung to her on the dance floor. Why hadn't she simply walked away? Her inquisitive mind was interested in his experiments, of course, but it did also seem as if she genuinely liked him. Or liked his Hyde side, at least.

Maybe it was simply a matter of her social skills. She was a courtesan. The ability to make anyone feel as if she liked them would be a valuable asset.

It also made her immune to Victor's charms, apparently, because she did no more than nod and smile at his flatteries, keeping her attention centered on Hal. She strode across the room and gestured in the direction of the dining room.

"Please, don't let me keep you from your breakfast. We can talk while you eat. How are you this morning in truth? Any lingering effects from the elixir?"

"No." Only from the liquor. As far as Hal could tell.

Callie sat down at the dining room table and poured herself a cup of tea. Hal joined her, nibbling at his toast. It didn't bother his stomach as much as he'd expected. That made one positive thing this morning, at least.

"I wrote out almost three pages of notes," Callie said, spreading her papers on the table. "I hope it's enough. I, too, was a bit tipsy last night, but after rereading this morning I believe they're accurate."

Hal nodded around a mouthful of bread. He had zero pages. Not even a line. Last night he'd stumbled up the stairs, barely managed to get his clothes off, and fallen into an exhausted sleep. A sorry excuse for a scientist, apparently. Why hadn't he taken the damned antidote?

"Shall I read them to you?" she asked.

Victor, who had been leaning in the doorway again, sauntered closer. “Please do. I would love to learn how the esteemed doctor comported himself last night.”

“Go away, Franklin,” Hal grumbled.

“And miss all the fun?”

Callie turned in her seat to look at Victor. “If you’re looking for scandal, Dr. Franklin, I’m afraid you’re out of luck. Dr. Jekyll was simply a gentleman enjoying a night of entertainment.”

“How disappointing,” Victor joked.

Unfortunately, it wasn’t a joke to Hal. His mind whirred as Callie read out her notes, comparing them with his own memories and trying to process the information. He didn’t like the conclusion it led to. Something about the formula was off. He’d gambled, but carefully. Flirted, but only with one woman. He’d broken several of his rules of behavior last night, but adhered strictly to many others. No cheating, unless using his ability to count and calculate counted. No lying, certainly. If anything, he’d been more honest than usual. Right now he sure as hell wasn’t going to admit to the feelings Miss Calliope Finch roused in him or the vivid erotic dreams he had of her.

Damn, damn, damn.

Hal bit his lip. The elixir had led to him swearing more, even if only in his head.

“Thank you, Miss Finch. This will be helpful as I move on to the next phase of testing.” Hal set down his fork and quaffed the last of his tea before rising. “If you’ll follow me, I will give you a tour of my laboratory.”

She hopped up to join him, taking hold of his arm. “So formal,” she teased.

“I’ll leave you two to your *science*.” Victor arched a

taunting brow at Hal. "I can see myself out. If I don't escape the teetotalers, douse my grave with a nice Bordeaux."

"Dr. Franklin is an interesting fellow," Callie remarked as Hal led her toward the passageway that connected his residence with the laboratory next door. "He's not what I would have expected from a friend of yours. But I suppose neither am I, and I hope we're becoming friends."

"I… yes," Hal replied. It was no use protesting. Miss Finch had somehow infiltrated his life, and he needed to accept the fact that he liked it. Her observational skills and interest in his work would be a great help to his research. He would simply have to restrain his baser impulses when around her and behave in a professional manner.

They emerged from the tunnel into what had once been the ground floor of a residence identical to his own.

"Ooh," Calliope murmured, her gaze sweeping over the large, open space. "This must have been quite the renovation."

"Yes. This house belonged to my uncle until his passing two years ago. When I inherited, I built the connecting hall and had this entire floor remodeled into a single room. I know it's rather empty." Warmth spread across Hal's cheeks as he waved a hand at his worktable and cabinets in the corner. He'd seriously overestimated how large his laboratory needed to be, and his workspace looked sad and small. "But I do have plenty of space to expand with additional equipment and storage."

"I like it. And it gives me ideas."

She didn't elaborate, but Hal's mind began to churn with thoughts about what she might mean. Ideas for what? Her own laboratory? A gambling club? A brothel?

Callie dropped Hal's arm and hurried over to his work area, peering intently at every item on every shelf.

"So you mix up your elixir here? May I open the cabinets?"

"Please," Hal replied, his voice coming out in a husky murmur that startled him so badly he jumped.

Dear God, what was wrong with him? Was he actually aroused by the sight of a woman poking through his scientific equipment?

Callie opened a cabinet, and another "ooh" of appreciation escaped her lips.

Yes. Yes, he was.

"Salamander slime?" she exclaimed. Her eyes shone with amusement. "You actually have salamander slime as one of your ingredients?"

Eddie squeaked in his cage and she whirled around.

"Oh, and you have a pet rat! How cute!"

Hal fought for composure. Desire coursed through his veins like an elixir more powerful than he could ever hope to create. Callie liked his slime and his rat. She had a massive library. She laughed and danced with him and studied him with a sharp, inquisitive mind. Fuck, she was the most beautiful thing he'd ever seen in his life.

But she was destined for some rich tycoon like Ackner, not for a hapless scientist with no social skills who couldn't afford to keep her in jewels and fine gowns. Hal could afford a night or two with her, but he doubted that would satisfy him. Assuming he could even bring himself to suggest such a thing without drinking his elixir. Worst of all, perhaps, a sophisticated woman like her was apt to be bored or frustrated by his inexperience and hesitancy. She wanted to be his friend. They would leave it at that.

Which meant he needed to get her out of his house. His self-control was stretched so thin it was likely to snap with the least provocation.

Hal strode toward her, steeling himself to tell her the tour was over. At the same moment she spun to walk toward him. He had no time to change course. Their bodies collided, the soft curves of her breasts crushing against his chest.

"M-miss Finch," he began, but the words he had meant to say vanished along with his resolve. "Calliope," he breathed.

Her arms wrapped around him. "I'll take that kiss now."

Chapter 10
Good to Be Bad

Calliope's lips were the softest, sweetest things Hal had ever tasted, her mouth warm and wet and oh-so-inviting. His left arm tightened around her waist, while his right hand slid over the smooth skin of the back of her neck, his fingers teasing wisps of hair loose from her upswept curls.

He couldn't stop kissing her, couldn't pause to rest, or think, or even catch his breath. All he could do was kiss her as if this was the last kiss he would ever have in his life. He had to make it last. Had to claim as much of her for his own as possible.

Her tongue toyed with his, tempting him to go deeper, crush her more firmly against him. Hal nipped at her lips in a greedy reply, then delved inside, again and again, over and over, gorging himself on the taste of her. Unable to get enough.

Callie broke the kiss, withdrawing just enough to look him in the eye. Her gray eyes gleamed, almost silver in the electric lamplight. Moist lips glistened, pink and swollen from his attentions. She lifted a finger, brushing it gently over his mouth. His own lips were sensitive, half-bruised. Her finger came away damp.

"You are a very enthusiastic kisser, Dr. Jekyll," she murmured. The low purr in her voice shot straight to his already eager cock. "I think you have less need of that elixir than you think."

"It's not for me." His own words were so raspy they sounded like an innuendo. "It's for the betterment of humanity."

Oh, God, how he wanted to kiss her again. Wanted to feel the slide of her lips over his and the practiced flicks of her tongue. The rules said he ought to desire a demure, virginal lady to take as a wife. But he only wanted Callie. Callie who kissed like she'd kissed a thousand men and knew exactly how to bring them to their knees.

Which was probably close to the truth. And he loved it. God, he loved it, and every muscle and bone in his body begged for more of her.

"So humanity is better if it's not stifled by propriety and resistant to fun?" she asked, the corners of her mouth twitching as she smiled. "I agree."

"I'm sorry?" Hal frowned at her in confusion, his mind still clouded by lust. "Oh. No, no. The purpose is to draw out the negative aspects of a personality. To separate them from the good side. Ideally, one could then eliminate those negative traits, either by applying a treatment or by allowing the inappropriate desires to run their course in a safely-controlled environment."

Callie released him, stepping back to regard him with hands on hips. "I don't think that's how personalities work, Dr. Jekyll. We're not X parts good and Y parts evil. We just are."

"I have done a great deal of reading on the subject, and several prominent theories suggest we are indeed made up of disparate parts. And you've seen the effects of the elixir."

She shook her head. "Hal, the elixir doesn't make you

even the slightest bit evil. All it does is make you a little less starchy."

Hal wanted to make an indignant reply, but unfortunately, she spoke the truth. He was a prude and the elixir wasn't what he'd hoped. Strangely, her arguing had done nothing to diminish his lust. If anything, it made him want to kiss her all the more. He pushed the urge aside and made himself continue the conversation.

"I realize my formula is imperfect. I hope your assistance will allow me to remedy that."

"Hmm." Her hands dropped from her hips, and she lifted one to skim across his chest. "I suppose we'll see. At the very least, we will make an interesting study of the human mind."

Hal clasped his hand over hers, his thumb stroking her smooth skin. His heart beat steadily in time to the lusty voice in his mind. *Kiss her, kiss her, kiss her.*

"That we will." Gathering all his self-control, he removed her hand from his shirt, released her, and took two steps backward. "I must return to work. Please, allow me to show you to the door. Shall I send you a message when I am next ready to test the formula?"

Callie pursed her lips, as if considering. "Yes, please do. I have business of my own to see to, but I look forward to our next meeting."

Hal waved her toward the door, not trusting himself to offer his arm. If she touched him, he might not be able to pull away again. He walked her through the tunnel, into his house, and all the way to the front door in silence, ideas of what to say to her warring in his head.

Thank you for the kiss.

Please stay.

Don't come back. I can't take it.

How much for a night in your arms?

Hal pulled the front door open, only to spring back in alarm from a raised fist. The man on the outside—who Hal belatedly realized had been intending to knock—likewise flinched.

"Jekyll," he said. "Pardon. I didn't realize you had company. I was here for the parade and stopped by to offer you a sample."

"Ah… thank you, Mr.… Becher," Hal stammered, struggling momentarily to put a name to the tall, redheaded man. "You were at the Pikes' dinner the other day, yes?"

"Indeed." Becher thrust out a bottle of the tonic water his company produced. "I know you're skeptical, but I'd love to change your mind. Starting here. Once you see how nicely my soft beverages can replace liquor in social situations, your worries will ease. Try it. Becher's tonic is good for what ails you."

"I don't have malaria."

Callie chuckled.

Becher squinted. "Beg pardon?"

"Quinine. Treats malaria. Flavors your drink?" Becher continued to peer at him from beneath a furrowed brow, so Hal shook his head and accepted the bottle. At least Calliope had appreciated his jest. "Never mind. Thank you."

"Enjoy. We'll talk. Good day, Doctor." Becher gave a nod and hurried off to join the retreating crowd of temperance marchers.

"There you go." Callie reached out and tapped a finger against the bottle of tonic water. "Now you can mix up your own gin and tonics."

"I don't have any gin."

She laughed and pressed a kiss to his cheek. "I'll send

you some." She stepped through the door, turning to wave goodbye. "Until our next experiment."

Hal gave her a polite nod. "Until then."

Callie moved as if to depart, then paused, casting an impish grin over her shoulder. "And, Hal?"

"Yes?"

Her mouth curved even higher, and his heart began to hammer once more.

Kiss her, kiss her, kiss her.

"Bring the penny."

Chapter 11
Third Time's the Charm?

Callie sipped her ice cream soda and flipped another page in her magazine. The buzz of the ice cream and soda machines mingled with the voices of the mostly female patrons lunching at Sanders' Woodward Avenue ice cream parlor. Outside rain beat steadily down, but inside lights were bright and customers smiling. The cheery atmosphere and her favorite treat had somewhat soothed her irritable mood, though not entirely. Nearly a week had passed without a single word from Dr. Jekyll. Not even an acknowledgement of the bottle of gin she'd sent to his house. Was he deliberately avoiding her? And why did she care so much, anyhow?

She returned her focus to the article in the medical journal, gathering yet another opinion on the workings of the human brain. Like all the others she'd read over the past few days, it was mostly conjecture. This was a subject science had only begun to explore, and the more she read, the more she understood how little was actually known.

This particular article, from a physician with a long string of credited writings, fell in line with Hal's view of the human psyche. Unfortunately, it offered neither proof nor suggestions for how to test such a hypothesis. Hal at least was running experiments and attempting to learn things.

This Dr. Willis merely stated his opinions as if they were facts, and in dry, long-winded prose.

Callie closed the magazine and checked her watch. Where was Mr. Valdez? The handsome porcelain manufacturer had finally declared himself ready to consider moving on from what had apparently been a painful split with his former mistress. He wanted to take things slowly, hence Callie's choice of the respectable and non-threatening sweets shop.

She stared at the numbers on her pocket watch. Twenty minutes late. Had he changed his mind? Third option gone before she even got to know him? Blast.

Her fingers skimmed across the medical journal. Maybe she'd take a break and spend some time with Dr. Jekyll before reevaluating her list of candidates. If he ever spoke to her again.

The bell above the door tinkled. Callie looked up just in time to see a dark-haired, olive-skinned man shaking out his umbrella before stepping into the shop. Valdez set the umbrella in the rack beside the door and surveyed the room, starting when he caught sight of her. He crossed the room swiftly.

"Miss Finch. It appears we are both here early. You're looking well today."

Early? Callie searched for the clock on the wall to verify what she'd seen on her watch, but the time was the same. Twenty past twelve.

Her brow furrowed. Had she told him twelve-thirty instead of twelve-o'clock? She couldn't really be that distracted by her foray into scientific research, could she? One glance down at her stack of magazines and papers answered her question.

"Can I get you anything?" Valdez asked.

"No, I'm fine, thank you."

He nodded. "I will be right back, then."

Valdez returned a short time later with a soda of his own, and took a seat in the place across from Callie, a warm smile on his face. "This is a pleasant place to pass a rainy afternoon," he said. "Thank you for inviting me."

"You're welcome. I'm glad you could join me."

Though not as glad as she ought to have been. She reached for the papers to clear them away.

"What's that you're reading?" Valdez peered closer. "Scientific magazines? Unusual for a lady. Are you finding them interesting?"

Callie's smile came more easily. "Some more than others. Depending on the author of each particular piece, they can either be fascinating or dull. As you might expect, I've enjoyed the articles aimed at a wide audience more than those intended for medical professionals."

"I'm only surprised you enjoy them at all. The only science that can hold my interest is the processes behind the production of my dishes and crockery. Now, articles about buying and selling, those I could read day and night. Which tells you why I do what I do, I suppose."

"It does indeed. So, tell me, what do you do for fun? Besides read the financial pages, that is."

Valdez happily took control of the conversation while Callie finished her soda. For the next half hour, he talked with a smile on his face and listened attentively to Callie's answers whenever he asked her a question. From this first meeting, he seemed all she had been looking for. Her library was within reach.

The satisfaction that her plan could move forward warred with disappointment. The more time she spent with Valdez, the less she would have to spend with Hal and his research. Plus there was the possibility that Valdez might prefer she not devote time to another man, regardless of any intimate connection. Considering his previous relationship had ended unhappily, he might be particularly sensitive to such things right now.

Valdez glanced over his shoulder out the window. "Ah. The rain has let up. It seems our conversation has dwindled at the perfect moment. Thank you for a lovely outing." He lowered his voice. "As I'm sure you've heard, I was rather more attached to Mrs. Baxter than she was to me, and as kind as she was when we parted ways, I am still smarting from the blow. Therefore, please do not take offense when I tell you I am not yet ready to begin anything too familiar. But, if you are interested, I would like to invite you to a show at the opera house this Friday evening."

"That sounds lovely. Thank you."

"Wonderful." Valdez rose from his seat and bowed. "Until Friday, then."

Callie waited until he'd disappeared from sight before gathering up her things and preparing to head for home. Beneath the shelter of her own umbrella, she walked toward her apartment, understanding why Jekyll liked to walk through the city sometimes, even with other transportation nearby. The exercise and time alone cleared her mind and gave her space to think.

The rain grew heavier as she neared home, and she jogged the final block to avoid a complete soaking. The rest of today would be reserved for a warm bath and a good book. Tomorrow she would devote to reviewing her inventory and adding to the list of books she would need to purchase for the library. It would be a good break from the medical journals. No more woolgathering about experiments with Hal, and no more reminiscing on how utterly charmed she'd been by his kiss.

Callie stepped through the front door, set down her umbrella, and shook droplets of rain from her skirts. Jackson, the daytime doorman, rose from his seat and held out a piece of paper.

"Letter for you, Miss Finch."

"Thank you."

Callie unfolded the paper as she ascended the stairs to her apartment. A short message in blue ink read, *I'm ready for the next experiment. Join me for a show tonight? I'll pick you up at 7. -J*

All the memories and daydreams she'd sworn to set aside flooded back into her mind. Such a strange thing, the human brain, telling her to do one thing while wanting another. Exactly what Hal was studying.

Apparently a change of plans was in order. She would still be taking that warm bath. But then she was dressing up. Tonight, she was going out on the town. For science.

Chapter 12
Just for Fun

Callie floated down the stairs from her apartment in her favorite blue gown, grinning at the undisguised admiration on Hal's face. She loved how genuine he was. Having spent years among actors who pretended for a living, and then mingling with the carefully-crafted public personas of the social elite, she didn't often encounter people who were simply themselves. Even when Jekyll was holding himself in check, he didn't prevaricate. He just closed his mouth, tensed his body, and—if those failed him—removed himself from the situation.

Hopefully the elixir tests would do him some good. Callie wanted to see him comfortable enough to express himself without fear of censure. The man who had kissed her knew how to have fun. He only needed to give himself permission to do so.

"Miss Finch. You look stunning, as always." He offered his arm when she reached the bottom of the staircase. "Is that the same dress you wore the day we met?"

"Yes. It's my favorite."

"Mine too. At least, of those I've seen so far. Shall we go? I have an autocab waiting."

They stepped outside, where the open-topped vehicle sat

huffing steam as it awaited its passengers. Callie looked at Hal with raised eyebrows.

"I thought you hated riding in these."

"Oh, I do. I was holding on for dear life on the ride from my house. But I can't have you walking to the opera house, and my bicycle only carries one."

"You didn't want to ride with me sitting atop your handlebars?" she teased.

His eyes widened. "You'd do that?"

"Maybe. But not in this dress."

Hal helped her into the cab, then took a seat beside her, reaching for her hand. She twined her fingers with his, giving him a squeeze. "Thank you for arranging this. Where are we off to tonight?"

"Whitney's Opera House. Remember how you told Dr. Franklin a temperance drama was showing?"

Callie blinked and twisted in her seat to stare at him. "You're joking."

"Nope. *Venom in a Bottle.* It's the latest hit around the country. 'Gripping and heartfelt,' the advertisements say. I had thought to take you to a concert or some such, but after I drank the potion, I decided this will be much more fun." He slipped his free hand into his jacket and withdrew a pair of stoppered vials. "I mixed us up some gin and tonics to secretly drink while we watch."

Callie's laugh rang through the street. "You might just be wicked after all."

"I ought to be. I spent the week going over all my research and calculations to make sure I had the proportions correct in the formula. Yesterday I mixed up an entirely new batch, and when I drank it today I took a double dose."

She shifted closer to him. "I'll pay close attention, then. We want to catch every detail for comparison."

Hal's voice dropped to a low murmur. "I can already tell you I want to kiss you even more than usual."

Callie suspected that particular desire had nothing to do with the elixir and everything to do with the kiss they'd already shared. She was hungry for a repeat too. She may even have tried it, if they weren't in a public vehicle in full view of downtown.

The autocab turned onto Woodward Avenue, chugging past shops closed up for the day and saloons just beginning their busiest hours. Pedestrians young and old roamed up and down the street beneath the glow of the sky-high arc lamps. A gentle breeze tugged at Callie's hair, while the mixture of voices and mechanized carriages hummed in her ears.

She sighed in pleasure. "Don't you just love a night out?"

"I don't know," Hal answered. "I've always liked the theater. But it's been ages since I've seen a show. I suppose I never really felt I had any place to go or anyone to go with. I've enjoyed all the times I've been out with you, though."

"I'm glad. Don't you go out with your friend Dr. Franklin?"

Hal shook his head. "Victor did go out often during our college days, but now he stays in most nights. It's his favorite time to work. When you saw him last week, he was probably about to go to bed rather than just getting up. We usually see one another at our club in the afternoons, and sometimes for dinner."

The cab turned a corner and slowed, joining a line of other vehicles waiting to drop passengers off in front of the theater.

"Shall we walk the rest of the way?" Hal asked.

Callie suspected he only wanted to get out of the vehicle as soon as possible, but she nodded. Hal dropped an extra coin into the fare box, thanked the driver, and hopped out, giving Callie a hand down in proper gentlemanly fashion.

"I do like the lights and the sounds," Hal said, setting a lively pace down the sidewalk. "There's something almost magical about it, which I suppose sounds silly for a man of science."

"Not at all. I feel the same. And I love to watch the people."

"Yes. I much prefer to watch than to bore them with my lack of conversational skills."

Callie gave his arm a squeeze. "You converse with me easily enough. At least once you've had your elixir."

"You're easy to talk to," he declared, then promptly fell silent.

The audience gathered for tonight's performance was what Callie expected, considering the subject matter: gentlemen in formal black and ladies in elegant but modest dress. The bold blue and low neckline of her gown stood out almost as much as if she'd been dressed all in scarlet. Hal, too, looked out-of-place among the tailcoats and white bowties. Did he even own any formalwear? Given what Callie knew of him, it was entirely possible he didn't. His tidy gray suit and bright green ascot tie became him well, despite being unusually casual.

The seats he'd procured for them were several steps down from her usual theater experiences, but still afforded a good view of the stage. Once they were settled and the lights dimmed, he slipped one of the vials from his pocket and pressed it into her hand.

"Enjoy," he whispered.

Callie tucked the bottle into her cleavage for safekeeping. She adored the idea of secretly imbibing during a temperance play. Hal's wicked streak was exactly the sort she liked. Not evil or harmful, but playful and mischievous. She also loved that he'd used his scientific equipment to store his contraband cocktails. Most men would have used a flask—another thing Hal probably didn't own.

The play began with an over-enthusiastic protagonist cheerfully working an unspecified desk job while making eyes at his employer's vapid daughter. Five minutes in, a dissolute acquaintance disrupted his worry-free existence, tempting him to a raucous party and plying him with drink. Callie struggled not to laugh. The actors were playing up the melodrama, and the crowd was captivated.

Hal leaned toward her. "The acting is a bit much, I think," he whispered.

"They've performed this show dozens of times. They have to have fun with it to keep from being bored."

A collective gasp rose from the crowd as the protagonist stumbled drunkenly offstage, lured by the unseen voice of a lady of the night.

"And people love it," Callie added.

Hal made a huffing noise and took a discrete sip of his gin and tonic.

Predictably, the life of the main character spiraled out of control as he drank more and spent increasing amounts of time in the company of various low-lifes, including the "sultry whore," who had clearly been chosen for her bosom alone. The first act ended with him lying in a puddle of filth, having lost his money, his job, and his home. As the curtain closed, the audience gave a thunderous applause.

"What do you think?" Callie asked, when the lights came on for intermission.

"Honestly, it's the worst show I've ever seen," Hal replied. "It's predictable, the dialogue is stilted, and the characters lack depth entirely, except perhaps for that well-endowed fly girl."

"Oh, she's definitely my favorite character. She's stuffed her pockets with the money of every single man in the show, except for the puffed-up boss. That girl has *goals*."

Hal grinned at her. "Like you do?"

A twinge of guilt twisted in Callie's gut at the reminder she wasn't currently focusing on her own ambitions. She shoved the feeling aside. It was fine to have more than one goal in life, and there was absolutely nothing wrong with making one of those goals to spend time with friends and have fun. Everyone deserved to claim a bit of happiness.

Hal assessed her with that tilt-headed gaze of his. "You seem thoughtful. Is the play causing you to reflect on your life choices and swear to drink only Mr. Becher's tonic water for the rest of your days?"

The false gravitas in his tone made her laugh. "Impossible. I enjoy ice cream sodas too much."

His eyes lit up. "Do you? So do I. I'm especially partial to a well-blended Boston Cooler. I'd love to take you out to the soda shop one day."

"I'd like that." Callie's gaze fixed on his lips, imagining the taste of the sweet drink in his kiss. The tip of his tongue darted across his bottom lip and she almost groaned. God, how she wanted a taste of him. Right here, right now.

She straightened up abruptly. This was not the sort of place for amorous advances of any kind, or for anything but the most subtle of flirtations. She prided herself on level-headed, situationally-appropriate behavior. The money she'd earned had come directly from knowing what roles to play and when.

Hal, though, had a knack for making her lose her

composure. When they were together, she forgot the world was watching.

The moment the lights went down for the second act, Callie pulled out her gin and tonic and took a healthy swig. To her surprise, the mixture was well-proportioned and quite tasty. Where had Hal learned to mix a drink? He continued to be a man of surprises.

The melodrama took a turn for the worse as the hero went begging to his former employer, offering to perform even the lowliest of jobs. Rather than offering assistance to a man he'd professed to have affection for, or pointing him in the direction of someone who could help, the employer simply handed him a temperance pamphlet and walked away. Hal snorted and gulped more of his cocktail.

The protagonist shot to his feet, declaring in a stentorian voice, "I see this now for the truth it is! From this day forth, I am cured of my poisonous desires!"

Hal nearly spit out his drink. His coughing drew looks of annoyance from several nearby patrons. Callie hid her drink in her skirts and gave Hal a quick pat on the back.

"That's not how it works," he whispered, once he'd recovered. "As a man with a medical degree, I highly object to the claim that one can resolve alcohol dependency without proper treatment."

He sulked for a time, then launched into a mumbled narration of the remainder of the play. "Our lady of the night has renounced her sinful profession for love of her former drinking companion, but, alas! In a turn of events that has stunned perhaps one person in the entire theater, she has contracted some dread disease and dies tragically in his arms. Handkerchiefs are all aflutter. Now the supposed hero of this drama returns to his former place of business. Amazing! His job is restored to him. Will he marry the boss's daughter? The answer is a resounding yes. The crowd is agog. Truly a plot twist for the ages. Miss Finch, have you been snickering?"

Callie laughed aloud, the sound muffled beneath the applause of the crowd. "Me? Snickering? I am appalled at the very suggestion."

She and Hal rose with the rest of the crowd, clapping heartily for the actors and their hard work on what was without question a very silly play. Silly, but fashionable. The audience had thoroughly enjoyed itself, and Callie had little doubt the show would garner many positive reviews. For her own part, she would say the cast had done a fine job with a highly unoriginal script.

"The saucy whore was one hundred percent the best character," Hal opined as they made their way slowly down the stairs toward the exit. "And of course they killed her off. Did she even get a name?"

"Mary?" Callie shrugged. "Or maybe Molly. I think they said it once." She took a quick glance around, then downed the last swallow of her gin and tonic. She handed the vial back to Hal. "Your drink was excellent. How did you learn how to make it?"

He grinned, tucking the bottle into a pocket and then offering her his arm. "I had a book in my library. *The Bon-Vivant's Companion*. I believe it belonged to my father. It didn't have a recipe for gin and tonic, but I used an average of the ratios of alcohol to mixer for other gin cocktails. I expected it to be horrible, but it wasn't."

Callie laughed. "You'll have to show me this book. I might want a copy for my library."

"The library in your apartment? It seemed quite full."

"No. The—" Callie bit off her words. She'd never spoken

of this to anyone, not even the other women in her building. "The library I plan to open," she said at last.

"You're opening a library? Sounds brilliant. You'll have to tell me all about it."

"Perhaps," she replied, not yet ready to confess all. "But not tonight."

"Maybe when I take you out for ice cream. Are you free later this week? Thursday or Friday?"

"Um…" Words failed her. She wanted to say yes. Wanted to make plans as if they were an average couple going courting. Where was her head tonight? She was supposed to have been paying attention to his behavior and making notes for the experiment, not daydreaming about kisses and arranging entirely non-scientific outings.

What had she noticed about him tonight? Nothing. Nothing except the way his laugh warmed her body and the way his eyes sparkled with delight when he was being mischievous.

"Choose any time you like," he continued. "You can send me a note whenever you're ready. I do all my work in my laboratory, so my schedule can accommodate whatever you need. And I will drink sodas with or without the elixir, so you needn't worry. But enough about that. Right now I have a more important question."

"Oh?"

Hal reached into a vest pocket and flashed a shiny penny for the briefest of seconds. "What are we going to do *now*?"

Chapter 13
Questions

Hal fidgeted, awaiting Callie's answer. She'd become strangely quiet. He'd thought she'd enjoyed the show, ridiculous as it may have been. Now, though, she'd lost her usual composure. Her expression had an uncertainty he'd never seen before. Undoubtedly he was the cause.

"Shall I hail a cab?" he asked.

The crowd spewed from the theater doors, sweeping Callie and Hal along with it. All along the street vehicles waited, horses nickering or boilers puffing. He'd never be able to snag one of the cabs among such a mob, but it seemed the gentlemanly offer to make. Callie was surely used to men with private vehicles. Another sign he was not of her world.

"Let's walk," Callie suggested, probably realizing how hopeless the situation was. Maybe if they went far enough they could find an available autocab. "Would you like a drink? There are a number of saloons nearby."

"A drink sounds excellent."

Which was the truth. Strangely, though, getting drunk didn't appeal to him. Why not? With a double dose of the elixir, shouldn't he not care what consequences he faced when he woke as ordinary Henry Jekyll? Or was it merely a sign of selfish concern for a body he possessed?

"Have you noticed any indications that the elixir is more

effective today than in the past?" he asked, hoping Callie could lend weight to the "selfish" theory.

She shook her head. "I'm sorry. I haven't been paying as close attention as I ought. I've been distracted, I suppose."

"Oh. Yes. Perhaps the theater wasn't ideal for the experiment."

He'd enjoyed it, though, sitting close to her in the dark. Trading secret whispers. Swigging gin among the teetotalers. They'd been co-conspirators in his scheme, and it had been delightful.

"Why don't we do an interview?" Callie asked.

Hal blinked. "An interview?"

"I ask you questions, then we record your answers and see how they deviate from the answers you would give without the elixir."

"Ah! Brilliant! We'll grab a quiet table at the nearest saloon and get started."

A quiet table proved to be something of a misnomer. Their booth against the wall meant noise didn't come at them from all directions, but the small room and large crowd created a constant rumble of voices that seemed to vibrate even through the bricks themselves.

For ease of conversation, Callie seated herself beside Hal rather than across from him, putting her body so close his own heated in response. The penny in his pocket beckoned. He would happily trade it for another kiss.

"Let's get started," she said, the unusual primness in her voice dashing his hopes. She was all business. He'd definitely done something wrong.

Hal took a sip of his mint julep. Interesting. Different than the gin and tonic, but pleasant. He would enjoy his drink, even if it wasn't what he most wanted to be tasting at the moment.

He took out the small notebook and pen he always carried in his coat and handed them to Callie. She turned to a fresh page, pen poised, her mouth pinched in a studious line.

"Question one: Why did you drink the elixir today?"

"To do the experiment," Hal replied immediately. He paused a moment. "Was that the right answer? Too obvious? Do I need to elaborate?"

"It was perfect. Don't think. Just say whatever comes into your head first."

Hal nodded. Good. That made things easy. He wasn't certain he'd be able to do much more than that anyway, considering the distraction of her presence. He did his best to sit straight and not lean into her. She didn't want that right now, no matter how much he did.

"Why did you invite me out tonight?" she asked.

"Because you offered to help." Though only God knew why. Callie was the sort of amazing woman who could have any man she wanted, and he was certainly not her usual sort. Now she wasn't even flirting with him anymore. Yet she was still here.

She jotted notes on the paper. "What do you think of Dr. Franklin?"

"Victor? What about him?"

"Do you like him?"

Hal squinted at her through the lenses of his spectacles, then took them off and polished them with his handkerchief. "Of course I like him. He's my friend."

She tapped the end of the pen against her bottom lip as she nodded. Hal took another sip of his drink and fingered the penny in his pocket. They should be kissing right now. If he'd done things right, he'd be kissing her.

"What about Mr. Becher and his temperance friends? What do you think of them?"

"They're wrong."

Completely wrong. They would disapprove of him sitting here, drinking with a woman. They would disapprove of Callie entirely. He couldn't agree with anyone who did that. She was marvelous.

"Do you enjoy drinking? Alcohol, that is?" Still the studious voice. Still the unsmiling face. Had he driven all the fun out of her?

Hal shrugged. "It's all right." Right now the drink was merely something to occupy him while his mind turned over everything he'd said and done that evening. He wanted flirtatious Callie back, dammit!

"How late do you want to stay out tonight?"

"I don't know."

The penny was warm from the heat of his body. His finger rubbed across the ridges and lines, feeling the image stamped into the metal. When she'd left that day, she'd asked him to bring it. Which meant she'd wanted to kiss him. Somewhere between then and now things had gone wrong. She'd flirted at the beginning of the evening. Something had happened tonight. No matter how he tried, he couldn't figure what that something could be.

"If a runaway trolley is headed down a railway track, certain to kill five people, but you have the chance to pull a switch and send it down a different track where it is certain to kill one person, do you pull the switch?"

"What?" Hal blurted, jolted from his musings by the ghastly question. "That's awful!" He pulled his hand from his pocket and twisted to stare at Callie. For the first time since they'd sat down, she was smiling.

"Which do you think is the better choice?" she asked.

"I don't want to kill anyone. I sound an alert or use some other signal to warn them to get off the tracks."

"They can't get off. They've been tied to the tracks by a villain."

He folded his arms across his chest. "This is a horrible question."

Callie laid the pen down atop her notes. "Hal, I don't think your potion works."

He frowned at her. "Of course it works."

"No, it doesn't. You're not any different than your everyday self. You think the same things, feel the same things, believe the same things. There's no evil side of you coming out. You're just you."

"Nonsense. Without the elixir I'm a bore. With it I'm fun. I drink and swear and go to parties, and I don't give a damn what anyone else thinks."

"Not true. Did you openly mock the temperance drama? Of course not. You laughed with me but allowed everyone else to enjoy it their own way. You were a complete gentleman all evening. You could easily have shoved your way to an autocab if you didn't care about being rude, but that never even entered your mind, did it?"

"No, but…"

"You're not evil, Hal. Not even the tiniest bit. The elixir is an excuse. You tell yourself it does something, and then you can do what you want without feeling guilty about it."

Hal's gut churned. She couldn't be right. All this time, all his experiments couldn't be for nothing. He was different with the elixir. He was. He had to be.

He jabbed a finger at the notes she'd written. "That's not proof. You're asking the wrong sorts of questions."

"Fine. If you could do anything you wanted, right now, what would you be doing?"

"Making love to you instead of arguing."

His face flamed.

Callie smirked. "And that, right there, is the *exact* answer I would have gotten from elixir-free Dr. Henry Jekyll, M.D."

"But..." Hal could barely even manage a protest. Everything was falling apart. Callie didn't want him. His experiment was a failure.

Callie placed a hand on his shoulder. "Let me give you some proper proof. Take me to your house. Let me drink the elixir."

Tingles of desire radiated out from the place where her fingers touched him. Callie in his house. At night.

He shouldn't agree. He didn't understand the elixir well enough. Hadn't conducted enough tests. But he'd come to no harm from it. And she was right: he wasn't evil. Even if it affected her, she wouldn't be, either.

"I'll hail a cab," he said.

Chapter 14
Cause and Effect

"Don't drink it until I've had the antidote."

Callie set the small bottle of green liquid back on the laboratory table. She could let him have this. Regardless of any possible effects of the elixir, it was probably better for both of them if he was less anxious about the situation.

Hal gulped down his remedy and closed his eyes, taking a deep breath. "All right," he said after a few seconds. "Go ahead. By the time the elixir begins to take effect for you, my antidote will have me fully restored to my usual self."

Callie refrained from repeating her skepticism regarding his potion, and drank down her own small sample. The syrupy liquid slid down her throat and her nose wrinkled at the faint taste of soured fruit.

"It's not the most pleasant of drinks," she observed, "but it could be worse."

"One grows accustomed to it." Hal gestured to the chair by his desk. "Would you like to sit?"

"I'm fine, thank you. Perhaps I'll do a bit more perusing of your shelves. When should I expect to feel an effect?"

"Anywhere from a few seconds to a few minutes. It's near to instantaneous for me."

Callie nodded and wandered over to his laboratory bookshelf, running her finger across the leather spines. A whole collection of science books. Medicine, physics, mathematics, modern chemistry, and even alchemy. He'd arranged them by size, rather than subject. Her inner librarian itched to pull them all down and group them properly.

"How do you find anything?"

Hal adjusted his eyeglasses. "Pardon?"

"If you want a particular book, how do you find it when the books aren't categorized?"

"I remember what the book looks like and where I put it," he answered, frowning in puzzlement.

Callie turned away from the shelf, shaking her head. "Of course. No need to be logical when one has a good memory. And I imagine you like the way the books look. It's aesthetically soothing."

"Er, yes, I suppose it is."

"I believe in subject-based classification and relative indexing," Callie explained. "You noticed, I assume, that the books in my apartment were arranged according to subject matter. If you did a more thorough study, you would see they're grouped by category, then subcategory, and then alphabetical by author. It's a relatively simple system, but in a larger collection where you might have many levels of subcategories, a decimal system such as the one developed by Mr. Dewey can allow for a precise arrangement of books as well as the flexibility to add and remove volumes in any category. Patrons can easily browse for reading material, and specific books can be found quickly. The system pairs well with a card-based catalogue."

Jekyll was staring wide-eyed at her. "Uh, Miss Finch…"

"I'm sorry if it sounds like I'm criticizing your shelving. You're welcome to have your own books arranged however you like. But I'm rather passionate about libraries and access to reading material, and I've done extensive reading about how booksellers and librarians can improve the experience for their patrons. I want my library to be easy to use. A comfortable place to be with books, discover new books, and find the information one wishes to find. I told you I would tell you about my library later, didn't I? I suppose 'later' is 'now.'"

"Miss Finch," Hal repeated. "I believe the elixir has taken effect."

"Has it?"

Callie paused to take stock of herself. Nothing felt different. No strange sensations in her body, no unusual urges. She certainly didn't feel any compunction to commit crimes or cause trouble, and the "immoral acts" she would like to engage in with her companion were the same ones she enjoyed on a regular basis.

"You are talking a great deal and rather rapidly," he replied. "In my experience that is a sign the formula is working."

"It's a sign I'm passionate about something. My library is a lifelong project, and I have very strong opinions regarding it. So, yes, I am talking a lot, but that doesn't mean it's the fault of your elixir. Shouldn't I feel something more? An urge to rebel or break the rules? Where is my 'wicked side,' Dr. Jekyll? Because as far as I can tell, I'm my usual self."

Hal shrugged, his expression uncertain. "Maybe you don't have a wicked side. Apart from your sexual liberation, which you have already embraced. You've always seemed to me a very kind and good-natured person. Are you certain you don't feel anything? Not even the slightest desire to do something abnormal?"

"No. Nothing like that."

"Damn," he muttered, then shook his head. "Oh, pardon me. Too much time with the elixir leads to bad habits, I'm afraid."

"Or you've become comfortable enough in my presence that you no longer pause to rehearse everything you say before you say it."

"A bit of that, perhaps."

Callie walked over to Hal's desk and took a seat, picking up a pen, and grabbing a sheet of paper from the next stack in the corner. "When in doubt, make more notes. Tell me what I should look for. How do you feel when you drink the elixir? What does your research say should be happening? How did you ever know it was ready for testing in the first place?"

Hal moved to her side, leaning against the desk. "See? Talkative. I first tested the formula on Eddie."

"Who's Eddie?"

"My rat. I gave him small doses of the formula as I developed it. This version was the first that noticeably affected him. He became noisier and more aggressive. After repeating the test several times with the same result, I tried it on myself. I was much freer with my tongue, almost immediately, saying the things that came into my head rather than holding them back for the sake of propriety."

"Hmm." Callie tapped the pen on the paper. "I truly don't feel any more uninhibited than I ordinarily do. Is there anything else you can tell me about how the elixir affects you? Anything at all?"

"Do you know that voice in your head? The one that tells you to stop and think or to behave sensibly rather than giving in to whatever impulse you're feeling?"

"Yes," she replied. "I know what you mean." The voice that kept her focused. That told her to remember her date with Valdez for Friday night and the money she needed for her library. The voice she'd been ignoring all evening.

"The elixir makes it quiet. I can do what I want because it's not nagging me."

Callie gazed up at him. Behind his tinted spectacles, his brown eyes were serious and sincere. His kissable lips were set in a straight line. The desire to flirt until he smiled swelled inside her. Her gut knotted with the knowledge she would be making him frown instead.

"Hal, I'm so sorry. The elixir isn't working on me. Not at all."

"Why do you say that?"

She took a deep breath. "Because I want to kiss you more than just about anything right now. But that voice you talked about? It's telling me loud and clear all the sensible reasons I shouldn't."

His mouth opened, but he said nothing, frozen for a moment in surprise. Slowly his expression twisted into bafflement, then contemplation, then disappointment. He leaned heavily against the nearest cabinet, letting out a sigh.

"I should have known it was too good to be true." He raked a hand through his hair. "I've probably been going about everything all wrong. I shouldn't have been trying to draw out the baser urges. I should have been trying to find a formula to suppress them. I thought…" He turned away from Callie, his shoulders slumping.

She rose from her seat and walked to his side, laying a hand on his shoulder. "What? Tell me. It might help."

A long moment passed. "I thought my way was better. I imagined some safe environment where the bad side could carouse freely, leaving a person refreshed, in a sense. 'Dr. Jekyll's Resort and Spa,' Victor called it. I believed it would be better for a person's mental state to relieve the urges instead of pushing them deeper and deeper down."

"Hal." Callie's hand stroked his arm. "If this can be done at all, I think your way is the better choice. You're right that it's not good for a person to bottle everything up inside. Don't be too hard on yourself. You're young. You have plenty of time. And science isn't easy. No one gets it right the first time."

He turned, gazing down into her eyes with an ardent expression that made her heart leap in her chest. Her body tightened. Her skin heated.

"Calliope," he breathed, his arms encircling her waist. "Must you listen to that voice? Because I brought your penny."

Her own arms wrapped around his neck. Maybe the elixir worked a little bit, because right now she was having a hard time hearing any reason to not become further involved with him.

"I could possibly extend the sale on kisses for another day or two."

Hal's lips descended, just brushing against her own, when the shriek of splintering and twisting metal shattered the silence.

Chapter 15
Letting Off Steam

Hal yanked back the curtains and peered out the window at the wreckage that had once been his front gate. A motorcar, twisted and broken from the crash, lay on its side, tangled in the mess of bent iron rails. Curls of rising smoke wreathed toward the sky, limned by the flickering light of gaslit street lamps.

The curtain dropped from his fingers, and he sprinted for the front door, heart pounding. The disabled vehicle could explode at any moment. What if the driver was trapped inside?

"Hal!" Callie raced after him, but he couldn't stop to talk to her. "What's happening? What was that?"

He threw open the door and bounded down into the yard, waving smoke away from his face as he raced toward the wreck. No, not smoke. No harsh burning smell assaulted his nose. Only steam, billowing from the damaged engine. Thank God.

"Hal!" Callie called out again. "Is that a steam car? How did this happen? Is anyone inside?"

She was definitely more talkative since imbibing the elixir. Not that he could dwell on that right now. Not when there was a victim or victims to rescue. Maybe nothing was on fire now, but that didn't mean the fuel couldn't ignite at any moment. And who knew what sort of injuries the crash itself could have caused? Hal didn't see patients on any regular basis, but he was still a trained physician and it was his duty to help.

He scrambled over an undamaged portion of fence. His clothing snagged on one of the decorative finials, and he heard the distinctive sound of tearing fabric as he jerked himself free. Blast.

"Hello?" Hal called. "Can you hear me? Do you need help?" He raced around the car to where the driver should have been. The seat was empty. No body, dead or alive, lay in the vicinity. "Hello?" he called again.

"Where's the driver?" Callie blurted.

Hal crouched down beside the broken steam car, trying to focus on the problem at hand rather than wondering how she had climbed over the fence in her evening gown. The passenger seat was also empty, and Hal saw no sign of anyone trapped beneath the car or tangled in the fence. He moved closer, to make as thorough an inspection as possible, wincing a bit as the hot steam touched his skin.

"This doesn't make sense," Callie puzzled. "I've never heard of a car that doesn't need a driver. How did this happen? Did someone crash and then leap out and run away? I would expect such a collision to result in injury."

"I would too." Hal straightened up, backing away. "But there's certainly no one here."

The front door of his house flew open. His housekeeper, Mrs. Sterling, burst onto the porch, clutching her wrapper across her chest.

"Oh, Dr. Jekyll!" she exclaimed, hurrying down to the bottom step. "Thank the Lord you are unharmed. I heard the most horrendous crash." She surveyed the damage. "What happened? You don't drive. Oh! Dear! Is anyone hurt?"

"No, not at all." He walked to the fence, intending to help Callie over, but she stuck a toe into the decorative scrollwork, grabbed hold, and hoisted herself up and over with a great deal more finesse than Hal had shown. He took his time following her, managing to avoid any further damage to his suit.

"Goodness!" Mrs. Sterling exclaimed. "Are you certain you're unhurt? Shall I send for a doctor?"

Hal waved a hand. "No, no. We weren't in the vehicle. We were in the laboratory working on an experiment when the crash happened. It appears the car had no driver. Perhaps someone lost control and fell from the vehicle and then it veered into the fence." He turned to look out at the street. Another steam car appeared from around the corner. Hal could just make out the markings in the dim light. A police car.

"The police?" Callie asked. "Already?"

"Someone must have telephoned," Hal reasoned. Who on this block had a telephone? Maybe he needed to get to know his neighbors better. He looked back at Callie and Mrs. Sterling. "Please excuse me. I should speak with the police and check the street in case someone did fall from the vehicle. Do you think you could put up Miss Finch in a room for the night?"

"Oh, of course!" Mrs. Sterling exclaimed. "Certainly we can't have a young lady walking herself home at night, and you'll be busy some time. I'll put her up in the room Miss Majhi uses when she stays. Come along with me, dear. We'll find you a nightgown and get you settled in."

"Who's Miss Majhi?" Callie asked. "Dr. Jekyll never mentioned having a lady friend. Is she…" The remainder of the sentence was lost as Callie disappeared into the house. The elixir might not be having a large effect, but it was making her blurt out whatever was on her mind. Maybe his tweaks wouldn't have to be as drastic as he'd feared.

Hal climbed back over the fence to give a report to the police. Not that he had much to say. He told them what he'd heard, then made a slow sweep of the street while they examined the crash site. The empty cobblestones glinted in the gaslight. Perhaps it was too dark to see specks of blood, but Hal doubted he would have found any, even in broad daylight. Nothing, anywhere, indicated that a person or persons had jumped or been thrown from the vehicle.

"No one here," a police officer said to Hal when he returned. "The steam's all blown out now, and the engine's shut down, so no need to worry about an explosion. A man will be by tomorrow morning, and we'll let you know if we hear of any runaway cars."

Hal gritted his teeth at the skepticism in the officer's voice. *They think I crashed the car and lied about it.*

"Our report is finished," the officer continued. "You can have the vehicle hauled away at your leisure."

"Thank you," Hal replied evenly, stamping down his feelings, as he so often did.

At my leisure? You want me *to pay the expense of removing this mess, when it is* my *property that has been damaged?* My *evening that has been disrupted through no fault of my own?*

If he'd been drinking the elixir, he'd probably have shouted at them, and possibly gotten himself arrested in the process. He needed to check on Callie. Maybe give her the antidote before bed, in case she had started to feel something more than simply chatty.

"I appreciate your assistance," he said to the police. It was almost the truth. He at least appreciated that they'd confirmed there really wasn't anyone trapped in the wreckage.

Hal waited until the men had driven away before climbing over his fence again—why had the cursed machine had to run into his gate of all places—then securely locked up his front door and the door of the laboratory. He poured one dose of the antidote into a vial and started up the stairs toward the guest bedrooms.

Two steps from the top, a flash of white caught his eye. Callie came barreling down the hall, barefoot and clad in a too-small nightgown. He grabbed the railing to steady himself.

"Hal!" His name was a whispered hiss. "What happened? Did you discover anything? I was watching out the window, but didn't see anything suspicious. No one appeared anywhere along the street except yourself and the police."

"No, nothing," he sighed, trudging up the last steps into the hall. "It appears to be a strange accident." The frustration boiled inside him again. "One I apparently must pay to clean up myself."

"I'm sorry."

Callie's sympathetic expression snapped the last of Hal's barriers. Words spewed from him like the steam from the damaged boiler.

"Those men had no care for the truth. They hardly listened to my story, made no mention of attempting to identify the vehicle, and only paid lip service to the idea of investigating further. I'm left with the work to do and the money to pay. And what of the owner? *Someone* must own that car. What happens if I hire a scrap dealer to haul it away and then the owner comes looking for it? Did the police even check for a registration plate? We have no answers. Only a giant mess in my front yard."

He let out a long breath. Some of the tightness in his

shoulders had eased. The problem hadn't resolved itself, but he would manage.

"Thank you for letting me rant. I think I needed that."

Callie grinned at him. "See? You can let yourself free without the elixir."

Hal held out the antidote to her. "Here. Drink this. Just in case it's had more of an effect on you than a tendency to speak without restraint."

"I don't think it has, but I'm happy to reassure you." She accepted the vial and drank the antidote. "It tastes better than the elixir, at least."

Hal nodded, glancing down to take his eyes off the droplets of moisture lingering on her lips. Bad idea. The nightgown stretched tight across her chest and the top few buttons were undone, giving him a glimpse of the tops of her breasts.

He sucked in a breath. Her evening gown had exposed more, but this was worse. This was indecent. Illicit. Dear God, what had he been thinking to invite her to stay the night in his house?

"I suppose we ought to turn in for the night," Callie said, her head bobbing slightly in the direction of her room. "We'll want to take a look at the wreckage tomorrow during the daylight to see if we can learn anything else."

"Yes. I…" He pointed back over his shoulder. "My room is that way."

That could be taken as an invitation, Hal realized. Had a part of him meant it as an invitation? Did he want it to be an invitation?

He took a step toward her. Yes. He absolutely wanted it to be an invitation.

"You appear to be walking in the wrong direction, Dr. Jekyll."

One more step. He was close enough to touch her now. "Am I?" This was a bad idea. A terrible idea. But his pleasant evening had been upended, and all he wanted was to smother the frustrations with something happy.

Callie reached for him, her fingers delving into the pocket where he'd stashed her penny. His penny. Their penny.

"Goodnight kiss. One cent." Her husky voice slithered under Hal's skin, turning his blood to fire. He lifted a hand to brush his thumb across her cheek.

"How much for the whole night?"

Chapter 16
The Price of Honesty

"One hundred dollars," Callie answered, watching Hal's face to gauge his reaction. This close, she could see his eyes widen, even in the dim light of the corridor.

"That's... quite a lot." He didn't step away, but he shifted, subtly widening the space between them.

"I cater to very wealthy clients. One hundred dollars is standard. I'm assuming you're not interested in anything unusual."

He blinked rapidly. "Unusual?"

Ah, yes. This was conservative Dr. Jekyll. He probably had no inkling of the astonishing range of human appetites.

"Why don't we talk about this in my room? It'll be more comfortable."

"Er..." For a moment she thought he was about to say he'd changed his mind, but then he steeled himself. "Yes. That sounds reasonable."

Callie walked to the end of the hall and opened her door. She'd left the electric light on, illuminating the emerald green papered walls and the gold trim accents. Already she was fond of the little jewel of a room.

"This is a beautiful room," she said, perching on the edge of the bed and motioning for Hal to take the armchair in the corner. "The green is so vivid."

"No arsenic in the paper."

Callie's eyebrows shot up for an instant before her surprise gave way to laughter. "I didn't think there was. You seem much too conscientious to allow a known hazard in your home."

"I appreciate that. Your response is much nicer than the, 'Are you trying to poison me?' I got when I first showed it to Nemo."

"Nemo?"

"Ah. Another scientist friend."

Callie nodded. "Your housekeeper mentioned a friend named Miss Majhi stays here. Is she a lover of yours?"

Hal jerked so hard his chair thumped against the wall. "What? No." He needed a moment to compose himself. "You met her the other day at the club. Nisha Majhi. She suggested I try the gin and tonic."

"Oh, the woman at the bar who was wearing trousers?"

"She's an engineer. She prefers clothing that won't tangle in anything while she works."

"Sensible. You and she never…"

"No," he answered vehemently. "We attended university together and are scientific colleagues." He straightened his spine. "Sometimes I invite my friends here in the evenings, and sometimes they stay the night. I do not invite ladies here for—" He broke off, his prim facade crumbling. "I didn't mean… That's not why I…"

"You were being a gentleman. I know." Callie leaned forward, resting her elbows on her knees and her chin on her hands. From his seat Hal would have a perfect framed view of the way the ill-fitting nightgown stretched across her breasts. She gave him a seductive smile. "Although I suspect a part of you was hoping the night might take an intimate turn."

"I'm a cad."

"Not at all. You know perfectly well I'm a courtesan. It's only natural you should proposition me."

Hal heaved himself up out of the chair. "Not in my house. Not when you're an invited guest."

Callie crooked a finger and beckoned him closer. "Come here. You don't get to run away that easily."

He didn't move.

"I'm going to be perfectly frank with you. This isn't going to go away if you walk out of this room. It will still be there tomorrow when we wake, or whenever we see each other next."

"I know." He pushed up his spectacles and rubbed the bridge of his nose. "Perhaps we shouldn't see one another anymore."

"You keep saying that and then ignoring your own advice. And, honestly, I'm no better. I like you. If I didn't, I'd have refused your offer. Immediately. No price given, no invitation to my room. I know not everyone can afford to be so choosy, but I can. So no telling yourself you're taking advantage of me."

Hal nodded. "Very well. I did *not* give you a room here for the purpose of intimate activities, but then I found myself desiring to take advantage of the opportunity."

Callie turned on her seductive smile again. "There. Now that's proper honesty. Which brings me to an important point. Before we make any decisions regarding particular acts or prices, we need to discuss the matter of your experience. Are you a virgin, Dr. Jekyll?"

Truthfully, she had no idea. Usually she had a better inkling of such things. Much of his behavior suggested chastity, but he certainly didn't kiss like an innocent. It was possible he was one of those men who'd only had one or two long-standing affairs with lusty widows, but that didn't feel quite right, either.

He coughed awkwardly. "Does that affect the price?"

"No. It just gives me a better idea of how to go about things. So, are you?"

Callie gave him time to prepare himself, and at length he answered, "Technically… yes. In a more, er, comprehensive sense, not at all."

Ah. "You've experienced sexual activity of the oral variety," she surmised. That did make sense. And most likely he'd paid for that pleasure, which explained how he'd managed to overcome his self-restraint to proposition her. "Is that what you're interested in tonight, or were you hoping for full penetration? I'm happy to provide either, and you needn't worry about any consequences, as I use a daily contraceptive draught from Mr. Robert's apothecary. So, the choice is yours. What would you like to do?"

Hal cringed. "I'm sorry. This was a mistake. Please excuse me." He inclined his head. "Goodnight, Miss Finch."

Callie hopped from the bed and jogged after him. "I took your penny. At least let me give you your kiss."

He paused with his hand on the doorknob. "I don't think that's wise."

Hot and then cold. Lusty then reserved. Never had a man baffled or frustrated her this much. "Might I ask what I did wrong?"

"Nothing. You've been entirely sensible about everything." He hesitated, then continued. "My desire is simply not as uncontrollable as I thought it was."

Understanding flashed through Callie's mind. He needed spontaneity. In his Hyde persona he didn't stop to think, just let himself feel and do. Out in the hall, he'd acted on impulse. Laying out the situation between them in clear terms had been important, but it had given him too much time to question his behavior. To doubt himself.

"Isn't it?" she asked. "Or are you simply resigned to frigging yourself while you imagine me naked?"

Hal went completely still. Callie moved as close as she could without touching him. Tonight was her best chance for a night with him. If things went well on Friday and Valdez made her an offer, he would want exclusivity. It was now or never.

"Because if that's your plan," she whispered, "I'd like to watch."

He spun around and pulled her into a crushing embrace.

Chapter 17
A Satisfying End

He would simply have to kiss her forever.

Hal clung to Callie, molding their bodies together. He deepened the kiss, drinking her in, savoring every nuance of her mouth, her lips, her wicked tongue that tempted him to further debauchery.

He could avoid that, though. He could avoid everything if he never stopped kissing her. All he needed to do was hold her here, their mouths moving together, their bodies aligned. Then he'd never have to concern himself with his elixir or the wreck in his front yard. He'd never have to fret about what might come next. He'd live here, in the glory of kissing her, until the sun went cold and the world crumbled to dust.

Callie made a faint noise of pleasure, and his cock throbbed in response. Seemed his body had other ideas.

"Calliope," he groaned, sliding his lips across the smooth skin of her jaw. Maybe he'd kiss her neck. And then her breasts. That was still kissing, right?

Dear God, but she tasted divine. And her scent. His head whirled from it. Whatever perfume she'd dabbed on made her smell like vanilla, and Hal wanted to lick her from her elegant neck down to her slick, hot cunny.

The thought of her moaning as he pleasured her sent

another spear of longing down to his groin. When Callie wriggled against him, he gasped.

Fuck. It had been too long. Ages and ages since anyone but himself had touched him there.

"Do you mean you want to fuck?" Callie asked. "Or is something wrong?"

Hal climbed slowly out of the haze of lust. Had he said that out loud? He opened his mouth, but no words came out. Doubt began to claw its way free, tangling with his desire.

Callie urged him away from the door, pushing his coat off his shoulders so it slithered to the floor. "Come to bed. Tell me what you'd like to do."

Before the doubt could seize control, her dexterous fingers set to work on the buttons of his vest. Hal shivered at the gentle caress of her hands. Another layer between them, gone.

"Anything." The word was harsh, ragged. "Everything."

He moved with her toward the bed, yanking his shirt free from his trousers, desperate to feel her touch against his bare skin. She reached for his waistband, and he jerked away.

"I won't last long if you touch me there." Hal was too far gone to succumb to the embarrassment of such a statement. She knew he was painfully unsophisticated, yet she wanted him anyway. Or was good at pretending she did. Right now he didn't care which.

"How about this instead?" Callie asked. She unfastened the remaining buttons of her nightgown. It slipped from her shoulders, fell open to expose her breasts, then dropped to a puddle on the floor.

"Hell and damnation." Hal grabbed a bedpost to steady himself. He'd seen various body parts exposed before. Had touched women in intimate places. But never before had he had the privilege of seeing a woman completely and fully nude before him. His skin was on fire. His cock so hard he was certain he could finish himself off with a few swift strokes. Calliope was every bit as spectacular as her Greek namesake. His free hand twitched, yearning to cup her round, rosy-peaked breasts, smooth over the curve of her hips, and squeeze her luscious derriere. Curls of sandy-brown hair guarded her sex, and he imagined stroking them on his way down, sliding a hand between her thighs to bathe his fingers in her arousal.

"Hell and damnation," he repeated. He didn't have to imagine. She was here, and she'd offered him whatever he wanted.

Callie grinned at him. Not her devastating come-hither grin, but one of light and laughter. "I guess you like what you see."

"You're gorgeous." He kicked off his shoes and shucked the remainder of his clothing. He was doing this. He was actually doing this, and it didn't seem to be one of his erotic dreams. "Mesmerizing."

Her gaze swept him up and down. "You're not so bad yourself." She sat on the bed and patted the place beside her. Now her sultry smile was back, and Hal was powerless to resist. "Join me."

He half-sat, half-fell onto the bed, and in seconds they were lying tangled together, mouths clashing in a frantic kiss. Hal's hands were everywhere: exploring her skin, kneading her breasts, scrambling to feel every inch of her. His fingers delved between her legs, finding her wet, drawing a sigh of pleasure from her as he stroked over and into her.

Callie rolled fully onto her back, coaxing him to settle between her thighs. The tip of his cock brushed against her core and his head swam.

You shouldn't be doing this, that pesky voice nagged, but it was faint beneath the force of his desire.

He'd had a double dose of the elixir. Should he have taken a double dose of the antidote? Did it even work? Did it matter?

Callie's hands moved up and down his back in long, gentle strokes. She nuzzled his neck, her tongue darting out to taste his skin. "I'm all yours," she murmured. "Whenever you're ready."

No, it didn't matter. Nothing mattered but her and him and whatever this madness was that had overtaken him. Hal thrust forward, sinking into her body as if it were the most natural, most inevitable thing that had ever happened. She lifted her hips, taking him in fully, her arms winding around him to hold him in place.

"Callie," he choked out. No other words were possible. He was lost, drowning in the perfect friction of her body around him. His fingers clenched in the bedsheets and he squeezed his eyes closed, willing himself not to spend immediately. Slowly, achingly slowly, he withdrew, then thrust again. A groan tore from his throat.

Callie's hands groped their way down to his backside, pressing him into her, encouraging him to thrust faster, harder.

"Take me," she moaned.

Was she enjoying this? Dear God, he hoped she was enjoying this.

"Ride me," she urged. "I want to watch you come."

The last tiny shred of Hal's self-control dissolved. He clung to the sheets and pounded into her as hard and as fast as he could, until his whole body convulsed in the most shattering orgasm of his life.

He collapsed. "Fuck," he gasped.

"Indeed." Callie's fingers brushed a damp strand of hair from his brow. "Well done."

* * *

Callie stroked her fingers through Hal's hair and pressed a kiss to his temple. What a beautiful thing, to watch so rigid a man come completely undone. He'd deserved that moment of bliss, and it warmed her heart to be the one to give it to him.

"You can sleep now, if you like," she murmured.

His lashes fluttered. "No. Can't." He pushed himself up on one elbow. "We're not done."

Her gaze dropped to his cock. It hadn't gone fully soft, but he certainly wasn't ready for another round yet.

"*You're* not done," he clarified. "You didn't… finish."

Good on him both to notice and to care. Many men didn't do either. Callie hadn't expected an orgasm. Not during his first time. But she was close enough to take care of that quickly, and would have, if he'd gone to sleep. Hal seemed to have other ideas.

His fingers caressed her inner thigh, and she spread for him again, letting him touch her as he pleased.

"I'm so sorry," he said. "I should have done this first."

His finger teased her clitoris, and she let her eyes drift closed. If he wanted to please her, she wasn't going to complain. And if he had any difficulty, she'd help.

The bed creaked as he moved, climbing over her and down between her legs. Her eyes flew open just in time to see when he pressed his lips to the mound of curls above her sex.

In an instant, his mouth was on her, his tongue licking her up and down, dipping inside her while his finger continued to circle her clit. Her breath caught in her throat. This was not the fumbling exploration of a curious man. Hal knew what he was doing. And he was good at it.

Callie's back arched when his mouth replaced his finger, suckling at the sensitive nub. Good God in heaven. The pressure was just right. The position just right. His fingers curling inside her stroked the perfect place to send her flying.

How? He… He…

All thought vanished in the storm of pleasure. Callie pressed her hands to the headboard, trying to anchor herself as her urgent desire spiraled higher and higher. Desperate, pleading noises tore from her lips. Her hips bucked and she cried out, her body contorting in a long, glorious climax.

When the tremors at last subsided, she opened her eyes to find Hal kneeling between her legs, a lopsided grin on his face, and moisture glistening on his lips.

"There," he said, his voice full of satisfaction. "That's much better."

Chapter 18
The Morning After

Hal stirred his porridge and flipped to the next page of the newspaper, attempting to reach some midpoint between staring across the breakfast table at Callie and ignoring her completely. He wasn't much of a blusher, thank God, but he was a champion of awkward body language. He hoped Mrs. Sterling and his cook hadn't noticed anything amiss.

"Did you sleep well, Miss Finch?" he inquired.

"Yes, I did, thank you. How about you?"

"I… yes," Hal managed. During his mad dash to his room last night, clutching a bundle of discarded clothing, he'd been certain he'd be up all night, contemplating what he'd just done. Instead, he'd fallen rather quickly into a deep, dreamless slumber.

Callie took a bite of her breakfast, her spoon sliding between her lips in a perfectly ordinary way that he nonetheless found alarmingly erotic. He quickly shoveled another spoonful into his own mouth and tried to actually read from his newspaper, rather than staring uncomprehendingly at the printed words.

"The porridge is excellent," she remarked. "Is it sweetened with maple syrup?"

"Yes. Made locally. We've been buying it from the same family since I was a small boy."

"That's lovely." Callie's smile was sweeter than any syrup ever produced.

Hal's heart thumped in his chest. He was sitting at breakfast with the courtesan he'd just bedded, and yet there was something entirely wholesome about her presence across from him. Something warm and cozy. Proper, even. As if he'd been waiting his whole life for a suitable companion and she'd finally filled that hole.

Ridiculous. That's what he was. This was only a temporary flare of passion between them. She had her own life and her library project. He had to return to his elixir. And take care of the mess on his lawn.

He resolutely turned another page in the newspaper. A bold headline caught his eye and he jerked, dropping his spoon. The sound of metal clanking against porcelain echoed through the dining room.

Callie leaned over the table, reaching a hand toward him. "What's wrong?"

"T-this article." Hal cleared his throat and read aloud, "Unchecked Drinking Leads to Runaway Cab. A group of rowdy youths booted from a saloon for overindulging caused a new kind of mayhem last night when they attempted to hire an autocab at the corner of Woodward and High Street. Thinking to drive the vehicle themselves, the besotted crew knocked the driver from his perch and set the cab into motion. Inebriated as they were, they did not realize until too late that the steam car was barreling down the street unchecked. 'It came right at me!' reported a terrified pedestrian who had to jump from the path of the runaway vehicle. 'Wouldn't've happened if it weren't for that unholy liquor,' the cab's driver was heard to say. As of the writing of this article, the final whereabouts of the autocab are unknown."

"Woodward and High Street?" Callie's brow furrowed.

"That's several blocks from here. Plus the cab would have had to turn a corner. Which doesn't seem possible for an unmanned vehicle."

"I agree. But it seems like too much of a coincidence that this story and the crash in my front yard would both happen on the same night."

She nodded. "It should be easy to confirm. Now that it's daylight, we should be able to find the vehicle's registration plate in the wreckage, and if it's an autocab, the company badge as well. We'll take a look as soon as we've finished breakfast."

Hal scooped up another bite of porridge, though his appetite had waned. Surely this was a positive turn of events. He could contact the cab company to take care of the situation. They could demand restitution from the men who had set the vehicle loose. It would be out of his hands.

If only he could shake the nagging sense of wrongness.

They finished their meal with little further conversation. Before heading out, Hal fetched a key from his study so he could unlock the gate in front of his laboratory. He preferred to keep it locked to prevent anyone knocking on the wrong front door, but he couldn't very well continue climbing over the fence until his primary gate was restored.

The moment the gate was open, Callie hurried to the wreckage, running her hands over the misshapen hood of the car as she bent to study it.

"A registration plate ought to be affixed to the front," she said, placing a foot on the car's tire and hoisting herself up for a better look.

"Please be careful."

She ignored him. "I don't see anything, but it's possible it was knocked off and trapped beneath. The front is quite mangled. Why don't you check the back? Look for a round metal disc with a number inscribed on it. I'm going to hop down and take a look from the other side of the gate."

Hal walked around to the back of the cab, where the passenger seat and trunk space remained mostly intact. A registration plate would be easy to spot. Given his dislike for machinery, he didn't pay much attention to autocabs or steam cars of any sort, but he thought most of them had number plates affixed to the back. A quick scan told him this one did not.

"I don't see anything." He squatted to examine the car's bumper. The metal strip running across the back was marred with dents and scratches. And not in a way he might have expected if the vehicle had been bumped from behind by another car. Instead, two distinct areas, one on either end, had been indented, while the center appeared smooth and shiny. Claw-like gouges along the top and bottom of the bumper made him think something large had grabbed hold. "Callie?" he called.

She appeared at his side in a rustle of skirts. "What did you find?"

He gestured at the marks. "I don't think this was a runaway cab. I think it was pushed."

Their eyes locked. The silver color of hers had turned hard as steel.

"Hal. If that's true…"

"I know." He stared at the car, groping for some other explanation, but coming up empty. "It means this wasn't an accident."

Chapter 19
Uncertain

Callie paced back and forth across Hal's lawn. "I don't like this at all. Who would do something like this to you?"

He leaned against his fence, heaving a sigh. "I have no idea. Someone who is angry with me? But for what? I suppose I did win all that money at cards the other day. But I don't think any of those men knew my real name. And then there was that obnoxious fellow I threw in the river." He grimaced. "Goodness. I've been quite the menace as Hyde, haven't I?"

"Hardly. I've seen men lose far more money than that, and Hinsberg fully deserved the soaking you gave him."

"Regardless, I'll have to be more careful when I test the next version of the potion." His frown turned contemplative. "What if it's someone who doesn't like what I'm doing? Someone who wishes to hamper my work?"

"A rival scientist perhaps? Do you know anyone else doing similar experiments to yours?"

He shook his head. "And not many people even know about my work. The Society, of course, and you. But I don't know if I've spoken of it to anyone else except in passing."

"The Society?" she asked. "Is that a scientific organization of some sort?"

"Er..." His shoulders moved in a little shrug that she

now recognized as a sign he was embarrassed. "More like a small club. My friends and I meet once a week to talk over our work and the latest scientific news. Part business, part social. We call ourselves the Mad Scientists Society."

Callie laughed. "It suits you. Though I don't believe you're actually mad. Overly ambitious, perhaps, and idealistic. How many people are in your Society? Any who might have done this sort of thing?"

"No!" Hal cried, looking offended. "My friends would never. And it's only the three of us."

"Hmm. Well, we can hope it was a one-time prank. I am somewhat comforted by the fact that it happened when no one was around. I don't believe this was intended to harm you, only to inconvenience you. I'd hate to leave you thinking you were in danger."

"Thank you, Miss Finch. You are a truly good and kind-hearted person." Hal gave her the same crooked smile he'd worn last night after sex. It was dangerous, that smile. Altogether too endearing. It made Callie want to hug him and then snuggle in bed for hours.

"I'll head for home, then, unless you need more help of any kind?"

"I don't, but, please, allow me to walk you home. Or take the trolley." He glanced at the mangled steam car. "I think it might be best to avoid cabs today."

"A walk is fine. It's no more than a mile."

"Excellent." Hal offered his arm and led her down the street, with only a single, forlorn glance back at the debris in front of his house.

As they walked, they talked of happier things. The fine weather. Their mutual love of reading. Whether the startled looks people gave them were because Callie's dress was completely out of place for a morning walk or simply because she stunned them with her beauty.

"You know full well they're all thinking, 'That woman is a whore,'" she asserted. "Because why else would I be wearing last night's dress?"

"It's entirely plausible that an incident could have occurred that required you to stay away from home unexpectedly, but at the house of a man who is not as weak-willed as I am."

Callie laughed. "That would have been a great deal less fun. I'm not ashamed of who I am. The fault lies with our society. It fears a woman who embraces her sexuality."

"Or a woman who embraces science, or business, or anything besides marriage and motherhood."

She gave his arm an affectionate squeeze. "You understand. You'll approve of my library, then. It's meant to be a ladies' lending library, but one that doesn't restrict or censor its collection. A place where women can go to read all the books they're told not to read. I want women to walk away from my library thinking, 'I can be a scientist *and* a mother. I can be a wife *and* an artist. I can be all those things. I can be none of those things.' I want to give women knowledge, education, and a place they can learn confidence and comfort with their true selves."

"That is an extremely noble goal, Miss Finch," Hal replied. "I applaud you." His gaze dropped to the sidewalk in front of them. "Might I hope my hundred dollars will contribute to your cause?"

"Every penny of it."

"I'm glad. I will make a note to report it as a charitable donation."

Callie laughed so hard she almost choked. "Henry Jekyll, that is the most scandalous thing I have ever heard you say!

See? You don't need any sort of elixir. You're perfectly delightful all on your own."

"Perfectly terrible, perhaps. I wouldn't have said that to anyone else."

"Then I'm glad you're with me."

He didn't reply, sinking into his thoughts as he so often did. They had reached Callie's block, and she didn't press him for further conversation until they stood in front of her apartment building.

"Thank you for walking me home, and for last night," she said. "I truly enjoyed it, from the show, to the bedroom, to our time together this morning. I'm very sorry about the crash, and I hope you don't have too much trouble having it cleaned up. Please let me know if you discover anything else, or if you need any assistance."

Hal nodded. "I'll send you a note if I learn anything."

"And if it looks like there's any danger, telephone the police," she insisted.

"I don't have a telephone."

"Well, report it somehow. And let me know immediately. I don't want to sit here thinking you're in danger."

"Thank you, Miss Finch. You are too kind, and I am honored to call you my friend."

She folded her arms across her chest and gave him a mock frown. "You also need to call me Callie."

He shifted, embarrassed again. "Callie. Might I take you out for an ice cream soda tomorrow? I promise to give you a full report on the crash cleanup."

Tomorrow. Friday. A last moment before Valdez took her out and she would need to shift her priorities.

"That sounds lovely, thank you."

"Two p.m.? I'll pick you up. Maybe on my bicycle if you're willing to try that handlebar stunt?"

“I have my own bicycle. We’ll ride together.”

Hal’s wide smile once again sparked the urge to throw her arms around him and not let go. “Wonderful!” he exclaimed. “Until tomorrow then.” He stepped back and bowed to her. “Thank you, Callie, for making what could have been a miserable night a beautiful one instead.” His grin turned bashful. “Maybe in the future I can contribute further to your library fund.”

She nodded and kept a smile on her face, but her heart sank. It would be months before such a thing was possible. By then, this fire between them would have long burned out. They were the victims of bad timing.

She waved to him as he departed. At least there would be ice cream.

Chapter 20
Falling Flat

It won't rain. It won't rain.

Hal hopped down from his bicycle and glanced up at the uniformly gray sky. No signs of a storm at the moment, but this wasn't the cheerful, sunny day he'd hoped for. He leaned his bike against the wall and started for the front door, but froze when a bicycle tire poked out from around the side of the building.

Callie wheeled her own bike toward him, her usual easy smile on her face. Hal's heart rate immediately quickened. She was stunning in her modern cycling suit. The light blue, pinstriped skirt had been lifted and buttoned up to allow her the freedom to pedal, exposing her calf-hugging boots and pale yellow bloomers. An elegant jacket in the same material as the skirt buttoned just under her breasts, and the blouse beneath matched the bloomers. She was the perfect picture of an independent woman.

"Miss Finch! Er, Callie. You look lovely. That's an ingenious outfit, with the way the skirt converts for riding."

"I'm fond of it. And it's comfortable as well." She mounted her bicycle, propping one foot up on the pedal. "Shall we be off? Best to have our ride before any rain comes along."

"Agreed. Would you like to ride down to the river for a bit? Work up an appetite before we have our ice cream?"

Her eyebrows twitched. "I don't think I need an incentive to drink a soda, but yes, a ride along the riverfront sounds lovely. And if the sky grows darker, we'll take that as a sign it's time for our treat."

"Perfect." Hal hopped on his own bicycle, and they started off.

For the next half-hour, they pedaled down the streets, dodging carriages and automobiles, enjoying the feel of the wind in their face. When a gentle mist began to form, they raced each other to the ice cream parlor, growing more damp from perspiration than from the moist air.

"That was wonderful fun," Callie declared, even as she leaned on her bike, catching her breath. "Thank you for suggesting it." She unhooked her skirt and shook it out to drape neatly to the ground. "I believe I'm ready for that ice cream soda."

Hal nodded in reply, no coherent words forming in his mind. She'd looked beautiful before, but now, with her hair mussed and her cheeks red from the exercise, she was nothing short of radiant. He wanted another night with her. Ached for another night with her. So much so that he was contemplating reviewing his monthly budget to determine exactly how many encounters he could afford.

Right now, though, he would simply enjoy this time together. He took genuine pleasure in her company, and hoped their friendship would continue to grow.

They propped their bicycles against a lamppost and headed inside to the counter to order drinks.

"I promised you an update on that car in my yard," Hal said as they waited. "Unfortunately, I have little to report. It's been removed, along with the broken sections of the fence. No identifying marks found, no registration plate. Now I get to decide whether to repair the fence or have it replaced entirely."

"I'm sorry." Callie's hand on his arm made him shiver. "It's entirely unfair that you have to pay for this in both your time and your money."

Hal shrugged. "At least no one was hurt. Where shall we sit? I'd like to go back to talking about nice things."

"By the window. I like watching the rain. And then we'll see right away when it lets up."

"A sound strategy. Why don't you sit? I'll bring the drinks."

The soda jerk set Hal's Boston Cooler on the counter, and Hal took a sip, enjoying the fizzy tingle of the Vernor's Ginger Ale on his nose. Callie's strawberry soda appeared moments later, and he scooped it up and set off to join her.

The bell above the front door jingled and a man stepped inside, throwing back the hood of his cloak. Hal would have recognized those ginger mutton chops anywhere.

"Jekyll!" Becher exclaimed. "How are you? Did you enjoy my sample?"

"Yes, it was excellent," Hal lied. He'd hardly touched the stuff except to make the tiny batch of gin and tonic he'd smuggled into the temperance drama. He glanced at Callie, inching in her direction, but Becher didn't take the hint.

"Wonderful, wonderful. I'll have another bottle sent 'round." He clapped a hand down on Hal's shoulder, shaking him enough that a bit of soda sloshed over the side of his glass and trickled down between his fingers. "And how about the union? Changed your mind? Ready to join us now?"

"Er..." He looked again at Callie. "Excuse me, Mr. Becher, but I..."

“Important cause, you know,” the tonic water tycoon ran on. “Got to stop all these sots and their drunken antics. You’ve read the papers, I’m sure. Runaway cabs. Destruction of property. Disturbing the peace.”

“Yes, of course,” Hal babbled. “Thank you, but I’d prefer to focus on my own work. I have someone waiting for me, excuse me.” He darted for the table without waiting for a reply.

Behind him, Becher huffed and muttered, “Terribly rude fellow.”

Shaking off the unpleasant encounter, Hal slipped into his seat and handed Callie her soda. Without thinking, he licked the spilled ice cream from his fingers.

Callie’s eyebrows rose and her smile turned flirtatious. “Be careful, Hal.” She leaned closer and lowered her voice. “I know what you can do with that tongue. Keep that up and it will get so hot in here all the ice cream will melt.”

The memory of the taste of her as she’d writhed beneath him sent his own temperature soaring. He glanced behind him, but Becher had moved on to talk with one of the store employees, presumably about his tonic water. Everyone else in the shop appeared preoccupied with their own affairs.

“Sorry. Becher startled me. Made a bit of a mess.”

“No need to apologize. I enjoyed the show. If we were in private, I’d happily watch you drink your entire drink in that fashion.”

Hal took a large gulp of soda, feeling the chill of the ice cream down his throat all the way to his stomach. It did nothing to ease the heat of his skin. “You’re right. It is growing rather warm in here.”

Again, he glanced around to check for other patrons watching or listening. He wanted to continue the conversation. Wanted to say flirtatious, suggestive, or even erotic things to her. But the need to maintain decorum and uphold propriety clawed at his gut.

Callie straightened in her chair. “Someday, I expect you to tell me how an innocent man could become an expert in that particular area.”

Her breezy tone was every bit as stimulating as a husky whisper would have been. Hal had no hope of ever being as comfortable speaking of carnal pleasures as she was, but he longed to become at least somewhat less embarrassed about it.

“A great deal of practice,” he answered, and picked up his soda for another sip. He couldn’t say anything more on the matter. Not in public. Even if he used euphemisms and carefully worded sentences, the mere act of explaining would make him squirm. Someone would notice, and he’d forever become “that man who discussed inappropriate topics in a respectable ice cream parlor.”

“Hmm.” Callie sipped her own drink.

He’d have to tell her eventually, but she would want more than a quick explanation. And he’d never told that story to anyone. Only his closest friends knew, since they’d been part of the… inciting incident.

“I can elaborate when we are, uh…” This time Hal caught himself before his gaze began to sweep the room. “Alone.”

“I hope you do,” she replied. “I’ve been dying of curiosity. You are a very interesting man, Dr. Jekyll.”

“Thank you.” He turned toward the window. A steady rain beat down on the cobblestone streets. “Perhaps when this lets up we can ride somewhere else. Your house, or mine? I…” He sucked in a deep breath. “I would be interested in an evening in private.”

“Oh.”

Hal's head snapped around at the sound of disappointment in her voice.

"What's wrong?"

She shook her head, looking down at her soda and sighing. "Hal, I'm so sorry, but I'm not available tonight. And likely not for many months to follow."

"Why? What's happened?"

For the first time since they'd met, she hesitated before speaking. "A friend is taking me out tonight. I expect he will make me an offer."

Oh.

"Well." Try as he might, Hal couldn't come up with any further words. She'd found herself a new rich protector. Sensible. Easier for her, he assumed, and more profitable. Really, he ought to have expected such a thing. He had no claim on her. They had a business arrangement and a bit of a friendship. Nothing more.

Which didn't stop the news from smarting like a blow to the gut. He hadn't had enough time with her. They'd only barely begun to explore the fire between them.

"I'd be happy to continue assisting with your research, however," Callie said. "In whatever way I can."

Hal nodded. He took another sip of his soda, but he'd lost all pleasure in it. He forced himself to give Callie a smile. He wouldn't let himself be foolish about this. She'd been his first. Naturally that would foster an emotional attachment. It would pass.

"Thank you. That would be nice," he replied. "I'll let you know when the new version of the formula is ready."

Again, he looked out the window. The rain continued on, relentless. If it didn't stop, he'd hail a cab for Callie and then walk her bicycle home for her. Right now a good, long walk in the rain sounded just the thing.

Chapter 21
Back to Work

Callie gave up on the toast and the newspaper at the same time. She pushed the plate away and let the paper fall onto the table. The empty table. Valdez never stayed for breakfast, scurrying off to work at an hour Callie considered only barely tolerable.

Two weeks she'd been here. Valdez was friendly and smart, and the sex was pleasant, but it all felt like work. Most days she existed in a state of restless boredom. She'd done everything she could on her library project. Scanning ads in the paper for houses for sale only reminded her how much more money she needed. The idea of continuing on like this for months made her cringe, and she scolded herself for being so negative.

This wasn't bad. Just bland, like the toast she'd pushed aside.

Callie picked up the paper again. There it was: the perfect sort of house. The right size, and in a good neighborhood. Seven thousand dollars. Ouch. Perhaps a little bit smaller would serve her well enough if she made careful use of the space.

Her eyes tracked down the list of ads. Brush Park. Hal's neighborhood. Her gut tightened. Two weeks without a word. No letters, no messages, no telephone calls—not that she expected him to use a machine when pen and paper would suffice. Every day she checked in with the doorman at her apartment, but every day she came up empty. He was probably tired of her asking.

"Face the facts, Callie," she told herself. "He doesn't want your help. He's done with you."

Saying it aloud didn't make it hurt any less. Which was just as well, she supposed. It *should* hurt. She'd completely bungled the situation. In all honesty, she probably should never have gotten involved with him. She'd been too easily swayed by her own desires.

When she had given in, she ought to have made it clear how temporary any association would have to be. She'd brought everything else out into the open, yet for some reason she'd neglected that. And then she'd hurt his feelings. Their parting had been awkward and uncomfortable instead of warm and affectionate, the way it should have been.

That day, Callie had cursed herself the entire way home for the foolish, hurtful mistake. She'd been too eager to become friends, as if she and Hal had a long-term arrangement instead of a single night between them.

Not that her current long-term arrangement was faring any better. And she had another half-year of this at least, if she wanted to earn the thousands she needed. Ugh. Hopefully Valdez wasn't as disillusioned with the relationship as she was.

Callie folded the newspaper and set it aside for good. No more moping. This wasn't helping anything. Maybe she would swing by the bookseller and begin placing orders for the volumes she would need for her library. She could fill her apartment with boxes of books and have them on hand the moment she secured a location. The money for inventory was already in the bank, aside from Hal's hundred dollars stashed in a drawer with her underthings.

She'd barely risen from her seat when a servant in a smartly tailored uniform strode into the room, carrying a silver platter with a piece of paper atop it.

"A letter for you, miss."

Callie reached for the note, her heart jolting. She recognized that careful penmanship. "Thank you," she replied, trying to calm her sudden burst of nerves. If Hal had written her, it was probably only to inform her that he no longer had need of her assistance. He'd put whatever was between them behind him, and this letter would confirm that. It was time for her to stop fretting and get on with her work.

The moment the servant turned away, she tore into the note, scanning the message quickly, then slowing to read it once more from the top.

Dear Miss Finch,

I trust this letter finds you well. I am writing to inform you that a new version of the formula is finished and ready to be tested. I would like to invite you to come by the laboratory this afternoon at one o'clock, if you are still interested in assisting with the experiments. If you are otherwise engaged, I fully understand. No need to reply unless you wish to schedule a different time or date.

Sincerely,
Dr. H. Jekyll

Relief flooded her body. He didn't hate her. And he still wanted her help.

Callie carefully folded the letter and tucked it into her bodice. This afternoon! She bounced on the balls of her feet, resisting the urge to twirl. Good heavens, what was wrong with her? Giddy was not a typical emotion for her.

It's relief from the guilt, that's all.

And perhaps relief from boredom as well. Callie had never been good at being idle. As a mistress, she only needed to keep a man's bed warm and look good on his arm, but she'd never used that as an excuse to while away her days doing nothing. She'd always gone places on her own, read enormous numbers of books, and plotted her future career path. She'd vowed on her seventeenth birthday to open her library within a decade. Studying and planning toward that end had kept her plenty busy.

Now Hal's project provided a means to remain occupied during this waiting period. Naturally, that would make her happy. And having a chance to atone for her prior behavior made it all the better. Apparently, that equalled giddy.

Callie changed into a simple dress suitable for scientific pursuits, then headed out to the bookseller, where she ordered one hundred dollars worth of science books for the library collection. Jekyll would be pleased. She bought lunch from a street vendor, then walked all the way to Hal's house, hoping the exercise would settle her restless body.

The giddiness persisted.

The lawn in front of Hal's house still bore marks where the crashed car had dug into the sod. The twisted sections of fence had been cleared away, leaving a large gap. She strode through, cut across to the front door of the laboratory building, and knocked.

Nervous excitement raced through her veins. Even after the long walk, she was still bouncing, still unable to quash whatever strange energy Hal's letter had unleashed.

After a few anxious moments, the door swung open. Hal stood just inside the entryway, looking as handsome as Callie had ever seen. His black hair had been recently trimmed, and was fixed in place with a pomade that gave it a glossy, but not oily appearance. The gray herringbone tweed suit he wore was well-tailored and neatly pressed. His eyeglasses poked from a vest pocket, leaving Callie with a perfect view of his soft, golden-brown eyes.

"Calliope." Her name on his lips was breathy, sensual, and her body tingled in response. "You came." He cleared his throat and stepped back, motioning for her to enter. "I'm so glad. Won't you come in?"

Callie stepped into the house and followed Hal to his work area in the corner of the large, empty room. This was the sort of renovation she would need for her library: one large room where she could arrange rows of shelves. A service counter in the corner. Smaller reading rooms upstairs.

More money needed on top of the cost of the property. She sighed.

"I'm sorry to have taken so long," Hal said. He shifted as he spoke, his gaze roving up and down her figure until he caught himself and focused on her face. "I've been distracted. First that crash, and then other troubles. Twice I tried to put up a temporary fence to fill the gap, and both times it was knocked down."

"I'm so sorry. Is it the culprit who caused the crash in the first place, do you think? Have you learned anything more about who might have done it?"

Hal shook his head. "I don't think these troubles are aimed at me, specifically. Strange things have happened throughout the neighborhood. Noises and disruptions in the night, talk of thefts, minor destruction of property. Reports are attributing it to drunkenness."

"What?" Callie's brow furrowed. "Drunken antics in a

quiet neighborhood with no saloons nearby? That sounds like nonsense."

"Agreed. I wonder if the owner of the paper is a temperance man, twisting stories to suit his purposes. I believe it's more likely to be restless youngsters feeling the need to be rebellious. Regardless, it's slowed my progress, and I apologize for that. I suppose I ought to have written with an explanation before now, but I didn't want to intrude."

"Nonsense. It wouldn't have been an intrusion at all. I was very pleased to receive your letter this morning."

Hal's answering smile made her belly flip flop, but Callie kept her expression serene, wrestling for control of the excitement that still hummed inside her. Her undiminished attraction to Hal had added more fuel to that particular fire, but she wouldn't let it control her. She was a professional.

"Well." He waved a hand over his worktable. "I did manage to complete the new formula despite everything, and here it is. Let me show you my notes."

At the same moment he reached for the papers, the window beyond the table shattered in an explosion of glass. Callie's mouth opened in a scream, her hands raising to shield her face from the oncoming projectile.

It never struck her. Hal's arm shot out, catching her around the waist, spinning her out of harm's way and into his solid chest.

"It's all right." His arms tightened around her. "I've got you."

Chapter 22
Sworn Defender

"I've got you."

Hal cradled Callie against his chest, keeping his body between her and the window. His pulse pounded in his ears. In the split second when that rock had come hurtling toward her, he'd sworn his heart had stopped in terror. He'd reacted instinctively, yanking her into the safety of his embrace without a thought in his mind. Even now, as his brain began to process everything, that primal need still thrummed through him.

Protect. Defend. Hold. Mine.

His gaze flicked to the rock lying on the floor amid fragments of broken glass.

"It was just a rock," he murmured, not certain how his tense body produced the soothing voice. "You're safe now."

Only then did he realize he was stroking her hair as he talked. Too intimate for the scientific friendship they were supposed to maintain, but he didn't care. In this moment, she was his to protect, and he would fight anyone who threatened her.

Callie looked up at him, her gray eyes soft and wide with worry. "Hal. I think someone means you harm."

"Nonsense. It was just some hooligan making trouble. Taking advantage of the hole in the fence to get close. I'll request a prompt repair so it won't happen again."

Her fingers clenched on his lapel. “No. You’ll notify the police. Ask for an investigation. This isn’t right. I don’t want to see you hurt.”

He pressed a kiss to her brow, his heart warmed by her concern. “I’m fine. We’re safe. I’ll protect you.”

“Hal…” Their eyes locked and they both froze. Her grip on his coat relaxed, and she melted against him. Lips painted a soft red tilted up at him, begging to be kissed.

How could he refuse? She was his queen, and he her sworn knight. He was hers to command. He lowered his mouth over hers.

Callie tore herself away just before their lips collided. “No. I can’t.”

Hal cursed and took a step backward, his hands falling away from her. His metaphor was too apt. He was the Lancelot to her Guinevere, and someone else was her Arthur. Surrendering would only lead to tragedy.

“I’m so sorry,” she said. “Marc is the sort of man who desires exclusivity, and I won’t hurt him with disloyalty.”

Hal squared his shoulders. Dammit, he was putting her plans at risk with his silly, lustful fantasies. “No, no, *I’m* sorry. I ought to have released you the moment you were out of danger. I would never want to interfere with your business.”

“Don’t apologize. I should be the one to apologize. I completely failed to explain the situation before we became intimate, and I’m certain I hurt your feelings, and now here I am, rejecting you again. Truly, I would love to kiss you, but I’m committed to my current arrangement.”

“Of course. For your library project.”

“Exactly. I estimate needing between eight and ten thousand dollars more to fund it.”

Hal cocked his head to one side. “Hmm. Why engage

in a long-term affair? At one hundred dollars a night, you could earn the money you need in just over three months."

Callie laughed. "It doesn't work quite like that. Every night isn't practical, for one thing. Then there's the limited number of men willing and able to pay that price. The number narrows further when you cross that with men whose offers I would be willing to accept. I have the luxury of choice and I employ it liberally. A long-term agreement gives me money to spend, plus gifts such as clothing, jewelry, and other saleable items. A single lover also provides far better protection against disease. It is the prudent choice in many respects."

"I suppose that does make sense." Hal suppressed a sigh. One night with her hadn't been enough. It would be a struggle for him to remember they were only scientific collaborators. But he'd manage. He wouldn't allow himself to stand in the way of her goals.

"Unless you happen to have enough to pay for, oh, say sixteen or seventeen nights a month?"

She said it jokingly, but Hal's mind immediately went to his carefully crafted budget. Impossible. He couldn't pull seventeen hundred dollars out of nowhere. Between the low-risk investments necessary to maintain his current standard of living, daily necessities, his mother's travel expenses, the salaries of his household employees, upkeep on the property, and funding for his scientific pursuits, little remained for frivolous purchases. A few hundred dollars each month, which he usually spent on books or added to his research budget.

"No. I don't." Hal turned back to his worktable. "Here. I'd said I would tell you about my work. Let's not let all this…" He waved a hand at the broken window. "Ruin that."

His change of subject was none too subtle, but what

other choice did he have? He was far too infatuated with her, and that could only detract from both his work and hers. He would handle it the way he handled everything: by behaving with the utmost decorum and restraint.

"I completely reworked the formula this time," Hal informed Callie, pointing at the notebook he'd left open on the table for her perusal. "Many of the same ingredients, but not all." He picked up the glass jug full of the elixir and held it up to the light. "Unfortunately, it looks like muddy water now."

"Repulsive," Callie agreed.

"I'm hoping the taste won't match the looks. But if it does, well, sometimes one must sacrifice for science."

Eddie squeaked in his cage. Hal poked a leftover bit of sandwich between the bars. Eddie pounced on it happily. At least there was one creature here who wouldn't need to sacrifice for science anymore.

"And you're certain this version will be more effective than the last?" Callie inquired.

The skepticism in her voice hurt, but Hal turned to face her, maintaining his detached scientist tone. "Not certain, but confident. I'd like to test it, and I believe that is best done in the presence of a trusted companion."

"Only one of us drinks at a time, while the other is fully sober and carries the antidote."

Hal nodded. "I will, naturally, test it several times myself before allowing you to sample it. I'd not have you come to harm if anything about the elixir is amiss."

Her eyes narrowed slightly, but she returned his nod. "Very well."

"Then the next course of action is to select an appropriate time and location for the test. Have you any plans for this evening or tomorrow?"

"Dinner tonight, and tomorrow Marc is taking me to a party."

"Perfect." Hal set the jug of elixir back on the workbench. "A swallow or two of this potion and I'll be happy to crash the party."

"No." Callie's response was so sudden and firm that Hal flinched.

"No?"

"You *cannot* crash the party. It's an extremely exclusive event at the Yacht Club and attendance will be strictly enforced. In truth, I shouldn't even be going. It should only be members and their wives. If you sneak in, you'll be arrested. It's impossible. We'll pick another time."

"When?"

She sighed. "I don't know. I'll think of something and send you a message. In the meantime, I want you to report this attack." She jabbed a finger at the rock on the floor.

"It wasn't an attack. It was random destruction."

Callie put her hands on her hips. "Hal. Report it, fix your fence, and *be careful.* Those are the terms and conditions of my assistance during your experiments."

"Fine, fine." It couldn't hurt to report the incident, and it would give her some peace of mind.

"Thank you. I'll pick a social event that will be safe for a first test and we can convene again in a few days. Do you need assistance cleaning up this mess?"

"No." Sweeping up the glass would keep him occupied for a time. Hopefully by the time he finished, Callie would be far enough away that he wouldn't feel tempted to follow her and offer to buy her ice cream or something equally foolish. "Thank you, though."

"I'll be on my way, then." Her gaze lingered a bit on

the scattered glass shards. "Our next meeting will go more smoothly," she declared, as if her firm tone could make it so.

Hal swallowed and nodded. Nothing with her would go smoothly until his unruly libido settled. He could only pray it wouldn't take too much longer.

He walked her all the way to the street, raising a hand in farewell as she headed off toward the nearest trolley stop. When he turned back to reenter his laboratory, he spied something sitting on the front porch of his house.

Hal jogged over to examine the surprise package. Two more bottles of Becher's tonic water. He rolled his eyes. Why couldn't the rock-throwing miscreants have smashed *those* instead?

Chapter 23
Willful Disobedience

Hal dropped the pen on the desk and pushed up out of his seat. No. He couldn't send a note. That was much too forward. She'd said she'd write. He only needed to wait.

He paced the open space of his laboratory, not allowing himself to look back at the desk. It hadn't even been two days. Tonight she was going to that party.

The party of the summer, it seemed. "All of Detroit's most celebrated names," would be there, according to the paper. The article had then gone on to gush about the menu and the imported French wines and how wildly expensive the entire evening would be. It had promised an update in the morning paper about what everyone was wearing. This was why Hal didn't usually read the society pages.

He whirled back toward the worktable. He needed to test the elixir. It sat there, mocking him. Yesterday he'd overseen the installation of a new section of fence. Today he'd done nothing. Not a single damn thing. He couldn't move forward on this project without testing the elixir, and he couldn't test it until Callie wrote to him with a date and time.

Hal stared at the bottle. Maybe he could at least fill up a few vials in preparation for the test. Better than pacing. He marched over to the worktable and began pouring.

One, two, three. That would do for now. He set the first

vial safely into a cushioned box, then did the same with the second. The third he held up to the light, contemplating the milky swirls in the light-brown liquid. He popped off the cork and sniffed it.

Not bad. The scent reminded him a bit of cinnamon, conjuring up pleasant memories of the apple pies his mother always made for his birthday. They'd had a cook for as long as he could remember, but his mother enjoyed baking sweets and her pies were a wonder. She'd be back in the fall to give Hal his usual birthday treat before starting off on the next leg of her grand tour of the country.

Hal closed his eyes and inhaled again. Yes, cinnamon and a bit of nutmeg, though he'd used neither of those things among his ingredients. Maybe this formula would taste good, too.

He paused and glanced around the lab. It couldn't hurt to take a small taste and record his reactions. He didn't have to go anywhere. Just a sip here, safely in the lab. He'd take some notes, accomplish something, and then not feel so frustrated about waiting. He lifted the vial and let a trickle flow past his lips.

Ooh. Well. That did taste rather nice this time. A slight bitter aftertaste, perhaps, but far superior to the original version. He smiled down at the vial in his hand. If the effects were improved even half as much as the taste, he would consider it a significant victory.

"And why not drink the rest of this dose?" he mused. "It's not as though it'll matter to anyone, and I'll get much better feedback if I've taken it all. Callie won't mind. I'll just stay here and have something to report to her."

Hal gulped the remainder of the vial and dropped the empty bottle onto the table. The bitter aftertaste was stronger now, but it was nothing compared to the rush of euphoria as the liquid settled in his stomach. All tension leached from his muscles. He felt energized, awakened, alive.

He glanced around the barren room. What a worthless place to spend his evening. This wouldn't do. He needed food, drink, merriment. Callie's party.

You'll be arrested, she'd said.

Hah! Fuck those snooty high-society bastards. They thought he wasn't good enough for them? Too damn bad.

Hal hurried into his house and up the stairs to his bedroom, where he dug his formalwear out of the very back of his wardrobe. A quick change later, he surveyed himself in the mirror. Not bad. The spectacles still marked him as unfashionable, but he wasn't going to go without his enhanced low-light vision. Not when stealth was called for. He adjusted his tie, smoothed out his lapels, and nodded. It would do.

He bounded down the steps, grinning. This would be fun. He'd surprise Callie, sweep her into his arms for a kiss, and maybe swipe some of that oh-so-fancy French wine.

Hal locked the house behind him and retrieved his bicycle from the carriage house. His tailcoat and matching trousers weren't especially suited for riding, but Belle Isle was much too far to walk, and hailing a cab was out of the question. Arriving in a horse-drawn carriage would attract unnecessary attention, and he had no intention of risking his life in one of those infernal steam cars.

The weather was clear, the evening a pleasant temperature, and Hal fully enjoyed his ride through the city. The contrast of his attire with his mode of transportation did attract a number of looks, but he only smirked in return. Defying expectations was fun. The few people who shouted at him were graced with the sight of his extended middle finger.

The party was well underway by the time Hal arrived. Despite its exclusivity, the event was too large and lavish for the small Yacht Club clubhouse. The Belle Isle casino building housed the affair instead, and private steam carriages lined the road leading to the three-story wooden structure.

Hal leaned his bicycle against a tree and approached carefully, using the steam cars to shield himself from view. A pair of porters flanked the main doors, ready to turn away any uninvited guests. In a large public building like this, however, entrances abounded, and not all of them would be guarded.

His gaze settled on the second floor balcony. The wide, gently-sloping roof beneath provided easy access. All he needed to do was shimmy up one of the many veranda columns or climb a well-placed tree.

After a circumspect circuit of the building, Hal chose the rounded corner porch, where he could step up on the railing and easily grasp the gutters above. A jump and a bit of pulling, and he wriggled up onto the roof. A quick scramble later, he stepped onto the balcony and sauntered through the open doors into the party. Easy. Now to find Callie.

Hal roamed the building as if he belonged there, keeping his stride purposeful and not engaging with the other guests. It wouldn't do to be thrown out before he'd had a chance for some fun.

A long table bedecked with an array of hors d'oeuvres made him pause. He piled a plate high with goodies, including the only remaining chocolate biscuits. The silver here was real, and shined to a perfect gloss, and he slipped half-a-dozen pretty teaspoons into his jacket when no one was looking. Chuckling to himself, he wandered down to the ground floor.

An increase in general clamor made Hal suspect he had reached the heart of the party. Sure enough, when he passed through the next door he found a large room packed with people. Busy bartenders popped corks and poured glass after glass of wine. Hal munched on a biscuit as he passed a refreshment table more depleted than the one upstairs.

"How's the food?" a voice asked.

Hal turned and quickly swallowed. The man who had spoken looked vaguely familiar, in that way of famous people who have had their photos printed in the newspapers.

"Tasty," Hal replied. "Which it had better be for the price, eh?"

The man chuckled. "True!" A crinkle appeared above his nose. "Have we met before? You don't seem familiar and I thought I'd been introduced to all the newer members."

"Oh, I'm not a member," Hal replied breezily. "I'm here with Marc Valdez."

"Ah, of course. He'd mentioned he was bringing a guest or two." The man looked around. "Where did he get to? He ought to have introduced us."

Hal smirked. "He might not want to do that. I'm really only here to steal his mistress."

The man laughed uproariously and slapped Hal on the back hard enough that he almost spilled his food. "You're a wit, aren't you, boy? And I admit, she is a pretty thing. Good luck with that." He waved a hand at another guest. "Gerald! How are you tonight?" He murmured a hasty goodbye and took himself off to chat with his friend.

Hal wandered further into the party, a broad grin plastered to his face. He'd successfully infiltrated this rich men's retreat. Better yet, Callie was somewhere nearby. He meandered through the crowd, scanning faces, lingering on every brightly-colored dress.

There!

No wonder it had taken him a bit of searching to find her. Her dress wasn't especially bright tonight. It was a lavender color, with bits of darker trim. And the neckline was disappointingly high. Much too prim for his brazen and beautiful Calliope. He marched toward her, contemplating his next move.

Announce himself loudly? Pull her into his arms and kiss her in front of everyone? Whisper in her ear and sneak her away for an illicit rendezvous?

Before he could decide, she caught sight of him. Her mouth dropped open, her gray eyes grew wide in shock, and her arm jerked so forcefully that the champagne she was holding sloshed from her glass, splattering on the floor at her feet.

Hal jogged to her side. "Calliope. As always, you are a vision of loveliness."

Her startled look hadn't changed. Her jaw worked up and down for several seconds before she finally blurted, "You! You..." Slowly, Callie's expression morphed from shock to anger. "Are in so much trouble."

Chapter 24
An Uneasy Compromise

Callie wanted to rage. Wanted to grab Hal by the coat and shake him and shout, "What are you doing here?" Especially with the way he stood there oh-so-calmly grinning like the fool he obviously was. Didn't he care that this was dangerous? That he could ruin his reputation and his career?

She took a long, slow breath, summoning every ounce of self-control she possessed. This needed to be handled calmly. Rationally. Anything that drew attention to his presence would only make the situation worse. She would get him out of here, send him home, and that would be the end of it.

"Callie, is something wrong?" Valdez asked, stepping up and lightly touching her arm.

Callie glanced down at the puddle of champagne on the floor. "I was only startled. No harm done." She turned to offer him her mostly empty glass. If she could send him off on an errand, she could seize a moment to talk to Hal. And hopefully drag him to the nearest exit. "Do you think—"

"Dr. Jekyll!" Valdez exclaimed at the same time, extending a hand to Hal. "What a pleasant surprise! I didn't realize you moved in these circles."

"I don't," Hal replied.

"Ah. First time guest? Nice to see some people value good sense over the almighty dollar when choosing friends."

Callie's jaw clenched. Hal had lost any claim to good sense the moment he'd made up his mind to come here.

"I'm glad you're here," Marc went on. "I'd been wanting to thank you for that speech you made a few weeks back at Pike's dinner. Your explanation for why you couldn't join the temperance union? It really made me think. I did some reading up on the matter, and I have to say, I absolutely agree with you. With all the smuggling that already occurs here at the border, I really can't condone anything likely to increase it. Especially when we have other, more pressing problems. I've decided to put my money toward fixing other social ills, such as poverty, poor working conditions, and the like. The very things that often drive people to drink in the first place. We need to raise people up, not heap more rules upon them. Apologies if I'm carrying on, but you were the one who led me to this path, and I've been wanting to thank you for it. Much better to do it in person, I think, than in a letter."

Hal stared at Valdez, his lips pinched into a thin line. "You agree with me." He sounded not quite doubtful, but perhaps puzzled.

"I do. In fact, I'd be delighted if you would join me for lunch sometime this week. We can discuss ways to improve our city. I understand you're conducting scientific research that might be relevant."

Hal's mouth curved into a self-satisfied smirk. "I'm in the middle of an experiment right now, in fact."

"Are you? Is that why you're here? Studying social behavior? I'd love to hear about it."

The smirk grew. Hal's gaze darted to Callie, then back to Valdez. "Are you sure about that?"

Callie seized Hal's arm before he could say anything

terrible and cause a scene. "Marc, if you could excuse us a moment? Perhaps fetch me a refill?" She handed him the empty champagne glass. "My friend and I need to clarify a few things about this particular experiment. We'll be right back."

She gave Valdez a bright smile and pushed Hal toward the nearest doorway, tightening her grip in case he tried to flee. To her vast relief, he came willingly, and a short while later they stepped out onto the mostly empty porch.

"Ow." Hal rubbed his arm where her hand had been clenched a moment before. "Why the ferocity, darling? Afraid some other woman will lure me away? Don't worry. I came here all for you." He leaned toward her and she ducked away.

"Oh, no. You're not distracting me with your flatteries." She placed both hands on her hips. "What do you think you're doing here?" she hissed.

Hal selected a bite of food from the plate he was still holding and popped it in his mouth. He chewed slowly, giving her anger plenty of time to simmer before he replied, "Testing the new elixir, obviously."

"You promised not to do that."

He snorted. "*Jekyll* promised that. He's a bore, remember? But Harry Hyde isn't afraid to go get what he wants." He eyed her from head to toe. "That's a lovely dress, but you look like you ought to be in church. I can't see your luscious breasts at all."

"This is a respectable event and calls for modest dress."

Hal rolled his eyes. "It's a gathering of hypocrites. Half the married men in there have mistresses, and I'd wager many of the wives are equally unfaithful."

"I don't care what these people do," Callie snapped. She

took a step closer, glaring up at him. "This is about you. You drank that potion."

"He thought he could get away with a tiny sip." Hal laughed. "But one taste and he gulped it all down. Have to thank him for that. Now I've come to steal you away. And have a bit of fun at the expense of the needlessly wealthy."

"You need to leave. Right now."

"No."

Callie swallowed back a retort as another couple strolled out onto the porch. She adopted an easy smile until they had passed safely out of earshot. Her stomach tightened. At any moment someone could come along and identify Hal as a trespasser. Concern for him rushed in to fill the place her anger had been. Concern for what this new brand of elixir might be doing to him, and the consequences he might face as a result.

"Hal," she began, her tone much softer now. "You *must* leave." She placed a hand against his chest, jerking when her palm encountered several hard ridges beneath his jacket. "What is that?"

After a quick glance to be sure no one was watching, she slipped a hand into his jacket, her fingers finding smooth metal protruding from the inside pocket. She pulled the object out and frowned at it.

"A spoon?"

"Indeed. Please, keep looking. There are more. Shall I put them in harder to reach locations? You may undress me as much as you like."

Callie held the spoon up in front of his face. "You're stealing silver?"

He shrugged and ate another hors d'oeuvre. The maddening fool! Didn't he care at all about any of this?

Her fingers clenched. No. He didn't care. Something

about this new elixir had made him reckless and indifferent. Reasoning with him might be impossible. But she had to try before he found himself in deep trouble.

"Why on earth would you steal spoons?" she whispered.

"Because I could. It was fun, being bad. Funny."

"No, it's not."

Hal pouted. "Oh, Callie, don't be a spoilsport. Here, try a chocolate biscuit. It's the last one." He held the sweet up to her lips.

"No, thank you."

"Then I'll eat it and you can taste it when I kiss you."

She took a step backward. "No kissing. You know that."

"Hmph. As if I care what Valdez thinks? I'm stealing you from him whether he likes it or not."

"And what about whether *I* like it? What about what *I* think? Don't you care about me at all?"

Hal flinched. He hesitated a long moment before replying, "You like me. You want to kiss me."

"I still said no."

He didn't reply. His brash confidence was gone, leaving him with a slumped posture and stricken expression. He was still in there, somewhere. She could reach a small part of the real Hal.

"It's time to leave," Callie said gently. "You should take the antidote."

"I didn't bring the antidote," he scoffed.

No, of course not. Bad Boy Hyde wouldn't want anyone ruining his fun.

"Is there anything I can do to convince you to leave?" she asked.

Hal sidled closer. "You could go with me."

"I can't do that. I came here with Marc. I'm obligated

to honor that commitment, and I also can't make a scene by leaving with another man."

"Then I guess I'm staying." He turned toward the door. "Where's the champagne? I need a drink."

"Hal." Callie grabbed his arm again, though not as tightly as before. "I'll allow you to stay if you listen to me. Do this for me. I know you don't want to hurt me."

He didn't turn to look at her, but he stood completely still and silent.

"Do as I say and remain where I can see you, and you can stay with me." She made the words soothing, affectionate. "But if you cause trouble," she added sternly, "or do anything to endanger anyone, I will shove you out the door myself. Do you understand?"

"Oh, fine," he mumbled. "I suppose you want me to put all the spoons back, too."

"I don't care about the spoons. Just relax. Have a drink. Act normal."

He whirled around, launching a piece of shrimp from his plate in the process. "Normal is Jekyll. Normal is boring. Nobody likes normal."

A pang of sadness gripped Callie's heart. That wasn't only the elixir talking. That was something deeper, and it filled her with sorrow to think he would ever consider himself unlikeable.

"You're not boring, Hal," she said firmly.

"Of course not. That's *him*." He turned away again. "Let's go get that drink."

Callie followed, unwilling to let him venture too far from her side. "You are *not* boring," she whispered to the man beneath the potion.

Chapter 25
Playing Nanny

A naughty child. That's what Hal reminded her of. Callie watched him out of the corner of her eye as she stood next to Marc and nodded at something one of his friends was saying.

Since they'd reentered the party, Hal had sprayed red wine all over the back of a woman's white dress, left a coffee urn slowly trickling onto the table, and eaten so many desserts Callie wondered how his stomach wasn't aching. Trying to keep him from mischief while socializing with Marc and the other guests had been impossible. Miraculously, no one had yet realized Hal didn't belong here.

She had to admit he looked like he belonged. He cut a fine figure in his perfectly tailored tailcoat. His handsome face and the roguish smile he'd worn all evening charmed the other guests. A short time ago, a Yacht Club member had engaged him in conversation, greeting him as if they were already acquainted. They'd been talking ever since, and despite the unyielding tension in Callie's muscles, the chat looked to be going smoothly. Hal's companion laughed often and was drinking enough he probably wouldn't notice any small slipup.

"That man has the devil's own luck tonight," Callie mumbled.

"What's that, dear?" Marc asked.

Callie replied with a small shake of the head. Her mouth was beginning to hurt from all the fake smiling.

Relax, she told herself. *Everything will be fine.*

Right now Hal was occupied and not causing trouble. She could wait this out. At the next lull in her own conversation—if she could even be said to be a participant—she would excuse herself and make another attempt to convince him to leave the party.

The later the hour, the more likely he would be to comply. The elixir would wear off as time passed, and given his juvenile behavior under its influence, he was likely to grow bored with the party eventually.

The self-propelled drink cart wheeled by, its mechanical arms reaching out to collect empty glasses. Callie handed it her champagne flute, but declined to take another from the tray atop the machine. She'd had enough to drink for one night. With Hal in an unpredictable state, she wouldn't risk becoming inebriated. The machine stashed her empty glass in its belly and trundled on.

"Hey, over here! I need a refill!" called the man chatting with Hal.

At the word "refill," the machine beeped and veered to honor the request. Hal's eyes widened and he shied away as the drink cart approached.

Callie instinctively took a step toward him. He'd made no secret of his dislike of machines. With the elixir affecting him, had that grown into a phobia?

One of the drink cart's claw arms stretched out, reaching for the empty glass Hal held clutched in his hand. He waved at the machine with his opposite hand.

"Shoo. I don't need your help."

The cart rolled closer.

"Stop. Go away." Hal gave the machine a small shove, probably only intended to change its course, but the cart wasn't as stable as it appeared. It wobbled, teetered, then toppled, sending glassware and liquor flying.

Callie was running before the shuddering crash of the machine hitting the floor reached her ears. The buzz of voices staggered to a halt. Eyes everywhere turned toward the noise. Toward Hal, mischief maker and interloper.

"I didn't mean to!" he protested, sounding every bit the petulant child.

Callie grabbed hold of his arm, as she'd done so many times tonight. "Hal, quickly, you must leave." The front entrance was too far. They'd never get out without being forced to field questions. She spun him around and headed for the porch.

The moment they were outside, she gestured at the rail. "Climb over. Quickly. Before anyone comes asking questions. Go home."

He stared at her, blinking, making no move to obey. "You're worried," he said at last. The same stricken expression from earlier that night came over his face. The one he'd worn when she'd sensed she reached the Hal beneath the potion. "I'm ruining things. Ruining your night. Ruining your plans."

Without another word, he vaulted over the rail and raced off into the night. Callie stared after him. The cool night air raised goosebumps on her arms, but she didn't turn away until she could no longer make out his shape in the shadows.

"Callie?" Marc stepped into the doorway.

She hurried to his side. "I'm so sorry. I didn't mean to run off like that. Hal wasn't quite himself tonight. I've been trying to assist with his experiments and I was concerned for him, especially after that machine toppled, and…" She trailed off. Babbling wouldn't help anything. "He's gone home now. Everything should be fine now." She glanced through the door and looped her arm through Marc's. "Shall we head back inside?"

Valdez covered Callie's hand with his own, giving her fingers a squeeze before letting go and turning to look her in the eye.

"Callie. You don't have to do this."

Her gut twisted. "Do what?"

"I completely understand that you feel the need to honor our arrangement. I like you, and I enjoy your company, but I won't hold you to any commitment. You don't need to be here tonight, and you don't need to be with me at all. You only had to ask, and I would have released you from any agreement we had made."

She could see her plans crumbling, the precarious tower of books she'd built toppling to the ground.

"No," she gasped. "I didn't mean—" *Didn't mean what? Didn't mean to put someone else above you? Didn't mean to pretend more affection than I felt?* Her mouth wouldn't form the lies.

Marc shook his head. "Callie, I'm not hurt. And I don't want you to be either. That's why I won't hold you to anything. I can't be someone who comes between you and the man you love."

Callie's mouth dropped open. Every hair on her skin stood on end. And this time she couldn't blame the cold air.

Chapter 26
Talk of Shame

Hal lowered himself to one knee and mimed holding out a bouquet of flowers. “I most humbly beg your pardon,” he implored. Grimacing, he rose to his feet. “No, no. That looks too much like a proposal.” A shudder ran through him. He was plenty embarrassed already. No need to do something likely to make Callie laugh in his face.

Hal held out the invisible bouquet again, remaining standing. “This unworthy wretch most humbly begs your—” He jerked and flailed when a head poked through the doorway. If he’d been holding real flowers, they would now be scattered across the floor.

“Hal?” a gentle voice queried.

“M-Mother?” He blinked several times as she strode into his laboratory. As usual, her gray hair was twisted into a perfect knot and her unembellished pastel gown hung elegantly on her slender frame. “I thought you weren’t due home for another month.”

“I’m not, dear, but I wanted to take Henrietta to Mackinac. And since that involved catching the train from Detroit, it seemed absurd to pass up the chance to stop in and hug my boy.”

Hal nodded and accepted the proffered embrace. He didn’t even cringe when she ruffled his hair.

"Now, what was all that carrying on you were doing in here a moment ago?" his mother asked. "Something about humbly begging? Are you courting a young lady? I hope so. You never did do well being alone. I know you have lovely friends, but you could use a permanent companion. Tell me all about her. It's not Miss Mahji, is it? I thought you two were only friends."

"I'm not courting anyone," Hal replied. This was a fitting punishment, he supposed, having additional embarrassment heaped atop his mortification over last night's behavior. "I was, er, contemplating possible apologies."

"Well, it sounded very heartfelt. What did you do to the lady?"

"What makes you think there is a lady involved?"

His mother waved a hand. "Oh, honestly, Hal. You were obviously speaking to a woman, and you sounded enamored of her. Tell me all about her."

She's a high-society courtesan with an interest in books and science. She rides a bicycle, loves ice cream sodas, intends to run her own library someday, and has a laugh like an angel. Oh, and I paid one hundred dollars for a night with her, and I'd do it again except that she has every right to hate me now.

"You're mistaken, Mother," Hal replied, trying his best to shove thoughts of Callie—especially thoughts of nights with Callie—aside. "It's an apology for a scientific experiment gone wrong. I made a terrible mess of things."

"But isn't that the way of science, dear? You make mistakes and then you learn from them?"

"Yes, I suppose it is."

He cast a glance at his worktable, where the jug of elixir sat. Maybe he needed to focus on the positive aspects of last night. The new formula clearly had improved upon the first one. He ought to be pleased by that. Maybe he would be if he could ever get past his own shameful behavior.

"Well, I'll leave you to it," his mother said. "I simply wanted to give you that hug and pass along this letter that arrived when I did." She slipped a piece of paper from her pocket and held it out. "I'm leaving again first thing in the morning, but I do hope we can have dinner together tonight."

"Of course." Hal took the letter, trying to still his trembling hand. Was it from Callie, announcing that she never wanted to see him again? Please, no. He needed to apologize in person. He'd never manage to convey the depths of his regret in writing. A new image joined his previous imaginings: him knocking on her door and begging just for the chance to begin an apology.

Hal's mother took a step toward the door. "I can see you have a lot on your mind right now. I'll see you at dinner and we can talk then. Don't fret too much, dear. I'm sure everything will be fine."

Fine. Yes, everything would be fine now that he'd completely lost his self-respect and was about to lose his friend and research partner. Just peachy.

Hal looked down at the letter. His nose wrinkled in puzzlement. The precise, square penmanship was nothing like Callie's hand. He broke the seal on the envelope and pulled out the paper inside. The note was brief and candid.

Jekyll,

I'm sorry we didn't have more of a chance to speak last night. I'd like to meet for lunch to discuss ideas for civic improvement and any ways your research might be of help. I am available at noon on either Tuesday or Wednesday.

-Valdez

Hal removed his spectacles, polished them with his handkerchief, then read the letter again. No, he wasn't hallucinating. Valdez still wanted to meet with him. Hadn't he noticed Hal's erratic and juvenile behavior? Or was this letter someone's idea of a joke?

A knock at the laboratory's front door caused Hal to whirl around. Now what? No one knocked at the lab door. Sighing, he crossed the room. He'd tell whoever it was to knock on the house door next time, and then go back to working on his apology. Maybe he needed to write it down on paper to get all his thoughts out before he practiced reciting it.

Hal yanked open the door, prepared to shoo away whatever salesman or neighbor awaited him. "I'm sorry, but—"

Callie.

His entire body froze. Heat crawled up his skin, his cheeks burning in a furious blush of shame. He'd been awful, and he had no excuse but his own lack of self-control.

"Miss Finch," he greeted her, summoning up his best polished manners. "I was not expecting you, but, please, come in." She stepped into the laboratory, and Hal closed and locked the door behind her. "Shall I send for tea or coffee?"

Callie regarded him in silence. She wore her cycling costume again today, with her skirt still tied up to reveal her bloomers and boots. Dark circles underneath her eyes suggested a lack of sleep, and her usually-smiling mouth curved the tiniest bit downward.

Jekyll, you goddamned bastard.

He'd done that to her. He'd broken his promise, ignored her warnings, and made a spectacle of himself in front of her friends. Why was she even here? To slap him across the face, perhaps.

Just when he thought the silence between them might linger forever, she asked, "How are you this morning? Has the elixir worn off? Are you fully yourself?"

"Yes, it's worn off," he replied. He turned away. "Miss Finch, I…"

No. Not like this. Already he was messing up again. Hal forced himself to turn back and look her in the eye. He wasn't prepared, but he would have to give it his best try.

"Miss Finch, I offer my sincerest apologies for my unpardonable behavior last night. I was a fool, a lout, and a cad, and I have no excuse."

"Why did you do it?" she asked, before he could continue. "Why drink the elixir?"

"I was frustrated and bored. And arrogant. I believed I could get away with a small sip. Now I know I was wrong. Please, do not feel obligated to continue working with me on this project. I have caused enough trouble for you."

The slight frown still marred her lovely features. Hal longed to wipe it away, replace it with the smile she deserved to always wear. Damn him to hell for being the one to put it there in the first place.

"You need to test the elixir, though," Callie said, her voice calm and sober. "And possibly future versions. You can't do that on your own. Not without putting yourself and your work at risk."

"I'm sure Victor or Nemo would watch me. I can make a swap to help with their projects." Except that both their projects involved machines. Hal suppressed a shudder. He could deal with that issue when the time came. "I will make do. You needn't worry. Please do not feel obligated to assist me further. I don't wish to burden you with my troubles.

Shall I walk you to the door? I'm sure you and Mr. Valdez have things to do this weekend."

She shifted her weight and her frown deepened. "I will no longer be seeing him."

"What?" Hal blurted, his control momentarily slipping. Another sin to pile on the growing heap. How could she even stand to look at him?

"We agreed that the relationship was not as beneficial to either of us as we had at first believed," Callie explained. Her gaze flicked slightly away. She was lying.

"But what about your library?"

"I'll make a new plan. It's only a minor setback."

Another lie. Hal's gut churned. This was his fault. He had to do something. He crossed the room to his desk in a few swift strides and opened the top drawer. Reaching in, he popped open the false back and withdrew a stack of banknotes.

"Here." He thrust the money in Callie's direction. "A donation. No obligations, no services requested. There should be one hundred fifty dollars there, or so. I will make arrangements to contribute additional funds once I have a chance to speak with my banker."

She made no move to take the money. "Hal, you don't have to do this."

"Yes. I do. This is my fault. I've ruined everything. Ruined our friendship, ruined your plans, probably ruined my experiment. I am one hundred percent at fault, and I must do something to help rectify that, even if it's only money, and even if it can only repair a small part of the damage."

Callie shook her head. "The split with Valdez isn't your fault. I… was unable to provide him as much affection as he deserved."

She shifted again, an unusually nervous movement for

someone normally so composed. Was it because she was lying? It was absolutely Hal's fault. He'd made a menace of himself and in doing so made her look bad.

Although, if he'd been so objectionable last night, why did Valdez still want to meet with him? Hal's nose wrinkled. The pieces didn't add up, but he couldn't find where his logic failed. He'd behaved badly and now Callie was out of a job.

"Cal—" No. He didn't deserve to address her so intimately. "Miss Finch. You are a kind and generous person, but I cannot allow you to excuse my role in this. Please, at least take the money. Buy books with it. Do some good for your ladies. I don't deserve your forgiveness, but I would like to atone in some small way."

She walked over to him and accepted the money, tucking it into an inside pocket of her jacket. "Thank you. I will put this to good use. I know you feel bad about last night, and you should, to an extent. You should never have sampled the potion on your own. But the things you did at the party? That wasn't you. It was different and strange. I know, because I saw glimpses of you breaking through it."

"That doesn't excuse what I did."

"No, it doesn't. But maybe it means you shouldn't be *quite* so hard on yourself."

Hal pinched the bridge of his nose. "I should have known you'd forgive me. You're too good. Much too good for me. What have I ever done for you except cause trouble?"

A bit of a smile crept over her face at last. "You make me laugh. You appreciate my books. You let me try new things." She waved a hand to indicate his laboratory. "You encourage my dreams. You treat me as a whole person and not just a whore."

Hal flinched.

"I'm not complaining," Callie went on. "I chose this

career path. I may be selective about my clients and my protectors, but I do make my living with my body. I'm not ashamed of that. But it does grow tiresome when people see me only as an object of physical gratification. You have never done that, and I appreciate it."

"I would never… Of course you are more than your job. No one is defined exclusively by their work. It would be ludicrous to think so. You have hobbies and passions and many interests. I like all those things about you. And I also like that you are sexually liberated. I…" He turned away, as a new and different wave of embarrassment washed over him.

"You what?"

Hal blew out a long breath. "I find it arousing," he admitted.

"Are you sure you don't want some services for those hundred and fifty dollars?" There was laughter in her voice, and Hal fought the urge to whirl around and kiss her.

"No, thank you. I can't understand why you'd even want to touch me after I caused a setback in your library plans."

"You didn't cause it." She paused. "Not directly, at least. It wasn't all about last night. I was never able to give Marc my full attention."

Slowly, Hal turned to face her. "Why not?"

Again, she fidgeted. Something was making her uncomfortable. *He* was making her uncomfortable.

"No, don't tell me. It's none of my business. Forget I—"

She flung her arms around his neck, stopping any protests with a ravenous kiss.

Chapter 27
Business as Usual

I couldn't stop thinking of you. I couldn't stop thinking of us. Of this.

Callie backed Hal up into the nearest wall, trapping him there with her body while she kissed him breathless. His jaw was freshly shaven, the skin smooth against her own. He smelled of soap and tasted of coffee. This was a man not long out of bed, and her body hungered to put him right back there.

She licked over his tongue and his lips, sliding into his mouth and then out again, leading him in a dance of pleasure. A prelude to the dance of twining, naked limbs.

This was foolish. It would only complicate an already unusual relationship. But she'd been yearning for him for weeks, and right now all she could think about was slaking her lust. She wanted to kiss the salt from his skin. She wanted his head between her thighs, tonguing her to glorious ecstasy. She wanted to ride him until he was shaking and moaning his own delirious pleasure.

Callie slid her hands down his chest, pushing his coat aside and working the buttons of his vest. Hal turned his head away and squirmed from her grasp.

"We can't. Not here."

She frowned at him through the fog of her desire. His

skin was pink, his lips reddened from their kisses. Behind his spectacles, his eyes gleamed, dark and full of desire.

"Why not?" They didn't need a bed. If he didn't like the floor, she could sit on his desk or they could brace themselves against the wall.

"My mother is here."

"Oh." Callie could think of no more to say. She'd never thought to ask about Hal's family. He always seemed such a solitary person, but naturally he would have other people in his life.

"She's here unexpectedly." Hal did up his buttons, then combed his fingers through his hair, mussing it more than Callie had done. "She could walk in at any time."

And proper Henry Jekyll would never want to be caught in flagrante delicto. Especially by his mother.

"Does she live nearby?" Callie asked, hoping the mundane conversation would help subdue her arousal.

"Technically she lives *here*," he explained. "My father died when I was very young and she was left to raise me alone. Now that I'm grown and self-sufficient, she is traveling the country with her 'particular friend' and living a grand life. She stopped in for a day's visit before continuing up north."

"Ah. I should probably leave, then."

A look of disappointment flashed across Hal's face. "Oh, no, you don't have to rush off. Er, unless you want to, of course. But I have no firm commitments until dinner. It's only that my mother could pop in at any time." He glanced at the passageway to the house next door, as if expecting to find her there. "We should, um, save any business of yours for another time."

That wasn't business, Callie wanted to say. Today she'd kissed him solely for her own pleasure. Which was a bit alarming, especially when combined with Marc's assertions last night.

It's only lust. Mingled a bit with friendship. I care for him. But that doesn't make it anything serious.

Still, the words echoed in her mind. *The man you love.*

No. She couldn't. This was a time to be rational. To think about her library and her future. Love wasn't something she could contemplate now. Whatever she was feeling, that wasn't it.

"I suppose we should discuss your business, then?" Callie suggested. There. That was her rational self. Cool and collected. No one hearing her would be able to guess that moments ago she'd had Hal flattened against the wall, tearing at his clothing.

He rubbed his nose, then removed his spectacles to wipe them clean.

"Yes, let's," Hal answered. His skin remained the tiniest bit flushed, but his voice was even and he strolled casually to his workbench. "I would like to make notes about my misbehavior last night." His mouth twisted in a momentary grimace.

"I want to discuss the procedure for future experiments," Callie insisted. "You are not to drink your elixir on your own again. Ever."

He leaned against the table. "Lord, Callie, I'm so sorry. I was awful last night."

She folded her arms across her chest. "I believe we already discussed this. If you wish to atone, the best way is to make a safe plan for the future and pledge to me on your honor that you will not deviate from it."

He nodded. "I can do that. You have some idea, I take it?"

"Yes. We take turns testing the elixir. Always together

for the entire duration of the experiment, and the sober person must have the antidote."

Hal's mouth tightened. "And what if I've drunk the elixir and I refuse to take the antidote? Thinking back on last night, I can't imagine I would have taken it at your bidding."

Callie tapped her finger against a bookshelf. "What if it was injectable? Do you have a syringe? Then, in the event of any emergency, the sober partner could jab the other with the syringe and administer the antidote."

"Good idea. And we should test the antidote before going out. I did adjust the formula based on the changes to the elixir, but we want to be certain. Especially given my, um, erratic behavior."

Callie gestured toward the desk. "Let's write all this down."

Hal pulled out the chair from the desk for her, then grabbed a stool from beneath the worktable to sit beside her.

"Callie's plan," he said, scribbling at the top of a blank notebook page. "Always together. Injectable antidote."

"Take turns," she added.

He wrote it down, but sighed. "I worry about endangering you."

"That's why we have the new protocol. Now, about last night. You write down your perspective on each part of the night, and then I'll add mine below."

Hal flipped a page and began to scribble. In minutes they had a whole page covered, falling into an easy back-and-forth as they rehashed every detail of the previous night's misadventures.

"Wait, you missed the incident where you sprayed wine on the back of Mrs. Roth's dress," Callie pointed out.

Hal tapped the back of his pen to his lips. "Mmm. That incident wasn't entirely selfish on my part, actually. I did it after I heard her make an insulting remark about a member of the waitstaff. The poor girl was doing her best. I decided the lady deserved what I gave her. Now, though, I'm worried that the dress may have been handed to some other underappreciated working girl who has to scrub out the mess."

"It's likely, I'm afraid."

Hal began to scribble again. "Never occurred to me at the time. I didn't think anything of cleanup at all, in fact. Or disposal of the gown. I just thought I'd made her look bad."

"Add 'shortsighted' to the list of effects, then."

He nodded and they continued on. By the time they'd covered all the night's events in detail, Callie's stomach was beginning to rumble. She consulted her pocket watch.

"Goodness! I've been here nearly two hours." She rose from her seat and Hal quickly did the same. "I should let you get on with the rest of your day, especially with your mother being here for a visit. No more experiments today, but perhaps tomorrow?"

"Tomorrow would be fine." He took a deep breath. "And, Callie, about that kiss. I *am* sorry I had to interrupt you, but I was also very serious about the money being a donation. You are under no obligation to provide me anything."

"It wasn't—" She paused at the sound of footsteps.

"Hal, dear." A tall, elegant woman with gold-brown eyes swept into the room, a bottle of tonic water in her hand. "Why do we have all these bottles—Oh! I didn't realize you had company." Her eyebrows lifted and a smile spread across her face. "You must introduce me to your friend."

Hal gave a stiff nod. "Of course. Mother, this is Miss Calliope Finch. Miss Finch is assisting me with some of my scientific research. Miss Finch, this is my mother, Mrs. Marjorie Jekyll."

Mrs. Jekyll glided across the room. "Such a pleasure,

Miss Finch. I love your cycling costume, and I'm so pleased to see my son has made a new friend. You must join us for dinner this evening."

"I wouldn't want to impose," Callie replied. She wracked her brain for an excuse, but could think of nothing. She had no plans.

"No need to fret, my dear. I've had dinner with all of Hal's friends at one time or another, haven't I?"

Hal's eyes had grown round with alarm. "Er..."

"It's settled," Mrs. Jekyll declared. "Bring Miss Finch to dinner, Henry. I want to get to know her." She waggled a finger at Hal. "See, I knew there was a young lady in your life. I'll leave you two to your conversation. Later on we can discuss why this is cluttering up Cook's cabinets." She plopped the bottle of tonic water on the worktable, then swished gracefully from the room.

Hal opened one of his cabinets, selected a bottle, and plunked it on the table beside the tonic water. It was the bottle of gin Callie had sent him, still mostly full.

"I need a drink," he declared. "How about you?"

Callie nodded. "Please."

Chapter 28
Motherly Love

Somehow, his life had turned into a farce. He was a character in someone else's play. That was the only explanation for how a man could end up sitting at the dinner table with his matchmaking mother and the woman he'd paid to take his virginity. He never should have gone to mock that temperance drama. This was surely his punishment.

"Is the wine not to your liking, dear?" his mother asked. "You've hardly touched your glass."

"It's fine. I'm not especially thirsty tonight." Hal took a small sip to make the lie more plausible. Drinking more was a terrible idea. He was already tipsy. Why had he ever thought it a good idea to mix up a whole jug of gin and tonic? He'd had a glass with Callie, walked her out to her bicycle, then headed straight back to the lab and poured himself another drink. And another.

He'd been drinking all day. Even now, he craved more. What the devil was wrong with him? He didn't do this.

Hal set down the wine glass and sawed off another bite of roast turkey. He didn't have much appetite, either. Eating was merely something to keep him occupied. A way to distract himself from the acute embarrassment he'd been wrestling with all day.

He'd hardly said anything during dinner, while Callie

and his mother had launched into an enthusiastic discussion on books. Usually such a conversation would hold his attention, even if he hadn't read the particular books mentioned. Tonight, he could only manage the occasional distracted nod, his mind too full of all the ways this gathering could go horribly wrong.

"I didn't find it all that scandalous," Callie said. Hal had missed what particular story they were discussing, but of course she didn't find it scandalous. She'd told him she read erotic books and she probably didn't find those scandalous, either. "I think, if anything, it was a realistic commentary on human nature. I can think of any number of people who wouldn't hesitate to live a life focused solely on their own pleasure if provided a magical portrait to suffer the consequences for them. In fact, plenty of people live such lives regardless of the consequences."

Hal's shoulders hunched. He wanted to sink into the floor and disappear. Of all the books in the world, naturally his mother had brought up one with a topic that was far too familiar right now.

Last night had been all about his own selfish pleasure. And self-pleasure, afterward, in his bed. Lying there, his cock in his hand as he remembered what it felt like to thrust deep into Callie's body.

Damn it all. Maybe he was more than tipsy, to be thinking lurid thoughts at the dinner table.

"So true, Miss Finch," Hal's mother replied. "People who think only of themselves can be found anywhere. Knowing that makes me value my friends all the more. And makes me grateful that Hal, too, has found friends who truly care for him."

"Well, I can see he cares a great deal for others in return." Callie reached quickly for her wine. Was she blushing?

Hal tore his gaze away before the women could notice he was staring, then glanced up at Callie as he took another bite. Spots of pink darkened her cheeks. Maybe it was only from the wine. Or the animated conversation. The unflappable Miss Finch didn't blush.

"Speaking of scandalous books," Hal's mother said, "have you read that book by the artist Mr. Whistler? *The Gentle Art of Making Enemies*, I believe it's called. So strange that an artist would sue a critic and then turn the whole public spectacle into a book."

"I haven't read it," Callie replied. "But it does seem that he's now more famous for the scandal than—"

An angry shout from outside interrupted her.

"Goodness!" Hal's mother exclaimed.

Another voice joined the first, then a third and possibly fourth person also began to yell, raising the noise to a furious clamor.

"More hooligans?" Callie asked, her tone suspicious.

"More?" Hal's mother echoed.

"I'll take a look." Hal rose from his seat. "Please excuse me."

He scurried into the front parlor, knowing the ladies would soon follow. Sure enough, the scrape of moving chairs and the rustle of skirts sounded from behind him.

Outside, the tinkle of shattering glass cut through the voices. Not his window, thank God. Hal could make out four figures in the twilight. They stood well beyond his fence, out in the street. The closest streetlamp had gone dark, whether by chance or foul play, he didn't know.

Callie pressed close beside him to peer out the window. "Looks like a fight," she observed. "More 'drunken shenanigans'?"

"Henry, what has been going on around here?" his mother demanded. "Is this connected to the new fence?"

Hal reluctantly turned away from the window. "I'm afraid so. We've had a rash of mischief-makers in the neighborhood. Our fence was broken, as well as a window. Others have suffered similar minor damage, and a few thefts."

"The papers blame excessive drinking," Callie added. "I think it's nonsense. The temperance leaders are practically dancing with glee. I would wager someone in that camp is responsible."

"Well!" Hal's mother exclaimed. "Regardless of the cause, you will not be returning home unescorted this evening, Miss Finch. Hal, you will see her safely all the way. I will subject no guest of ours to potential danger walking the streets alone at night."

"I agree," Hal replied. "I will be happy to see you home, Miss Finch." Callie was highly self-sufficient, and he doubted any of the men currently tussling in the street outside would pay her much attention, but he would never risk her safety. He quickly brushed aside his other reasons for wishing to see her home.

"I appreciate your thoughtful concern," Callie said, her smile giving no indication that she objected to the decision. Did she *want* him to come home with her, or was she only agreeing for his and his mother's peace of mind?

The trio returned to the dining room and resumed their meal, the conversation now more subdued. Hal participated even less than before. He managed to finish his food, despite the lack of appetite, but he abandoned the remainder of the wine. Even now, he was still craving another gin and tonic.

"It has truly been a pleasure meeting you, Miss Finch," his mother gushed when they prepared to leave at last. "I'm thrilled Hal has found another lovely friend, and I hope to see you here again in the future."

Hal's smile was so tight his jaw ached. His mother meant well, but her none-too-subtle implications had Hal wanting to bury his head in his hands and groan. He fought off the sensation with the knowledge that this was almost over. He'd made it through without embarrassing anyone and without jeopardizing Callie's plans for the future. Plans that in no way resembled his mother's fantasies of romantic courtship.

"Thank you for a wonderful evening," Callie replied. She reached for her wide-brimmed hat that hung on one of the wall pegs. "Shall we be off?"

Hal opened his mouth to reply, but at the same time, Callie grasped what looked like a decorative bauble on the hat and pulled. A six-inch-long blade slid free, the sleek metal glinting in the gaslight. Hal sprang back with a yelp.

"You have a knife?" he spluttered.

She laughed. "It's only a hatpin." Looking in the hall mirror, she positioned the hat on her head and skewered it in place with the pin.

"The hatpins I've seen before were all dainty little sticks. Yours could be a weapon. I thought you meant to do me in." He eyed the pin, now neatly concealed in the hat.

"Not *you*."

"A lady can never be too careful, can she," Hal's mother declared. "An excellent choice of accessory, Miss Finch. Pretty and useful. I knew you were a sensible girl. Have a good night. Hal, please escort her safely home."

He looked again at Callie's headgear. "Miss Finch might be the one escorting *me*."

"Nonsense, dear. You're a perfectly virile young man. Now out the door with you." She shooed Hal and Callie out, closing the door behind them.

Callie's laugh tinkled like a music box. "I like your mother."

"Did she really just call me a 'virile young man'?" Hal groaned. "I'll be over there, huddled in a ball, dying of mortification."

Callie gave him a playful nudge with her elbow. "Don't be silly. And you *are* virile. I have firsthand experience, remember?"

As if he could forget.

"My mother really doesn't need to know about that."

"Ah, but she probably suspects. Mothers always seem to know things. Mine does, at least. But, then, she also reads the gossip columns to discover who I've been linked with and then writes to ask after my intimate life." She adopted a sing-song voice. "Is he giving you enough orgasms, Calliope? Don't go faking it for his sake, or he'll never learn."

"Good God. You can't be serious."

"I am. But at least I know she cares. Oh, that looks like the trolley up ahead. If we hurry, we can catch it." She lifted her skirts and Hal jogged alongside her. The trolley was preferable to an autocab.

An uneventful ride and a short walk brought them to Callie's apartment just as one of the other tenants was stepping out for the night. Her red curls were piled atop her head, and she wore a flattering, low-cut gown. She smiled at Callie, then let her gaze rove up and down Hal's body.

"Hi, handsome," she greeted him.

"Good evening, Miss…?"

"Hill. But you can call me Betsy."

"A pleasure, Miss Hill." Hal tipped his hat.

Betsy laughed. "Oh, Callie, he's so proper! You'll have to shake him up a bit. Knock those spectacles askew so he can't see straight."

"The spectacles aren't strictly necessary," Hal explained. "They reduce glare in bright light, provide enhanced low-light vision, and have a small amount of magnification for reading." Ugh. He was babbling. Why couldn't he simply tell the ladies goodnight and head for home?

"Well, you two have fun! I'll see you in the morning, Callie, and you can tell me all about him."

Betsy bounded away, leaving Hal and Callie alone at the door. He turned to face her.

"Goodnight, Callie. You were perfectly lovely this evening, and I'm so glad that you got on well with my mother. I'm sorry for being a less-than-ideal dinner companion myself."

Callie opened the door. "Would you like to come in?"

Yes.

"Uh..."

"Let me rephrase that," Callie amended. "The night is young and I have a comfortable bed, an equally comfortable sofa, and plenty of naughty books. No one will be around to interrupt us. I'd like you to join me. Will you?"

"I..." His gaze drifted down her body, taking in the dinner gown that molded to her curves. He'd wanted this for weeks, and her kiss that morning had heaped fuel on the sizzling embers of his desire. She reached out a hand and pressed it to his chest, and the fire flared up into a conflagration. "Yes. I'd like that."

Chapter 29
Words of Passion

Callie locked her door, anticipation sizzling all along her skin. There would be no business tonight. Only pleasure. Her pleasure.

Tomorrow she'd be back at work, revising her lists and revamping her plans to earn what she needed for her library. If she branched out a bit from her original pool of applicants, she was certain she could find someone suitable. And in the meantime, she would have Hal. She'd indulge freely in his awkward charm and his impassioned desire, so when the time came to move on, she would be fully satisfied.

She turned to find him standing by one of her bookshelves, his fingers running gently across the spines. Her heart gave a little twinge. *The man you love.*

"Stop that," she muttered to herself. She could allow herself to consider those sorts of feelings later, after her library was established. Not now. Lust and friendship. Nothing more.

"I'm going to duck into the bedroom and change out of this dress," she told Hal.

His head jerked around. "Oh. I'm sorry. I didn't mean to get distracted. I'm still in awe of your library."

Callie gave him a winning smile. Smiling at him was

so damned easy. "Feel free to peruse the books. I'll only be a few minutes."

She hurried into her bedroom and quickly divested herself of her gown. One of the best parts about patronizing a dressmaker who primarily sold to the mistresses of the wealthy was that all the clothing was easy to get on and off. No rows of tiny buttons up the back, no difficult-to-reach fastenings. Callie's wardrobe was as functional as it was elegant.

She quickly stowed the dress away, dropped her shift and drawers into a basket for laundering, and wrapped a silk dressing gown around her naked body. She plucked the pins from her hair, brushed it out, and washed her hands and face. Splendid. Everything was ready for a night of passion, and she didn't want to keep Hal waiting.

Though she suspected he could occupy himself for some time with her collection.

Callie stepped into the library to find him next to her shelf of erotica, a magazine in hand. He wore a broad grin, a comforting change from the tense discomfort that had plagued him all day. By the time she was through with him tonight, he wouldn't even remember he'd ever been worried.

Hal turned a page, read a bit more, then laughed aloud.

"Enjoying yourself?" Callie asked.

He jumped, but smiled again when he turned toward her. "Yes. These magazines are funnier than I would have expected."

Callie strode across the room to his side and plucked another volume off the shelf. "*The Pearl* was as much about the humor as the erotica. It's a good choice."

"Do you have every volume?"

"I do. Even the Christmas special editions."

Hal looked back down at the page. "These limericks

might be my favorite part. 'There was a young man of Nantucket.'" He let out a snort of laughter. "I'm a little disappointed, though. They rhymed that with 'suck it' and not 'fuck it.'"

Callie laughed with him, laying a hand on his arm and sliding it slowly up and down. "I like hearing you say naughty words. Read more to me."

Hal cleared his throat, shuffling a little in that embarrassed way of his. Still, he plowed ahead. "Their wedding was deferred; but soon, impatient for the pleasure, he found his way into her room and swived her at his leisure."

Callie pressed her cheek against his shoulder, peering down at the text. "Well, that wasn't too terribly risque."

"I know." His eyebrows twitched as his grin grew. "I just wanted to say the word 'swived.'"

She opened the volume she held to a page of limericks and scanned the text. "Oh! Here's one I like. It reminds me of you, actually."

"Me?"

"Yes. 'There was a young man of this nation, who didn't much like fornication. When asked, "Do you fuck?" He said, "No, I suck women's quims, and I use masturbation."' Someday you need to tell me how you came to be a virgin with such a wicked, talented tongue."

He opened his mouth to reply, but she stopped him with a finger to his lips. "Not now." She returned her magazine to the shelf, then wrapped both arms around his neck. "Right now I want you to demonstrate those talents again."

Hal swapped the magazine in his hand for a different volume from the shelf. "I thought you wanted me to read to you. I saw a poem before that made me think of you. It sounded like the writer might have been speaking of a courtesan."

Callie tugged him toward the largest and most comfortable of her chairs. She pressed a kiss just behind his ear. "Read it while you kiss me."

"How can I—"

She cut off his question with a fierce kiss to the mouth, and then they were stumbling together, tongues tangling, hands grasping, a desperate clash of lips and bodies. She needed this. Needed it more than she remembered needing anyone, ever.

No more business. No more boring. Hal tasted like fire and sin and her every deepest desire. Her body was alive, her heart beating wildly beneath her breast.

Callie's legs hit the seat of a chair, and she flailed, letting go of Hal so she wouldn't take him down with her. She fell back onto the cushions, her robe splaying open to reveal the entirety of one bare leg.

Hal gazed down at her, his eyes dark with desire. His eyeglasses sat crooked on his nose. He removed them, folded them, and tucked them into a pocket. His other hand still clutched a volume of *The Pearl*. The way his finger spread the pages to mark his spot looked almost obscene. A throb pulsed between her thighs. She wanted those fingers spreading her open.

She yanked on the tie of her dressing gown, drawing it apart to expose herself and parting her legs. "Kiss me, Hal," she begged. "I need to feel that clever tongue of yours all over my body."

Hal dropped the magazine at her feet, open to the page he had marked, then removed his jacket and began leisurely rolling up his sleeves. He'd become eerily calm, as if he had all the time in the world. Meanwhile, she was nearly panting with arousal, merely from the heat of his stare.

What was this bizarre reversal? She was supposed to be

the cool one, the one driving men to distraction. Tonight, she was the one aching and pleading.

Hal knelt between her legs. Gently, he lifted her right leg, propping it on his shoulder. He pressed a kiss just above her knee.

"My sweet goddess Calliope," he murmured. "You asked me to read and kiss you, so I shall." He kissed her thigh an inch higher, while his fingers skimmed feather-light along her opposite calf.

"With her rich beauties I never am cloyed," he recited. "Fresh pleasures I find at her side." Another kiss, the slightest bit higher. "'I don't love her less because she's enjoyed, by many another beside.' See? His lover is free with her favors. I imagine her a dazzling courtesan like you." He crept higher still, sucking her skin until it prickled, then bathing the spot with his tongue. Callie's legs trembled.

"Hal," she gasped. Her fingers delved into his thick hair while her body warred with the twin desires to pull him closer or to let him continue forever.

"'Shall I try to describe all her merit, I feel that I'd never have done. She is brimful of sweetness and spirit, and sparkles with freedom and fun.' *That* is you, Callie. So perfectly you."

Callie sighed in response, letting her head loll against the cushioned back of the armchair. Her eyes slid closed, all her senses now honed in on the pleasure of his mouth against her skin and the teasing promise of his slithering fingers. Never in her life had she experienced anything so blissfully erotic.

"It is bliss then to hold her and win her." Hal's voice was thick, almost choked with his own desire. "She never proves peevish or coy."

Lord, he was so close to her core now. Callie was

dripping with arousal, her hips canting toward him. The merest touch of his tongue to her sex and she might explode.

"But the farther and deeper I'm in her," he whispered. "The fuller she fills me with joy."

His fingers parted her folds, and his tongue swept across her needy flesh. Callie bucked, gasping.

"Yes. Oh, God, Hal, please."

Her desperate words spurred him on. He feasted on her as though she were the finest of delicacies, missing nothing, making noises of pleasure deep in his throat. Callie's entire world had come unbalanced. Helpless mewls of ecstasy poured from her as he thrust his tongue inside her, his fingers stroking her clit until it was taut and aching. When he shifted to suckle that swollen nub, she cried out—maybe his name, maybe a blasphemy. It didn't matter. He understood. He sucked harder and she came apart, writhing and shaking, the climax going on and on until she was left weary and boneless. A puddle of perfect rapture.

"You are the most beautiful thing I've ever seen," Hal murmured reverently.

Callie opened her eyes. Her limbs still felt like jelly, but she managed to lift an arm and point at the sofa. "Get out of those trousers and have a seat."

By the time he managed to complete the assigned task, she'd recovered enough to move to the sofa and straddle him, slowly lowering herself down onto his jutting cock. She shivered, the feel of him stretching her sending new pulses of desire through a body still tender from her orgasm.

Their groans mingled, quickly squelched as she crushed her mouth to his. Hal's arms clasped her tight and he kissed her ferociously, thrusting up every time she rocked down on him. Callie reached down and fingered her clit, riding him hard and fast, bringing herself to a new peak. They came together, clinging to one another until the spasms subsided.

"Damnation," he gasped.

Callie brushed an errant lock of hair from his brow, smiling at his satisfied expression. He looked glorious, all flushed and disheveled. His answering smile sparked a burst of warmth and happiness deep within her chest. She snuggled against him, sighing contentedly. "That was magnificent."

Dreamy relaxation overtook her. She would gladly stay here for hours, locked in the comfort of his embrace. Hal kissed her brow and stroked her hair, his touch soft and soothing. This was glorious. Perfect.

"I never finished reading you the poem," he said. "And I can't see the words from here. But I think I remember the last stanza."

She reached to cup his cheek, caressing his jaw, enjoying the slight scratch of his evening stubble on her fingertips. "Tell me."

"Reclined on her breast, and clasped in her arms, with her my soft moments I spend." Hal kissed her fingertips and stared intently into her eyes. "And revel the more in her melting charms, because they are shared with a friend."

Callie's chest constricted. That last line was likely meant to imply that the writer enjoyed this woman more because she also laid with his friends. But the way Hal read it, the way he'd looked at Callie as he spoke, said differently. In his interpretation, the friend *was* the woman, and it was that friendship, that affection, that made their coupling so joyous.

"You are breathtaking, my sweet, passionate friend," he murmured.

Callie pressed her face against his shoulder, her own breath nearly stolen away.

I love you.

She didn't dare say it, but the words echoed in her mind, rhythmic as the ticking of her mantelpiece clock.

I love you. I love you.

She clutched him, trembling. Maybe with longing. Maybe with fear.

Chapter 30
Back to Business?

"It started with a gathering of science students that had devolved into heavy drinking," Hal explained.

"As is typical for intellectual gatherings, I understand," Callie replied, snuggling against him.

Her bed was as comfortable as she'd claimed and made all the nicer by her presence. She curled into his side, her cheek pressed to his shoulder, her hand over his heart. Hal hadn't expected her to be so cuddly, but damned if he didn't want to bask in this cozy feeling all night.

"Victor started bragging on his latest sexual exploits, forgetting there was a woman in the group."

"Your friend Nisha?"

"Yes. She said to him, 'I doubt you could find a clitoris if one smacked you in the face.' Which left him rather dumbfounded. I'd been reading medical texts, including a book that covered procreation and sexual intercourse. It had an entire section on the female orgasm. Being young and foolish and a bit tipsy, I launched into a discussion about everything I'd read. At which point Victor asked if I thought I—who had done no more than share a few kisses with the girl across the street—could please a woman better than he could."

Callie's laughter shook her whole body. "And you said

yes, naturally!" Her hold on him tightened. "Oh, Hal, I love your blunt honesty."

Hal stared up at the ceiling, his eyes tracking a crack that had been plastered over. He wasn't honest. He lied all the time. Suppressed his impulsive thoughts and feelings in favor of what was proper and expected of him.

He dragged a finger along Callie's bare arm. No one knew about this. No one knew that he'd enjoyed reading her dirty magazines or that he'd snuck alcohol into a temperance play. No one knew he was swearing a lot these days because he found the foul language cathartic. Only Callie knew this side of him. He wasn't honest. He was a deceitful cad.

Her fingers slid through the hairs on his chest. "So what happened?"

"The next day a woman showed up at my door. Offered me whatever I liked and said she'd been told I'd make it good for her, too. I never did find out who paid her, but I assume a group of my fellow students was somewhere laughing at me. With everything I'd been reading, I wasn't going to chance anything that could lead to a child. But she was attractive and I was a randy youth, and I wanted to prove myself to all those who were mocking me. I was clumsy and awkward, but I did the best I could for her with my fingers and my mouth and eventually I did bring her to a climax. A few days later, I discovered that everyone knew about it and now I had a reputation. 'Cunny licker,' 'quim eater,' et cetera, et cetera."

Callie hooked her leg over his and kissed his jaw. "As far as reputations go, that's an excellent one to have."

"Apparently. I soon met up with a young lady my own age who wanted to explore without technically surrendering her virginity. We were together a few months, during which we learned one another's bodies quite well. I assume she talked about us to her friends, because my reputation only grew from there. I still wasn't willing to risk intercourse, but I never lacked for companionship during my university days. It was only afterward that I became more moderate in my habits. So, there you have it. The story of my misspent youth."

"Well-spent, I think you mean," Callie replied. Her hand slid down his torso and his body stirred in response. "Why me? For your 'official' first, I mean."

"You're not only gorgeous and fun, you're also smart and responsible. And I was so damned tired of waiting, wanting, denying myself. The elixir was an excuse." He could be honest, here, with her. Maybe their shared bed was the one place he didn't need to prevaricate.

Callie straddled him and kissed him. "Want to have another go?"

He gave her the absolute truth. "I'll fuck you all night if I can manage it."

* * *

He couldn't manage it, of course. Eventually they both fell into an exhausted slumber, waking only when the bright rays of the sun and the insistent chirping of birds dragged them from their dreams. Callie looked wonderful in the morning, still dazed and sleepy. Hal kissed her gently before sliding from the bed to dress.

"Come over any time you're ready to test the elixir," he told her. "I'll be there. Waiting. Not touching anything. I promise."

She blinked at him, her expression uncertain. Had his shuffling around in bed woken her too soon? Or had he kept her up too late? She wasn't her usual cheery self this morning. Which was understandable. He could use a good strong cup of tea, himself.

"I'll be there this evening," she said, after a long pause. "Today I have… work to do."

Hal nodded. "Back to business."

"Yes. Business." Her tone was flat. Hal's jaw clenched. He'd forgotten. In all his lustful eagerness, he'd completely forgotten that he'd upended her plans. He needed to rectify that. Find a way to help her earn that library.

"I look forward to seeing you tonight," he said. "Until then." He picked up his coat and his hat and headed for the door.

Callie's friend Betsy walked through the front door of the apartment building as Hal was descending the stairs. He tipped his hat to her.

"Good morning, Miss Hill."

Her jaw went slack. "You were here all night? Callie doesn't let anyone stay all night. Even when she has a long-term gentleman friend, she only stays at his place. Never here."

Hal didn't know what to say. Had he overstepped his bounds? Violated some unspoken code of conduct? If he'd done yet another thing wrong, he'd need to work even harder to make amends.

"She must really like you," Betsy declared. "Bound to happen sooner or later. Growing up in the theater stuffed her head full of romance, if you ask me."

"Uh…" Try as he might, Hal couldn't come up with a good response. This was all business, wasn't it? He hadn't set out to romance Callie. That wasn't part of her plan. "Good Day, Miss Hill," he mumbled, and hurried out the door.

A brisk walk later, he stepped into his own house, determined to spend the day doing what he could to fix the damage he'd done. Callie helped him with the elixir, he helped her with the library. It was the only fair way. He'd bathe and change and have breakfast, then get to work.

He'd just reached the stairs when his mother's voice called out, "Hal! Where on earth have you been? You never stay out all night."

"Um…"

She glided up to him, frowned at his rumpled clothing, and straightened his tie. "You look like you just tumbled out of bed. Does this mean I should begin preparing to welcome Miss Finch to the family?"

Dear God, what had he done? He was making a mess of everything. "No, no. It's nothing like that. We're friends, and, um, colleagues."

His mother sniffed. "Miss Finch may be a modern woman with modern notions, but you shouldn't take that as an excuse to be anything less than a gentleman. I hope you aren't toying with her affections."

"Certainly not!" His horror must have shown on his face, because his mother's expression relaxed. "I only want her happiness."

Which is why I need to concentrate on helping her finance her library.

"I'm glad." His mother smiled and patted his arm. "Be a good boy while I'm gone and take care of that sweet girl. I liked her quite a lot. If anything of significance happens while I'm away, send me a message at the Grand Hotel."

"Yes, Mother."

Nothing that fit his mother's idea of significance would be happening at any time, but Hal didn't want to even attempt to explain that at the moment. Maybe he could explain far in the future. Or maybe never.

By the time he'd seen his mother out, Hal's stomach

had begun making horrible growling noises. He soothed it with meat, eggs, an entire pot of tea, and twice his usual amount of toast. Apparently his vigorous night with Callie had left him ravenous. Or maybe the food was a way to distract himself from his worries—including yet another article in the morning paper about the drunken antics in his neighborhood.

A bath, a shave, and fresh clothing did little to soothe his restlessness. Nothing would, he suspected, besides work. He gathered up as many relevant books and papers as he could find, carried them all to his laboratory, and started plotting.

Hours later, he sat on the floor, notebook open in front of him and papers scattered all around.

It was no use. He couldn't offer himself as an alternative to Valdez or her other potential clients. He simply didn't have the funds to buy her an appropriate piece of property in her desired timeframe. Not without depriving his mother of her retirement travels or taking a chunk from the savings that guaranteed their secure future. Neither was an acceptable option.

Hal flipped the notebook closed. He couldn't look at the words and charts he'd scribbled there any more. Pages and pages of possible alternatives. Ideas for funding a library that didn't involve Callie taking up with any man but him. Few of the ideas were viable. All were selfish.

Callie hadn't asked for this. He couldn't make decisions for her. Couldn't take away her choices merely because he wanted more of what they'd shared last night. She and she alone got to plot her future course.

The sense of failure gnawed at him. He wanted to help. Needed to help. Whatever form that help took, he would do it. But he had to ask her. He couldn't move forward without knowing *how* he could help. What he could do for her.

Hal began gathering up his papers. She'd be here sometime soon to discuss the next experiment. Better that she didn't walk in on his giant mess.

A knock sounded at the door. He was too late. Abandoning his task, Hal hurried to the door to let Callie inside.

She wore a pale green evening dress that hugged her figure. It lacked flounces and fancy trim, making the dress a mere accessory to the alluring shape of her body. Small diamond studs sparkled in her ears, and a matching pendant rested just north of the valley between her breasts. She was ready for a night on the town. Or a night with Hal's hands and lips all over those glorious curves.

"Miss Finch, please come in," he said, waving her through the door.

Liar, liar, he scolded himself. *What you really mean is: "Callie, darling, even now I haven't had enough. I long for you. Ache for you."*

Callie stepped into the laboratory, taking in the scattered papers and the notebook still on the floor.

"I see you've been working. On the elixir?"

Hal bent to grab the closest of the papers. "No, no. Thinking, mostly. Ideas. Primarily determining what I *can't* do. But never mind. Tell me about your work today. Have you made any progress toward your library? How can I help you achieve your goals?"

Her cheeks paled. "I can't talk about this with you right now."

His brow furrowed. "Is something wrong? Did *I* do something wrong?"

Callie looked away. "No. We... can't discuss it." She spun toward the workbench. "I'm here to test the elixir. Let's get on with it."

"Should we do the antidote test..." he began, but she

was already striding to the table and reaching for the jug of elixir. “I have premeasured vi—”

The metal cap rattled on the table as Callie lifted the jug to her lips and took a healthy swig.

Chapter 31
Rebellion

Callie wanted to forget. Just for a short time to push aside the worries and doubts that had plagued her all day. Her mind wouldn't stop, weighing her down with a barrage of what-ifs and if-onlys. Failed attempts to resolve anything haunted her like vengeful ghosts.

She'd burned two lists of potential protectors. How could she bring herself to lay under someone else when she would spend the whole time wishing it was Hal atop her. In her. With her. How could she keep it all business?

She didn't think she could. Last night had been too different, too intimate. And she'd let it linger long after she knew she should send him away. She'd fucked and cuddled and loved until she'd fallen asleep in his arms, taking comfort instead of giving it.

Now the thought of being with anyone else when she could be with him instead filled her with nothing but dismay. She wouldn't be able to enjoy it. It would be boring at best. Possibly worse. Unpleasant. Arduous.

When it feels like that, it's time to get out of the business.

Callie hadn't always been one hundred percent thrilled with all her clients. But she'd never disliked the work. She enjoyed sex. She enjoyed pleasing her partners. She'd taken on this career by choice, and while retirement had always been part of her plan, she hadn't expected it to be because the job had become disagreeable to her.

"Don't drink any more than that." Hal grabbed the jug from her hands, capped it, and stowed it in a cabinet. "Are you all right? How do you feel?"

He adjusted his eyeglasses, gazing at her with such intense concern that a hot flush crept over her entire body. This was precisely the problem. She'd let her sexual feelings and her emotional feelings become all tangled together, and now she didn't want to separate the two.

Maybe she only needed time. Time to take herself away from all of this. To clear her head of the impassioned feelings that had blazed in her all night.

"I feel fine," she answered. "Ready to go out."

"No odd urges yet?"

Only the urge to bend over the table, flip up her skirts, and beg him to take her from behind.

Make him an offer. Tell him you want to be his mistress.

No. She'd been over that this morning. And over and over. It was possible. Tempting. In some ways, it even seemed a fantastic plan. But it would mean changing her schedule. The library would no longer be able to open in the spring, as she'd hoped. She would fail to keep the birthday promise she'd made to herself all those years ago. That would hurt.

And then there was Hal himself. Hal who would be paying for what she really wanted to give him for free. Hal who would be determined nonetheless to see her fairly compensated for her work. Who still saw their relationship as business. Callie didn't want business between them anymore. Only passion. Only love.

What if he never loved her back? What if she changed all her plans, delayed the library, and, then, at the end of the arranged time he thanked her and left? It would be unbearable. How could she give her heart to someone for so long knowing it was only a transaction to him? It might be even worse than leaving him for another man.

"Callie?"

He probably wondered why she was just staring at him. Foolish man. Didn't he know how gorgeous he was? All the spectacles and tweed suits in the world couldn't disguise that. She licked her lips.

"Tell me how you're feeling," he urged. "Is the elixir working?"

She stepped toward him, debating what she wanted to do to him first. "It might be," she replied. Because suddenly she didn't much care about business or the library or what might theoretically happen in the future. She only wanted thrills. She only wanted now. "Come here and kiss me."

"No."

"No?" She pouted. "You're no fun."

"Not while you're under the influence of the elixir." He brushed past her to fiddle with something on the worktable. Callie leaned into him, pressing her breasts against his arm. He ignored her, finished whatever he was doing, then stepped away. "I would never take advantage of you."

She snorted. "You think I don't want it?"

"Your judgment is impaired," he replied coolly. "The things you are doing and saying cannot be assumed to be your true desires."

"You're boring," she sniffed.

"Yes, I am. And the real Callie likes me anyway. If you don't, that's only proof you're not yourself."

She grabbed hold of his coat and pulled him toward the door. She was tired of boring. Tired of unpleasant, heavy feelings. Tonight she was getting the hell away from all that.

"Let's go. It's time you learned how to have fun."

* * *

List of un-Callie-like behaviors, Hal catalogued mentally. *Pouting. Complaining.*

Those things fit with his own juvenile behavior from the other day, meaning the elixir had a similar effect on her. Which was good. Something positive he could focus on.

He scanned the room, taking in the finely-dressed patrons and the lavish foodstuffs that graced their tables. A nervous shiver raced down his spine. They should never have entered such an upscale establishment. Why had he let Callie choose their destination?

"You ordered the absinthe?" a waiter asked, setting the small glass in front of Hal.

Callie snatched it up. "That would be mine." She held it up to the light, grinning as she slowly swirled the green liquid.

"Er, and a Vernor's?"

Hal accepted his ginger ale with a nod of thanks. Callie gave the bottle a look of disdain.

Thinks I'm boring.

Hal couldn't prevent the pang in his chest that accompanied the thought. He sipped his drink, calling on his long-practiced manners. Tonight required a cool head. Whatever she said or did, he had to remember this wasn't the real Callie.

She took a drink of the absinthe. "You should have ordered something more fun. You won't be such a prude when you're drunk."

Her words were matter-of-fact, as if she was trying to offer genuine advice. They still stung like a slap to the face.

Maybe she really does think I'm boring and she's lost the ability to conceal the truth. She's well-practiced at putting people at ease and saying things they want to hear. Her job is to make people feel good. She's too kind to tell me I'm uninteresting to her.

He slid a hand into his pocket, feeling the syringe of antidote, a tactile reminder of his purpose here. Watch out for her. Protect her. Prevent any catastrophe. Exactly the way she'd done for him the other night.

"How's your drink?" he asked. Maybe if he encouraged her in this small rebellion he could stave off any troubles. Let her get drunk on la fée verte and then walk her home. They could take less crowded roads and she could dance in the street or turn tipsy somersaults or whatever she liked.

"It's excellent," she declared. She took another sip, her mouth puckering. She waved a hand to fan her face. "It has a powerful burn and I'm actually not fond of anise-flavored things, but that hardly matters, does it? The horridness is half the fun. I hope it causes me to have hallucinations."

Hal didn't believe the tales of the drink's supposed mind-altering capability, but he nodded. Her mind was already altered. It would be interesting to see what changes she attributed to the elixir and what to her choice of beverage.

Enjoys "horrid" drink. Rebellious?

"What sorts of things do you expect you'll see when you hallucinate?" he asked. Keep her talking. Ask scientific questions. He could do this.

"You. And me." She leaned across the table toward him. "Doing all sorts of delicious things. Maybe you'll crawl under the table and beneath my skirts. Or maybe I'll straddle you in your seat. Or we'll both be atop the table, and—"

"I think I understand," Hal interrupted, before her impassioned explanation grew loud enough for anyone else to hear.

Callie held out her drink to him. "Want to try it?" she cooed. "It'll make you more fun."

"No. Thank you."

She sat back in her seat, her shoulders slumping, and heaved a loud sigh. "You're going to be dull all night, aren't you?"

A woman at the next table over turned toward them, her gaze meeting Callie's.

"Hi," Callie said. She jerked a thumb in Hal's direction. "This is Hal. He's being frightfully dull tonight, and I'm so tired of it. He wouldn't even kiss me."

The woman and her two female companions gasped at the scandalous declaration. Hal cringed.

"Calliope, dear," he said gently, trying to draw her attention.

"And he doesn't have to be boring," she went on. "He's done not-boring things before. When *she's* here, he does plenty of not-boring things." She shivered, and a lascivious grin spread across her face. "If you can get him in the right mood, he's thrilling. His kisses will melt you, and he's so very good at—"

"Science!" Hal interrupted, nearly yelling to cover up Callie's inappropriate remarks. "I'm a scientist."

Callie kicked him under the table. "They don't care about that. The ladies want to know what you can do—"

"To help those less fortunate than ourselves. Yes, dear, I know you love to go on about our charity work, but we really ought to leave the ladies to their meal."

Callie scowled at him. "Quit interrupting me."

Hal dug a handful of coins out of his pocket and slapped them on the table. "I think it's time we went home, darling. Have to read the children their bedtime stories, you know."

He hopped up, took hold of Callie's arm, and pulled her up out of her seat. "Best be off before it gets too late."

She reached for her drink, but he dragged her away before she could get a hand on it.

"We're leaving," he hissed in her ear.

Callie wriggled in his grasp. "Why are you being so mean?"

"I'm saving your behind," he replied. "You can't go telling those ladies about my bedroom skills."

"Why not? It'll help your reputation."

Reckless, Hal added to his list. *Lacking in forethought.*

He steered her toward the exit. "I don't want a reputation. But you should take care with yours."

"I'm a whore," she scoffed. "I don't have a reputation."

"Oh? Don't you need some measure of respectability, or at least responsibility for your library?"

She flinched.

"Yes. You do care," he said. His muscles relaxed a bit, and he loosened his grip on her arm. "Let's go somewhere else. No more fancy restaurants."

"Fine," she agreed. "Let's go to a saloon. Ooh!" Her entire face lit up with delight. "Let's go to a saloon that doesn't allow women! I'll walk right up to the bar and demand to be served!"

Hal loved the idea. He could envision her striding in, confident and brazen, insisting on fair treatment. No sneers or insults would hold her back. She wasn't likely to succeed, but she would make a statement.

Which made it a terrible idea. With the elixir burning in her veins, she might say or do anything. She would give no thought to consequences, have no care for reputation or safety.

"I know just the place," she declared. She was dragging Hal now, away from the restaurant and down the street.

"Will anyone at this saloon know you?"

She made a noise of displeasure. "Of course not. I wouldn't consort with the type of people who frequent such an objectionable establishment."

Hal refrained from pointing out that the vast majority of saloons barred women or allowed them only in a limited capacity.

Callie took his silence as compliance and continued to lead him down the street. Hal didn't protest. A saloon was a reasonable choice. It would already be loud and busy. Probably no one would recognize her. She could engage in whatever outrageous behaviors the elixir prompted more safely than she could in most places. And if she was busy rebelling by shouting at men to serve her drinks, maybe she wouldn't bring up any more inappropriate sexual topics. Who knows, maybe her demands would even do a bit of good to further the campaign for equal rights for women.

Unfortunately, temperance turned out to be the cause of the night. Hal and Callie rounded a corner to discover half-a-dozen primly-dressed matrons marching up and down in front of the door to a bustling saloon. They carried signs denouncing the vice of drink, chanting in unison as they walked. Sashes slung across their dresses declared them to be from the Detroit Ladies' Committee Against Vice.

"Oh, balls," Callie muttered. A moment later, her face brightened. "No! This is good." She turned a devilish smile on Hal. "Watch this."

Head held high, she walked directly to the lady protesters. Hal kept close behind, his pulse quickening. This could go wrong so easily.

"Ladies," Callie said cheerily. "It seems our purposes align perfectly tonight."

The women didn't stop their marching, but all eyes turned to Callie.

"I came here, to this house of vice, intending to demand entry, as should be my right as a citizen of this country, regardless of my sex. You protest here, but inside the men drink and carouse, ignoring us as they ignore us every night. It's time to take our concerns inside. It's time to assert ourselves and show them they cannot stop the just cause of determined women!"

"Yes, let's!" cried one of the women.

"A good idea," said another. "They can't stop us if we all enter together. We'll take up their tables and order tea and coffee!"

In a flash, the women were pushing their way into the saloon. Callie and Hal followed the pack inside.

At once men began to shout, but the ladies were not to be deterred. They cleared a table, sat themselves down with their signs, and began to call out to every server, asking for soda, tea, coffee, and juice.

Callie walked up to the bar.

"Get out of here, you teetotaling bitch," the bartender sneered.

Hal tensed, but she ignored the insult. "Oh, I'm not with them. I'm here for a proper drink. I want an absinthe."

The bartender squinted at her. "You what?"

"One glass of absinthe, please."

Now too confused to be angry, he scratched his head. "We don't sell the green fairy here."

"A bourbon, then," Callie requested.

"Bourbon!" exclaimed one of the temperance marchers, approaching them. "What is going on here?"

Callie smirked at her. “I’m having a drink.”

“I thought you were on our side,” the woman retorted, suddenly hostile.

“No.” Callie almost spat the word, and Hal stepped closer, his body tensing in anticipation of danger. “We may both believe in suffrage,” she continued, “but your little club wants nothing to do with me and mine. You shame us and shun us, claiming to be champions for women while with the same breath you demean any women outside your class, your race, and your rules. When you raise your voice for a Jewish matron, a Black girl, an opium-addict, a whore, then and only then will I be on your side.”

The other woman gaped at Callie. “How dare you, you…” She eyed Callie’s form-fitting dress. “Insolent slattern!”

Callie grabbed a pint of ale right out of the hands of a man nearby and dashed it in the woman’s face.

The woman screamed. She grabbed a drink from someone else, but Callie ducked the attack, and the beer soaked the bartender instead.

“Sorry!” the woman blurted, whirling and racing back to her friends.

Chaos erupted. Liquid splashed across tile and clothing as men and women alike began to throw more drinks. Glass shattered. Insults flew. One of the temperance women jumped atop a table, screaming surprisingly foul words. Hal seized Callie’s arm. This was too much.

“Callie, we should go.”

She pushed his hand away. “I have a right to be here. I want my bourbon.” She dropped a coin on the bar.

“That had better be buying me a new beer,” snarled the man whose drink she had stolen. He and the bartender were both red-faced, and looked a breath away from joining the melee.

"Yes, of course it is," Hal assured him. Before Callie could argue, he grasped her around the wrist, tight enough he worried he might hurt her. "Callie, we must go," he pleaded. "This is getting out of hand."

She tried to free herself, but this time his grip held. "Let me go. I want to have fun."

Hal took a step away from the bar, but she resisted. Dammit. He couldn't pick her up and carry her away. That would only add to the madness.

"Callie, listen to me. Remember your library. This isn't—" He froze. Across the room, standing calmly in the midst of furious customers, stood a man with a pencil and a small notebook.

Hal's heart leapt into his throat. A reporter! If Callie ended up in the papers, it could be the end of everything. Even without her name, a description that could be connected to her could do damage. It was time to end this.

He yanked the syringe from his pocket, jabbed the needle into Callie's arm, and slammed the plunger down. She yelped and jerked.

"You stabbed me!" she cried, staring at him in disbelief. A moment later, she shook her head, her lashes fluttering. "Oh," she gasped. Her eyes darted back and forth. "Oh, no. We need to leave."

"Yes." He took her arm in a gentler grip and together they fled.

"Oh, my God," Callie gasped. "I was wild!"

Hal hurried her around the corner, where they resumed a more sedate pace. He glanced behind him, but saw no signs anyone was following.

"You were absolutely magnificent and also quite horrible. I'd love to see you champion good causes without the elixir muddling your mind."

"Thank you for the antidote. That woman made me so angry. Their club—the Detroit Ladies' Committee Against Vice—have been absolutely vile to women like me. And I had no good sense to stop myself from venting all my anger right then." Callie rubbed her temple. "I can't believe I threw that drink. If I get in trouble with the law, it could ruin my library. I can be scandalous, but I can't be untrustworthy. This library is meant for ladies who break the rules, or who want to. Those who don't or can't fit in. The ladies who will change the world for the better. They have to believe I will be discreet, competent, and committed to providing them a safe space."

Hal let his hand drop to grasp hers, giving it a squeeze. "And you will be those things. You *are* those things. Don't take the elixir again. I know you wanted to help, but it shouldn't put your library at risk. Your dream is grand, Callie, and you can achieve it. I know you can. Don't let anything stand in your way." *Especially not me.* "And whatever I can do for you, you know you only need ask."

Even if it meant watching her take up with another man. Even if it meant never holding her again. He would see her triumph. That had to be enough.

"Tonight, just walk me home, please," Callie replied.

Hal nodded. He wouldn't stay the night this time, no matter how he yearned for it. He was done letting his selfish desires jeopardize her future. He was moving on.

Chapter 32
One Thing After Another

Nemo propped an arm against the mantelpiece and frowned down at Hal. "Where have you been? You missed our last meeting, and we've had hardly a word from you about anything."

Hal shrugged. He reached for his teacup, which the autokettle had overfilled once again. "I've been busy." He took a careful sip, trying not to spill. "Doesn't this club have any normal teapots?"

"Of course not," Victor scoffed. "They pride themselves on their technology. That's why we chose this place."

"I thought we chose it because the membership fee was low and because…" Hal glanced up at Nemo, who nodded.

"They're progressive," Nemo finished. "But you've deliberately changed the subject. What have you been doing?"

"Yes, tell us." Victor leaned back in his chair, crossing his legs at the ankle. "How is your elixir? And more importantly, how is Miss Finch?"

"The elixir works. The new version causes a noticeable change in behavior for the worse. Recklessness, immaturity, lack of remorse. I intend to try it again to confirm the effects, but I don't plan to go out again during the experiment."

"And did the bad behavior result in a subsequent reduction in your 'baser urges'?" Nemo inquired.

Hal sighed. “Not at all.”

“What about Miss Finch?” Victor wondered. “Does she calm your baser urges? Or only inflame them?”

“Miss Finch is none of your business,” Hal replied, focusing on his tea.

“Ah, but she’s *your* business.”

Hal had to swallow hard to avoid choking on the tea. Victor couldn’t have known how those words would sting.

She’s not my business. Not anymore. I can’t partake of her business and she can’t partake of mine.

“So, tell us,” Victor went on, oblivious. “Does she know you’re a connoisseur of cunnilingus? Have you left her begging for more?”

“Stuff it, Franklin,” Nemo retorted. “Can’t you see he doesn’t want to talk about it?”

“He’s been so distracted by her he missed last meeting,” Victor protested. “He doesn’t have to give the gory details. I was only joking.” He looked to Hal. “Tell us the romantic part, then. Have you gone down on your knees and declared your undying love?”

Thank God the porcelain here was sturdy, or the teacup in Hal’s hand might have shattered, his fingers clenched so hard.

“No.”

And he never would. It didn’t matter that her smile could turn around his whole day. Or that he imagined sharing breakfast with her every morning and a bed every night. It didn’t matter that she would now forever be a part of his work, even if she never set foot in the laboratory again. He could not and would not tell her.

“You do love her, though.” This from Nemo, the shrewd observer. “It’s written all over your face.”

"Yes," Hal admitted, though he avoided saying the word, as if that somehow made it easier.

It was precisely because he loved her that he couldn't be with her any longer. Only her future mattered. Her happiness. Hal was nothing but an obstacle standing in her way.

Victor straightened up in his seat and leaned forward, his brow crinkling in a frown of concern. "What's the trouble, then? Are you feeling shy? Would you like me to woo her for you? I can send flowers on your behalf. Or diamonds."

All the tea in Hal's stomach suddenly threatened to come back up. Victor was the right sort of man for Callie. He had money to burn, and he was loyal and good-hearted, despite his cynical facade. He'd even learned to be a thorough, generous lover, from what Hal had heard. He was absolutely the perfect candidate to fund Callie's library.

Hal abruptly rose from his seat, abandoning the rest of his tea. "I should go. Excuse me."

Victor jumped up as well. "Hal, I'm sorry. I didn't mean to upset—"

Hal waved a hand to cut him off. "Forget it." He turned away and dashed for the exit before he did something he'd regret. Like stab Victor with a fork. Or tell him he'd found him the perfect mistress.

* * *

The temperance marchers were back. Or a small subset of them. Men, mostly, and they appeared to be not just carrying signs, but installing them. Hal picked up his pace, hurrying down the street for a better look.

"Liquor-Free Neighborhood," the nearest plaque proclaimed, above the printed image of a bottle with a large X across it.

Bzzt! Bzzt!

A man pushed a vibrating digger apparatus into the grass, and a moment later it spewed out a neat, round plug of dirt. He lifted the machine out of the way, and a second man plunged the wooden post that held up the sign into the hole. Together they kicked dirt into the hole and stomped it down.

Hal rushed past, not stopping until he'd reached his own front gate. The men continued on, carrying the digger to another location.

Bzzt! Bzzt!

Hal put a hand on the gate, but didn't open it. He didn't know whether this sign installation was legal or not, but he wasn't going to let them put one up on his property.

"Jekyll!" Mr. Becher came jogging down the street. He wore a large ribbon pinned to his chest that declared "Be a Liquor-Free Neighbor!" in the same font as on the signs. "Did you get the latest batch of tonic water? I set it right on your front porch."

"Yes," Hal replied. *Made a whole jug of gin and tonic.*

"Excellent. We've been working on some new advertisements. I would greatly appreciate it if you could give me an endorsement of its healthfulness. In your professional capacity, of course." Becher waved a hand at the men with the signs. "Glad to see so many people banding together to improve our neighborhood."

Hal blinked at him. "I didn't realize you lived near here."

"Indeed. Over on Winder."

"Ah." In one of the mansions, no doubt. Several houses on Winder were about twice as big as any on Hal's block. And none of the houses on this street were small.

The men with the digger approached. One of them lifted a hand in greeting to Becher.

"Please, no signs in front of my house," Hal called to them.

The men gave him stern looks, but continued on, pausing in front of the laboratory.

"That's my house, too," Hal said.

They shook their heads and kept going, grumbling something he couldn't hear.

Becher made a clucking noise. "You're not bothered by our neighborhood improvement plan, are you?"

The obvious answer formed automatically in Hal's mind. *No, not at all. But I don't like signs on my property. Not good for the lawn.*

The old Henry Jekyll, the prudish one who did everything by the rules and tried never to upset anyone, would have spoken those words as easily as he breathed. Today they stuck in Hal's throat. He was sick of this. Sick of not being himself. Sick of putting what everyone else thought above his own opinions and desires. He wanted to be free, the way he was with Callie.

Hal squared his shoulders. "Yes. I am. The signs are unsightly, useless, and a waste of money. No one who wants to have a drink is going to care whether you've declared the street liquor-free or not. No troublemaker is going to change his ways because of a sign. And that's assuming the recent disturbances were actually caused by drunks, which I doubt. This is a pointless endeavor, unless you mean it entirely for show."

As he said the words, he realized the truth in them. This *was* all for show. Becher's temperance union friends would pat him on the back for it. People loyal to their cause would buy his drink because he'd openly pandered to them. It was one big advertising scheme.

"I'm sorry if that bothers you," Hal added. Truthfully, too, since he really did dislike bothering people. "But I did already tell you my stance on temperance, and I'm afraid I haven't changed my mind. I wish you a lovely rest of the day, and I hope we can continue to disagree amiably."

A muscle twitched in Becher's jaw, and he gave a stiff nod. Hal returned the gesture, then turned and headed into the house.

The day's mail sat on the hall table. Hal scooped up the envelopes and gave them a quick perusal. Callie's curvy penmanship leapt out at him, and he tossed the other letters aside and tore into it.

Dear Hal,

Thank you for watching out for me last night. I must admit that drinking your elixir was among the strangest experiences of my life, and one I'm not keen to repeat. I wrote down everything I remembered for your notes, so I hope they will be of use to you. I will bring them by tomorrow morning, and if you are ready we can conduct the next test. We won't leave the laboratory, and I'll have the antidote in case anything goes wrong.

Why don't you mix up a new batch of gin and tonic? I'll bring some playing cards and chips so we can gamble. I bet you'll try to cheat! Maybe we can read the newspaper, too, and write down your reactions to the events and people. I'm sure you'll have some ideas for things we can do around the lab as well, and I look forward to hearing them.

I will plan to come by at 10:00 a.m. unless I hear otherwise.

Yours,
Callie

Hal read the entire thing twice, then folded it and tucked

it into his pocket. She was coming here tomorrow. Despite last night, despite her own business to see to, she was still committed to assisting with this project. She was so good, so loyal. He had to repay that with equal support. He'd watch her build her library, and then when it was open, he'd shout its praises from the rooftops. He knew scientific-minded women. They'd be interested, and they'd help spread the word.

Tomorrow would be his final experiment with Callie. When it was over, he'd tell her that this phase of the project was complete and he no longer needed assistance. All he had to do was keep his damned feelings to himself and avoid touching her at all costs.

He headed for the laboratory. He'd get the room prepared, remove anything valuable, and fill two syringes with antidote. By the time she arrived in the morning, he'd be ready for anything.

An image of the salutation of her letter flashed in his mind: the word "Yours" in her elegant, looping script.

"Mine," Hal murmured. "I wish you were. I wish you could be."

He'd be ready for anything. Except her.

Chapter 33
Elixir and Tonic

Would you like to go to dinner later?

Perhaps we should go out and relax afterward.

Gee, all this experimenting is making me hungry, how about you?

Callie put on her well-rehearsed social smile and tried to shake off the litany of possible questions running through her brain. When was the last time she'd been nervous about asking a man to take her out?

Never, that's when. Even adolescent Callie hadn't hesitated to ask the boys to go out walking or to sneak a kiss.

Maybe it was only the significance of the event. It wasn't merely dinner. It was the pivot point upon which her future rested. Time alone, only her and Hal, with no business to interfere. Time to ascertain his feelings. Could they run deeper than casual affection and lust? Did she dare gamble on that chance?

After tonight, she would know. They would talk, and that would tell her whether she could reconfigure her plans in order to win him or whether she needed to walk away and never see him again.

As usual, Hal waved her into the laboratory and locked the door behind her. A simple wooden table with matching chairs had been added to the room. A jug sat atop it, along with two empty glasses and an unopened deck of cards.

"Our personal casino," Hal said, one side of his mouth rising in a shy half-smile.

"Excellent." Callie opened her bag and withdrew her own supplies: a box of chips for wagering and two more decks of cards. "One of these has been marked," she said. "I won't tell you which."

"Ooh, fun." He shifted nervously. "And, no, I didn't take the elixir yet. The real me is actually looking forward to figuring out ways to cheat."

Callie laughed. He always made her laugh. Imagining a future where that never happened was becoming more and more difficult.

"Of course you are. It's the sort of thing that appeals to your curious mind."

He smiled at her, but only for an instant, before he returned to fidgeting. He was anxious today.

Or maybe you're projecting your own uncertainty onto him. Maybe he senses that something is off and is reacting accordingly.

Callie straightened her spine. Time to be all business. "Shall we begin, then? I think the gambling should keep you occupied for a time."

"I hope so." He walked to the worktable and picked up a pair of syringes. "The antidote. Two doses, to be extra safe."

Callie tucked the syringes into the pockets on either side of her skirt.

Hal lifted a small vial, filled with the swirly brown elixir. "Whenever you're ready."

She'd arrived ready. She would always be ready to help. Yet at the same time, she wasn't and would never be ready for him to drink the potion. Not when it meant losing him to the drug for a time. Time she could otherwise be spending with him, exactly as he was.

Callie waved a hand at the card table. “Let’s sit and then we’ll begin.”

They sat across from one another, and Hal poured out two glasses of gin and tonic. He downed the elixir in one long gulp, then lifted his cocktail.

“To my stalwart scientific partner,” he said. “For your much appreciated and undeserved assistance.” He took a long drink. “Damn, that’s good.”

Callie sipped from her own glass. “The help is deserved. You’re a good man with a noble goal of helping people who are unable to control their urges. It could reduce crime and improve lives. Why would you think that unworthy of help?”

Hal snorted. “Noble goals. I can’t believe you *like* him.”

Callie let out a slow breath. Hyde was back. Time to play. She reached for a deck of cards and began to shuffle.

“I don’t think you’re up for this,” she challenged. “The elixir makes you too rash. You’ll never beat me.”

“What?” His mouth puckered in a little pout. “I will. You just watch.” He took another drink, draining almost half the glass. “This is the best batch I’ve made.”

Callie tossed him some cards, then sipped her own gin and tonic. “I’ve noticed you say ‘I’ when it’s something you like. But when it’s something you don’t like, you say ‘him.’ You can’t have it both ways. Either you’re the same person or you’re not.”

“I make my own rules. I only take his fun parts.” He scowled at his cards. With that lack of a poker face, she would trounce him.

Callie nodded. “Let’s play.”

Cards proved to be a good choice for their experiment. The elixir made Hal hungry to win, but he wagered recklessly, pushing the stakes higher to make up for his losses. In this frame of mind, he would be a gambling den's dream customer.

Before she knew it, Callie was lifting her empty glass to her lips. Had she really drunk it all already? It seemed hardly any time had passed. She craved more. She held out the glass to Hal, who was already pouring his third.

"Only half a glass, please." She couldn't get drunk, in case he grew tired of games and decided a night on the town was just the thing.

He filled her glass to the brim, smirking.

Oh well. She didn't have to drink it all. She swallowed another mouthful. Even if it was astonishingly good.

Callie turned her attention back to Hal and the game. He had yet to figure out which deck was marked, but she was certain he was counting cards. That would have to be added to the notes: mathematical abilities not altered.

Hal dealt the next round, sliding cards across the table to her and deliberately letting his fingers brush hers. "I think I know what I want to do when we're done with cards," he leered.

"Not under the influence, remember?"

"Of course I remember," he snapped, in a tone harsher than she'd ever heard from him. "Do you think I give a damn about him and his rules?"

"No, but I think you give a damn about me." She'd always been able to get through the elixir's effects to him, even if only in tiny ways.

And like before, her words sparked a momentary change in him. A flicker of emotion in his eyes. This time, however, it looked less like recognition and more like… panic. Why? Had he read something in her own eyes? Did he know she was asking for love?

Callie picked up her cards, letting her uncertain emotions become her mask for the game. She'd let him see her doubt. Because she had good cards. Better than good. By far the best hand she'd had all night.

Hal examined his own hand, frowning slightly, but she caught the telltale hitch in his mouth—the way he almost smiled when something amused him and he was trying not to let it show. So. He had good cards too.

The wagering went back and forth, Callie hesitating a bit more with each increase. Hal grew bolder, adding more chips to the pile until at last they splayed their cards face-up on the table. He relinquished his with a confident smile. He did have a very good hand. But not as good as hers.

It took several seconds for his defeat to register. Hal stared at the cards as if they made no sense. Suddenly, fury blazed in his eyes.

"You cheated," he snarled.

Callie flinched at the ferocity of his anger. Was it the elixir? He certainly hadn't shown any signs of it during the previous experiment. "No. I didn't. I'm not the one using the elixir. I don't care about winning. It was only luck."

He swiped at the cards so forcefully, half of them flew off the table. "You must have cheated." He bit out every word, his cheeks coloring.

Something was wrong. Callie remembered her own bout of anger under the potion's influence. It had been exactly what she would have felt without the elixir. Only her foolish reaction had differed. But Hal looked enraged.

"I promise I didn't cheat," Callie said, making her voice as soothing as possible. "Shall we play again?"

He pounded a fist on the table, rattling the glasses and sending chips flying. Callie jolted in alarm.

"Don't lie to me, you stupid bitch!"

Callie scrambled up out of her seat. This was beyond wrong. He'd come unhinged. She plunged a hand into her pocket, fingers curling around the syringe of antidote.

"Hal, where are you? Are you in there?"

His eyes were wild, his pupils large. His hands clenched on the table, knuckles white. He pushed himself from the chair, the movement slow and menacing.

"Your beau isn't here, slut," he growled. "Tonight you get the *real* Harry Hyde."

Fear lanced through her. For herself and for Hal. What was happening to him? If he were damaged forever, it would shatter her heart. She spun the syringe in her fingers. He couldn't touch her. Not without getting close enough that she could stab him.

"Hal, look at me," Callie pleaded, staring straight into his eyes, desperate to find that flash of recognition again. "It's Callie. Look at me. Remember me."

His eyes didn't change, but his voice did. "How could I ever forget?"

"Shut up!" Hyde snarled. "No one wants you here."

Callie took one step to the side, considering how best to go after him with the syringe. "I want him here. You're the one I want gone."

His laugh was cruel, mocking. "Not true. You want all the bad parts. The gaming and the drinking and the fucking. All the parts that aren't him."

"They *are* him," she shot back. "He can enjoy those things without being a bad person."

"But he doesn't," Hyde sneered. "He frets and he wrings his hands and he feels oh-so-guilty. You don't want him. He's ashamed he's ever touched you."

"I will never be ashamed of her," Hal vowed, and in that instant she saw his true self flicker in his eyes.

Callie took the opening. She sprang forward, swinging her arm and burying the syringe's needle in his shoulder. By the time he cried out in pain, she had already depressed the plunger. She staggered back a few steps, gasping. They were safe. A few seconds and he'd be back to himself.

His eyes closed briefly, and when they opened again, Callie's heart contacted in absolute terror. That wasn't Hal.

Hyde bellowed in rage. He seized the table and flung it and all the contents aside. Wood splintered. The near-empty jug of gin and tonic shattered.

"How dare you?" he roared.

Callie backed away as he stalked toward her. She grabbed the second syringe, praying a second dose would be enough.

"You think you can throw me aside?" His eyes had turned to ice and his face was a mask of blinding hatred. Twisted. Ugly. He was wearing Hal's body, but he'd stolen away all the warmth and joy that made it so beautiful. "You think you can stop me with your little remedy? Hah!"

Callie ran for the door to the tunnel, but Hal had locked everything to slow any possible escape attempt, and her trembling hands fumbled with the key. Hyde stomped closer.

"Don't touch her!" Hal's voice. He was still there. He was fighting.

"You don't control me, boy," Hyde taunted. "You let me free, and tonight I do what I want."

The lock turned in Callie's hand. Hyde broke into a run.

"No!" Hal cried.

Hyde faltered for a moment, the fractional hesitation just long enough to give Callie time to escape. She dodged his grasping hand, threw open the door, and tore off down the tunnel. Heavy footsteps thundered after her.

"I'll make you both pay," Hyde raged.

Callie's heart pounded. She slammed into the door at the far end of the tunnel, also closed. Sweaty palms grabbed for the handle, pleading for it to turn.

"Too slow, bitch," Hyde taunted.

"No!" Hal screamed again, his voice—his true voice—filled with a fury beyond anything she'd ever heard. "I will kill you before you touch her!"

A thud echoed in the hall behind her. Then silence. Callie stopped and turned, her heart in her throat. Hal lay face-down in the center of the tunnel, unmoving.

A trickle of blood snaked out from beneath him, fiery crimson against the pale wood floor.

Chapter 34
Unwholesome Ingredients

Hal was a ghost, a phantom. In his body, but not. Reaching, grasping, flailing madly, yet unable to touch. Unable to act.

Hyde advanced on Callie, sending spasms of terror through whatever ephemeral specter remained of Hal. This, he could feel. His own fear. Hyde's wild rage. The agony that he might hurt Callie with his stolen body.

"No!" Hal put everything he had into the cry, but it wasn't enough. Hyde barely paused, stomping after Callie in his frenzied madness.

"Too slow, bitch."

He was running for her, reaching for her.

No, no, no. Hal couldn't stand it. Couldn't let her be hurt. He thrashed and screamed, fighting for control of the body that had once been his.

"No!" The word came again, louder now, more desperate. He wouldn't let this happen. He would die first. "I will kill you before you touch her!"

His body froze. Hal wrestled to seize control from the foul, evil thing that threatened his love.

Never.

He pushed harder, letting his whole heart fuel his righteous anger.

You will never hurt her. Never while even the merest shadow of me lives.

Something snapped. Hal sucked in a sudden gasp of air. Darkness descended.

"Hal." The pleading voice came to him from a distance. "Oh, God, Hal."

The darkness began to fade. He could sense the light now, behind his eyelids, feel the cold, hard surface beneath him. His muscles began to work again, flooding him with blessed relief. His body was his own. He hadn't killed it.

"You're alive," Callie gasped. "Oh, thank goodness."

A soft, caring touch swept across his cheek. Hal breathed slowly, in and out. His world was right. She was safe. He could have lain there forever, basking in her perfect, gentle caress.

"Hal," she murmured. "Are you with me? Is it you?"

He forced his eyes open, rolling to his side so he could look at her. Something wet trickled down across his left eye. He tried to say her name, but it came out only as a barely-there rasp.

"I'm me," he choked out. "He's gone."

"Don't move," Callie commanded. She wiped at his face with a handkerchief, clearing the blood away. "That's a nasty gash." She pressed the handkerchief over the wound, causing him to wince in pain. "Can you hold that in place?"

Hal lifted a hand to the cloth and nodded. Every movement of his body was like a gift. He was himself. He was whole. He pushed up into a seated position.

Frantic footsteps announced a new arrival. Mrs. Sterling materialized in the tunnel door, her hand going to her mouth to cover a gasp.

"Good heavens!" she cried. "What happened? I heard shouting. Should I send for a doctor?"

"It's not bad," Hal assured her, his voice still gravelly, but working now. "Nothing to worry about. We had a problem with an experiment. Sudden explosion. Broke a table, I'm afraid."

He climbed carefully to his feet, allowing Callie to assist him. His head was clear, his limbs sturdy. Whatever the elixir had wrought, it was gone. He lifted the handkerchief from his forehead. Blood soaked the white fabric.

"That's an ugly cut you've got there," the housekeeper fretted. "Are you certain you don't want me to call a doctor?"

"I'll tend to him, Mrs. Sterling," Callie assured her. "I'll walk him up to bed. Do you think you could send up a cold compress and a bit of lunch?"

"Of course, miss. Right away."

"I don't need a bed," Hal protested. "The study will be fine." Before either of the women could protest, he added, "Then everyone in the house will be close by in case I have need of anything."

Walking to the study under his own power appeared to ease a bit of Callie's worry. The tightness around her eyes faded, and her frown vanished. She insisted he sit on the sofa so she could sit beside him, inspecting his injury. A few minutes later, Mrs. Sterling brought in a medical kit. Callie immediately opened it and began to clean and bandage the wound.

"I don't deserve a friend like you," Hal sighed.

"I think we already had this discussion," Callie replied, her stern tone implying she would brook no argument.

"I'm so sorry. Sorry for dragging you into this. Sorry for that… *thing* that threatened you." Guilt clawed at him.

Callie would forgive him, of course, but he wasn't ready to forgive himself.

"It wasn't your doing," she replied. "Something went wrong. I don't think it was the elixir. I remember how it felt. There was nothing cruel or evil about me. I was merely a more selfish, less level-headed version of myself. This, though, today. That wasn't you at all. You didn't simply *say* you were two different people. You *were* two people. Thank you for fighting him off, however you did it."

"I'm not sure," Hal admitted.

Callie finished taping the bandage in place and sat back. "We need to determine what went wrong, to prevent it from ever happening again. Was anything different about the elixir this time?"

Hal shook his head. "No. I filled that vial I drank at the same time I filled the others. It was exactly the same formula and dosage."

Callie pursed her lips. "Did you notice anything different in how you felt after drinking it? Strange sensations while we were playing cards?"

"Cards?" Hal rubbed his temple. He could picture the cards and the chips sitting on the table, but had no memory of picking them up or playing. "I… don't remember."

"That's not good." Callie's eyes widened in alarm. "Before you always remembered everything clearly."

"I know. But now, everything is hazy. I…" He shook his head, which did nothing to clear it. "The details are fading quickly. I remember anger, not my own. Fear, danger. Fighting my own body. Nothing clear. Nothing more."

"You lost at cards," she explained. "It made you angry and you spoke nasty words to me. Things you wouldn't say. Your eyes changed, too. Becoming hard and cruel. You began arguing with yourself, out loud. One voice was you.

The other was something else entirely. He's the one who threw the table and came after me. You got him to stop. Do you remember any of that?"

"Very little. Feelings mostly. But I remember everything from before. I remember you coming into the lab, and setting your things on the table with mine. We sat down before I drank the elixir. We had the cards and the jug of gin and—"

They both froze.

"Did you ever drink the gin and tonic before?" Callie asked. "With this elixir?"

She spun something around in her fingers. The syringe of antidote. Hal's gut tightened. Of course she didn't trust him. He barely trusted himself.

"Not at the same time," he answered. "We had a small amount together with the old elixir at the temperance play. And I had the gin and tonic on its own the day we had dinner with my mother. I craved it. Drank almost an entire jug in a single day." Thinking about it stirred a craving inside him. Not as powerful as when he'd been drinking it, but there just the same.

"I'm still craving it," Callie admitted. She turned the syringe over in her hands once again. "I drank the first glass today so fast and I wanted more. I don't think it's out of my system. And you had at least twice what I did."

Hal gripped the arm of the sofa, his muscles clenching. "If that's the culprit, I could lose control again at any time."

"Possible. I think it must have been the combination of the drink with your elixir."

Hal rose from his seat. Callie sprang to her feet as well, putting out a hand to prevent him going anywhere.

"You should go home," he said. "Be safe. I can't stand the thought of hurting you."

"No. We should stick together. What if whatever was in that drink affects me too?"

Hal pinched the bridge of his nose. "Dammit. There's no good option here, is there?"

Callie reached out a hand to stroke his arm. "There is. We find out what was in that drink and how it might have gotten there."

The pieces fell into place. "Becher," Hal blurted. "The jug was clean. The gin was from you. But the tonic water… It came from Becher. Samples, he said. He wanted me to try it and endorse his product." Hal began to pace the room, running his hands through his hair. "Fuck! It's all part of his scheme. His ridiculous temperance advertising; promoting his drink as a healthy alternative. He's probably the one behind the neighborhood mischief."

"But why target you?"

"I don't know. I'm sure he's been annoyed with me since we met and I refused to support his cause. Beyond that? I couldn't guess." Hal sighed. "Now I might have made it worse. I saw him the other day and I didn't hold back my thoughts. I bluntly told him I disliked what he was doing. He might be furious with me now. Fuck. I don't know what to do."

He turned away from Callie, but she gripped his shoulder, spinning him to face her. "Do you have any more of the tonic water?"

"Yes. There's one more bottle in the kitchen."

"Get it," she commanded. "We're going to see the apothecary."

* * *

"Dr. Jekyll, Miss Finch, how lovely to see you both."

Mr. Robert looked at Hal and a single eyebrow twitched. "Together. What can I do for you?"

Hal set the bottle of tonic water on the counter. "We'd like to analyze the contents of this drink, if possible. We believe there may have been an addictive and potentially mind-altering substance added to it."

Both of Robert's eyebrows rose now. "That's no small thing. One moment." He slipped out from behind the counter, locked the shop's front door, and placed an Out to Lunch sign in the window. He gestured with his head toward the back room. "Follow me."

Hal had known the apothecary would have more ingredients on hand than he would ever have in his own laboratory, but the knowledge didn't prepare him for the sight of row after row of shelves crammed with bottles and boxes. He goggled at the array, spotting ingredients he'd never heard of and long scientific names he only vaguely remembered from school.

"The bottle?" Robert requested.

Hal jumped. "Oh, sorry. I, uh, got caught up reading the labels." He handed over the container of tonic water, and Robert placed it atop a long, narrow countertop.

Callie's fingers brushed Hal's arm. "I'm glad to see you being your usual self," she murmured.

"Me too."

Robert uncorked the tonic water and poured a dozen samples into a series of tiny cups. "Any idea what might be in here? You said it was addictive. Opium? Cocaine?" He wandered between the shelves and returned with an armload of ingredients. "We'll try those and a few other possible culprits."

The apothecary dripped one substance into the first cup and stirred. Nothing happened. He tried again, with a second substance. “No chloroform. No opium.” He continued on. “No alcohol. Yes to quinine.” He pointed at the cup where the water had taken on a slightly bluish tint. “So it is at least nominally tonic water.”

“What about cocaine?” Callie asked. “I know some people think it’s a wonder drug, but the way Hal reacted to this drink…” She trailed off, clearly not wanting to reveal too much.

Robert dropped something into the next cup. “Hmm. Inconclusive. Let me try a different test.” He unscrewed a small vial and poured a couple of drops of clear liquid into the tonic water. Immediately, the mixture turned bright red. A second later, it began to bubble and steam.

The apothecary took a step back. “Well,” he said, “there’s your culprit.” When the smoke from the reaction died down, he returned to the opium test, adding another few drops to it and nodding when it darkened. “Yes, definitely. Sobridyne.”

Callie and Hal looked at one another in puzzlement.

“What’s that?” Hal asked.

“Recent patent medicine. Made with no alcohol and marketed to the temperance crowd.”

“So Becher would know how to get his hands on it,” Hal mused.

“It’s nasty stuff,” Robert went on. “High concentration of cocaine, a bit of laudanum, castor oil, creosote, tobacco. Wasn’t in stores long because people tended to overuse it and wind up dead. Wouldn’t ever hear of having it in my store. It’s been banned in many cities, but not everywhere.”

Callie shuddered. “Are we in danger from drinking the tonic water?”

“I’d say no,” Robert replied. “Not unless you’ve been drinking it every day for years or you’ve had multiple bottles of it in a single sitting. The concentration in the water wasn't very large, or we would have had a much bigger reaction."

Hal looked at the cup of red liquid, which was still bubbling a bit. A few wisps of steam rose from it. "A bigger reaction?" he wondered.

"Oh, yes. Could have been explosive." The apothecary looked at the tonic water bottle. "Do you mind if I keep that? I'd like to run some more tests."

"Feel free," Hal answered. "If you discover anything else unusual about it, I'd like to know."

"Of course. And for the future, I'd recommend drinking a different brand. Too much of this could be harmful."

"Thank you. I very much appreciate your assistance."

"Happy to help, my boy. You're one of my best customers. And how could I ever refuse a pretty lady like Miss Finch? You kids run along now. I'll let you know if I make any more discoveries."

Hal thanked him again, then he and Callie headed for the exit.

"That's our answer, then," she said. "Becher has poisoned his drink to make it addictive. How horrid!"

"Revolting," Hal agreed. "And with that list of ingredients, it's no wonder it caused a bad reaction with the elixir." He cringed. "I'm lucky I'm not dead."

Callie stepped close to him. "I'm a bit worried some of it may still be in your system. What if you take ill or collapse?"

"You drank it too," Hal pointed out. "You really shouldn't be alone tonight, in case you have an adverse reaction."

She took hold of his arm. "Exactly. I'll stay at your house."

Hal swallowed hard. So much for the plan of keeping away from her. He'd have to suffer through this one last night, and then he could send her safely on her way.

Callie moved closer as they walked, her body pressing into his. Desire spiraled through him. Who was he kidding? He wasn't going to suffer. He was going to enjoy every damn second she was with him. Because after tonight, their business arrangements were over for good.

Chapter 35
Affair of the Heart

Whoever had designed Hal's study had done a masterful job creating a warm, inviting space for reading. The wide windows admitted plenty of natural light, and electric sconces placed strategically around the room provided ample illumination after the sun had gone down. The sofa and the two matching armchairs were sturdy and comfortable, and situated so as to take advantage of the best of the lighting. Half-height bookcases with glass doors protected the volumes from dust and dirty fingers.

He didn't own as many books as she did. To fit her collection, the shelves would have to be swapped out for floor-to-ceiling models.

For heaven's sake, Calliope, you aren't moving in with him. Stop fantasizing.

That was no easy task. In fact, after a lazy afternoon reading out back in his garden and then a delicious dinner together, her fantasies had gone quite wild. And while she could tell herself her happiness stemmed from the fact that he appeared to have suffered no lingering effects from either the elixir or the tonic water, she knew it for a lie. She was happy because they were together. Because he smiled at her in a way that made her heart thump. Because he showed genuine interest in whatever she had to say. Because he made her feel not just admired or desired, but adored.

"This room is a bookworm's paradise," she said, imagining herself stretched out on the sofa, reading while Hal sat beside her, idly running his hands up beneath her skirts. "You must spend a lot of time here."

"Not particularly. I always tell myself I will, but then I get so caught up in the laboratory, or meeting with this or that person who wants the advice of a scientist. Never enough time in the day, I suppose."

"You mean you don't take enough time for yourself. Don't get so caught up in caring for other people that you forget to take care of yourself."

A wry smile touched his lips. "I'm working on that. What about you? You're so kind and generous. I know you love to help people and to please people. Do you struggle with self-care also?"

"All the time. It's why I planned to retire as a courtesan and open the library. It's as much for me as for the members I hope to have. It's a future surrounded by books and knowledge. I can have them for myself and give them to others at the same time." Callie cast a suggestive look in Hal's direction. "And anything else I choose to give, I can give freely, with no care whether it's good business."

His Adam's apple bobbed in his throat. "That does sound like a satisfying future."

"I hope so." Callie ran a hand along the edge of the large wooden desk that stood near the window. The polished surface was entirely bare, without even a pen or an inkwell. "I can tell you don't use this desk."

"No."

"Too bad. It seems very… sturdy." She hopped up to sit

on the desk, tugging up her skirts a bit as she adjusted her position.

No one could call Henry Jekyll a prude any longer. He recognized the invitation immediately, closing the distance between them with swift strides. Callie spread her legs, and he fitted himself between her thighs. He pushed her skirts up, letting his hands rest just above her knees as he leaned in to kiss her.

"Calliope." His lips grazed her mouth, her jaw, then higher. "I want to give you everything you desire." He sucked gently on her earlobe, drawing a delicious shiver from her. "But I'm afraid all I'm doing is taking what *I* desire."

She slid her hands up under his coat, popping open the buttons of his vest. "You're a talented man," she murmured. "I think you can do both at once."

His fingers crept up her thighs. "I'll try."

Their lips came together, and they kissed deeply, hungrily. Callie's body ached in response, as if she'd been weeks or months without him, rather than mere days. She urged him closer, groaning when the hardness of his cock rubbed up against her. She canted her hips and he pressed closer in response.

"Christ, Callie, you make me wanton," he growled. "And I love it. I could take you right here on the desk, or on the floor, or anywhere."

"Mmm," she agreed, tugging his tie out of the way and kissing his throat. "So many options. You have that beautiful private garden out back. And rooms I haven't even seen yet. Perhaps we can try them all, one-by-one. Where would you like to start?"

Hal pulled back and stared at her, his expression so full of naked longing that her breath hitched. "My bedroom," he replied, a note of desperation creeping into his voice. He grasped her around the waist and lifted her down from the desk. “It has to be my bedroom.”

“Why the bedroom?”

Before he answered, he scooped her up into his arms, like a husband carrying his new bride across the threshold. “Because it’s not often a mere mortal has the opportunity to have a goddess in his bed. Where he can worship her all night, bathed in moonlight, then wake to behold her golden and glorious as the sun.”

“Have you been reading poetry?” Callie teased, the breezy words a mask for her churning emotions. Did he love her? This goddess would visit his bed every night. All he had to do was ask.

“No. But you conjure up thoughts of beauty.”

He strode through the house and up the stairs. His bedroom door was ajar, and he nudged it open with his foot, carried her inside, and laid her on the bed. The room was simply decorated, with practical furniture and no unnecessary ornamentation. The bedside table held a stack of books three high, each with a bookmark jutting from it. Exactly the sort of quiet, comfortable space she would have expected from him.

Hal didn’t join her in the bed, but stood above it, gazing down at her intently. “I want to undress you very, very slowly.”

“Please.”

He came down on top of her, undoing the buttons of her bodice, then peeling it away to expose her underthings. His hands caressed her through the remaining layers, up her torso, over her breasts, leaving fire in their wake. At this pace, she would be burnt to ashes by the time he finished. Not a bad way to go.

Callie had to turn over to give him access to her corset

laces. Hal kissed the nape of her neck as he worked the knot open, and her whole body trembled in a ticklish shiver. Goodness, had she always been so sensitive in that spot? He kissed her there again, and she gasped aloud.

Hal tossed the corset aside and moved on to her skirts, kneading her buttocks between each layer removed.

"I could touch every part of you forever," he murmured.

Yes, yes, please.

He slid her drawers and stockings off, then paused to let her sit up so he could tug her shift up over her head. When she was naked, he stilled, perching on the edge of the bed to gaze down at her.

Callie fluttered her lashes and gave him a coy smile. "Well? What would you like to do?"

He shook his head. "No. What would *you* like to do?"

She caught herself before she could reply with, "Anything you want," or that sort of phrase. Hal wanted to please her. At least as much as she wanted to please him. Maybe it was that mutual desire that made them so good together.

"I want what you offered," she said. "For you to touch every part of me." *Forever.*

"As my lady desires," Hal answered, reaching for her.

Callie put out a hand to stop him. "But I want you naked first."

His grin was wolfish. He quickly stripped out of his rumpled and partially-unfastened clothing, then climbed atop her, capturing her mouth with his. His hands trailed up her arms, over her shoulders, along her neck, then down to her breasts, cupping and squeezing until she sighed her pleasure into his mouth.

His lips quickly followed his hands, kissing little by little down to her breasts. Callie's eyes closed. Her arms splayed out at her sides. This was heaven, where the world shrank to nothing but the soft, worshipful touch of the man she loved.

Or maybe it was all too earthly, she amended, as the throb between her legs grew more urgent, more insistent.

Hal's tongue made a slow, teasing circle around Callie's nipple at the same time his fingers slipped between her legs. He sucked gently at first, then harder, the caress of his hands matching the rhythm exactly. Callie's back arched.

"Hal," she pleaded. "I need you."

He paused.

"I want you in me. Now. Please."

His brown eyes were as soft as fur and as warm as a crackling fire. "Anything for you, darling," he replied.

He shifted his position and they joined, both gasping as their bodies came together. Hal moved in careful, measured strokes, purposefully, as if trying to stretch the moment out into eternity. Callie wrapped her arms possessively around him.

I accept. You. Me. Eternity.

Soon, though, their bodies were clamoring for more, picking up the pace, bucking and thrusting, straining for blessed release. They crashed together, clutching one another until the storm passed.

They separated only briefly before curling into a happy embrace, sharing soft kisses and gentle touches. Cozy. Intimate. Loving. If she was his goddess, he was her god. Equally matched. A perfect pair. A two-parts-working-in-harmony couple, rather than those awful squabblers like Zeus and Hera.

She giggled.

"What's so funny?" Hal asked.

"Just thinking about how terrible the Greek gods were."

He grinned. "True. Not my Calliope, though."

Callie ran her fingers over his chest in lazy strokes. “I don’t remember any myth about Calliope and the Doctor.”

“We’ll have to write one, then. Long ago, in the days when gods still walked among mortal men, a young physician snuck his way into a grand symposium. There, great minds had gathered to take inspiration for their art from the muses themselves.”

“The moment he entered the room,” Callie continued, “he caught sight of Calliope, and desire jolted like Zeus’s thunderbolt in his chest.”

“No other woman could compare with her poise and beauty. But the lowly doctor knew himself far beneath her notice.”

“Or was he?” Callie laughed. “This is fun. I’m going to write all the bawdy parts.”

Hal chuckled, but it soon morphed into a yawn. “I’d love to act them out, but maybe a nap first.”

She snuggled closer, pulling the blankets up around them. “I am happy to sleep with you both literally and euphemistically.”

He kissed her brow. “Me too.”

* * *

“What’s your plan for the day?” Callie asked. She finished buttoning her bodice and then checked herself over in Hal’s mirror. Good enough for the trip home to change. “Finish writing our epic story of Calliope and the Doctor? Or do scientific pursuits take precedence?” Her lips pinched together. She didn’t like leaving Hal to potential danger. “Or do you need to do something about Mr. Becher? Do you think he means you harm?”

Hal fussed with his cufflinks. “Assuming he’s responsible for the crashed steam car and the other troubles, it seems he only wants to annoy me. I plan to avoid him. And there's no more tonic water in the house. Nor will there ever be. I'm swearing off the stuff."

"Temperance?" Callie's teasing smile was a little too stiff. Hard to be lighthearted when she was concerned for him.

"Something like it." He gave up on the cuffs and let his hands drop. "Today I have to clean up the laboratory."

"Would you like some help?"

"No." The response was brusque. "Thank you. It was my doing. I will take care of it."

"And the elixir?"

He turned away. "I don't know."

"Perhaps Mr. Robert can help you run some tests to determine what exactly went wrong. Let me know what you discover."

"Callie." Hal raked a hand through the hair he had just combed. "Please don't fret over me. You have your library. I don't wish you to neglect it in favor of my work."

"Yes, the library." She stepped closer to him, gently touching his shoulder. He remained facing away. "I think we should talk about that."

Her mind was made up. She would delay the project. Hal could contribute whatever amount he felt comfortable giving, but only as a donation. She wouldn't charge him for anything else ever again. Together, they could think up ideas for raising funds. A loan might be possible. Or sponsorship from progressive ladies who would approve of Callie's mission.

Missing her deadline would hurt. But she would be retired. Free to take up with any man of her choosing, purely for her own happiness.

Hal's shoulders rose and fell as he took a deep breath. "I know the library is very important to you."

"Yes, it is," Callie agreed. "And I'm determined to make it the very best it can be. But I want you to know—"

"You should talk to Victor," Hal blurted, jerking away from her touch.

Callie's nose wrinkled at the seeming non sequitur. "Your friend Dr. Franklin? Why?"

"He's rich. High society rich. Victor is descended from Benjamin Franklin on his father's side, and his mother brought in loads of money from the Astor fur-trading fortune."

Her entire body went cold. Hal couldn't mean that the way it sounded. She'd been so certain he loved her. He wouldn't casually pass her off to a friend, as if…

Her own words echoed in her mind. *You treat me as a whole person and not just a whore.*

"I know he can seem a little obnoxious on the surface," Hal continued, "but he's a genuinely decent fellow, and I'm sure he'd be very—" His voice broke, the rest of his words coming out clipped and harsh. "Kind and generous to you."

No. No, no, no. Callie backed toward the door, her body trembling. How could he be so… so horribly businesslike, when last night he'd been all passion and sweetness?

"Callie." He turned around at last. "I want you to have—"

"No!" She almost shouted it. "Don't. Stop. Don't say anything else." She reached behind her, groping for the door handle, desperate to get away, yet still unable to look away from him. Was that sadness in his expression, behind the determination? Damn her foolish heart for hoping for what she couldn't have.

Her fingers found the knob, and she threw the door open.

"I want to help," Hal insisted. "However I can."

Callie's hand flew to her mouth to cover a sob. She had to get out. Now, before he offered to pay her for last night and destroyed what was left of her aching heart.

Whatever he felt for her, it wasn't enough. On some level, to him the relationship always had been and always would be business. For Callie it wasn't. It never could be again.

The truth was like a stone in the pit of her stomach. They were over. Whatever she'd imagined last night was a dream, slipping away in the harsh reality of morning.

Hal took a step toward her.

"Stay away," she commanded. The tears were coming now, building in the corners of her eyes, threatening to stream down her cheeks. "I can't see you anymore. Ever."

Callie turned and fled.

Chapter 36
Tidying Up

He'd made her cry.

Hal stood in his laboratory, staring at the mess he'd made when the elixir had gone so horribly wrong. None of it registered. The memory of Callie overshadowed everything. All he could see were the tears trickling down her cheeks. All he could hear was the pain in her voice when she'd told him she never wanted to see him again.

He'd made her cry. He'd hurt her. How had he gotten it all so terribly wrong?

"Jekyll!" called a voice from the tunnel.

Hal cringed. Victor. Of all the people he didn't want to see at the moment.

And of course there was no stopping him. Victor strode into the laboratory like he owned the place, Nemo following close behind. They stopped just inside the lab, flanking the door, as if preventing Hal from fleeing.

"What the hell is going on?" Victor demanded. "Your housekeeper sent an urgent message. Apparently you got clonked on the head, possibly poisoned, and now you're wandering the house like a lost soul. What did you do?"

Hal traced a finger over the gash on his forehead. He'd removed the bandage, but the area was still tender.

"I fucked up," he admitted. Many times. This morning

was only the final straw in a long series of mistakes, he was certain.

Victor looked at Nemo. “See? He’s skipping out on meetings, swearing, going out at night, consorting with—”

Nemo cut him off. “Hal, tell us what happened. You can start with this mess of a room and then explain why you look like someone ripped your heart out.”

“It’s Miss Finch,” Victor opined. “He’s fallen head over heels for her. Clearly she’s broken his heart.”

“I think I broke *hers*!” Hal burst out. “She ran off. *In tears.* I hurt her, and all I was trying to do was help.” He kicked at a poker chip, sending it skittering across the laboratory floor. “I did everything wrong. I dragged her into my work, made a fool of myself multiple times in front of her fancy friends, put her in danger—both socially and physically—and chased away all the men who would have been much better for her than me. I thought… I thought I was finally doing the right thing.”

Nemo walked closer. “Maybe give us a bit more detail? How were you trying to help?”

Hal pushed up his glasses and pinched the bridge of his nose. “She has this dream project. A library. It’s a wonderful idea. A worthwhile one. It’ll be amazing. I know it will, because she cares deeply about books and knowledge and sharing those things. I wanted to see her succeed. I wanted to see her shine. But all this…” He waved a hand at the wreckage. “Everything I did interfered or threatened to ruin her plans. I can’t destroy her future because I’m selfish and want to spend time with her. I can’t be the one to stand in her way if she can earn what she needs somewhere else.”

Victor grimaced. “With *someone* else, you mean.”

Nemo muttered something in Bengali that Hal suspected was profanity.

"Shit, Hal, most fellows just tell a girl they love her," Victor sighed. "Give her flowers or chocolates or something. Why couldn't you do that?"

"So I was supposed to ruin her dream?" Hal demanded.

"Tell us precisely what you said to her," Nemo requested.

"I said she should talk to Victor because he's rich and a decent guy and—"

"What?" Victor shouted. "Are you out of your damned mind? You told her to proposition me? Not just any guy, but *me*? Jesus Fucking Christ. I'm not going to bang the woman you love! What kind of friend do you think I am?"

Nemo cursed again, in both Bengali and English. "The poor woman. You absolutely broke her heart."

Hal sat down on the floor in a pile of scattered playing cards and put his head in his hands. "I thought I was offering her a way to get what she wanted."

"She wanted *you*." Nemo's voice was softer now. "And whatever you meant, what she probably heard was, 'Oh, I don't care if you move on to someone else.'"

"Of course I care! I hate it! I hate it so damn much to think that I can't have her and that I can't be the one to give her everything. I wish I had the money to buy her a thousand libraries! But I don't."

"You should have told her you love her," Victor said. He crossed his arms over his chest and glared down at Hal. "Now you're going to have to apologize. Preferably in a loud, public, embarrassing way. Also, I'm never going to forgive you."

"Doubt she will, either," Hal sighed.

"Find a way to apologize," Nemo suggested. "A way that includes telling her how you feel, being genuinely contrite, and letting *her* decide whether she wants you or someone else. Right now, I'm guessing she wants neither."

Hal thought he might be ill. He'd ruined Callie's plans and broken her heart all at once. She was one hundred percent right to say she never wanted to see him again. The thought of her all alone, crying over what he'd done, made his chest hurt. Whatever happened, he couldn't leave her believing he didn't love her.

"I'll tell her. She deserves to know the truth and that I'm sorry. I doubt she'll ever want me back, but I owe her an apology regardless."

"Good." Nemo surveyed the room. "Do you want help cleaning up this mess?"

"No, thank you. I'd rather do it myself. I think it'll help clear my head."

"The head that got clonked," Victor pointed out.

"I had a bad reaction to the elixir. I won't take it again, don't worry."

"I hope not. Because right now I'm really questioning your decision making."

Hal slowly rose to his feet and faced his friends. "Thank you for coming to check up on me. Clearly I needed to talk that through."

Nemo and Victor both nodded.

"Damn right," Victor said.

"I'll let you know what I decide to do and how it all goes," Hal promised. "You have my word on that."

"And you'll let us know if you need help," Nemo added. "No going it alone anymore. You know we're here for you."

"I know." Hal clasped hands with each of them in turn. "Thank you."

Hal saw his friends out the door, then returned to the lab, determined to set everything right. First the physical mess, then the mess of the rest of his life. One thing at a time.

He picked up the box where the poker chips were stored.

Chips went into the box, sorted properly by color. Next came the cards, divided into their individual decks, shuffled, and packed into their boxes. The broken table he dragged out to the front yard. It could be broken up further and used as firewood. Lastly, he swept up the remnants of the jug of gin and tonic and the shattered glassware, depositing the debris in the trash.

Better.

Hal stretched. His muscles were more relaxed, his nerves less frayed. He'd made mistakes, but like in his scientific experiments, he could see his errors and was ready to begin anew. On to step two: the elixir.

Hal didn't have to think particularly hard about this step. It had been coming for a long time, though he'd stubbornly hung on to his belief in the experiment. He opened the cabinet and took out the jug of elixir, carrying it over to the small sink beside his worktable. Popping the stopper, he upended the jug and watched the liquid flow down the drain.

Eddie gave an encouraging squeak.

"That's right, my friend. Good riddance."

The sadness Hal expected as months of work trickled away was tempered with a profound relief. This was the right course of action. Failure was common in the scientific world, and he could see now that this project was never meant to be. The world didn't have a strict line between good and evil or order and chaos. Sometimes society's rules needed breaking. And no one should be forced into a lifestyle that didn't suit them merely because of what others thought.

The antidote followed the elixir down the drain. When both were fully washed away, Hal cleaned and dried the equipment. The sight of the empty bottles filled him with a renewed sense of purpose. No more Mad Scientist life. He had the skills to do real good in society. Nothing flashy. No fame or fortune. Just sensible, useful work.

Hal's gaze drifted across his laboratory. He would never need all this space. Not for the remedies and medicines he intended to concentrate on in the future. Maybe he was better off selling this house and taking down the tunnel. He didn't need a great deal of space for his work area, a desk, and a couple cabinets. The only other thing in the room was the bookshelf with all his scientific texts.

Hal froze, a vision flashing through his mind of more shelves—row after row, turning the empty room into a cozy, happy place.

"Hell and damnation," he cursed.

He'd had the means to fund Callie's library all along. And now he knew what he needed to do.

Chapter 37
Irregular Visits

Two weeks later

Hal took the corner at a nearly-reckless speed, allowing himself to enjoy the wind whipping through his hair and the sun on his face. These daily bicycle rides had become cathartic, even though Callie still refused to see him. He'd left his letter and thanked her doorman. She hadn't yet told him to stay away, and as long as that was the case, he had hope.

He pedaled swiftly toward his house, only to slam on the brakes when he saw a large black steam car parked out front. The vehicle was one of those fancy sorts that wealthy owners trundled about in: fully enclosed, with shades to cover the windows and a separate front seat for the driver. Perfect for a secret tryst or a criminal meeting.

Hal approached slowly, steeling himself. Whoever this was, he was telling them to get the hell away from his house, and he was using those exact words. No more Doctor Nice Guy.

A door swung open before he could even dismount from his bicycle. A large man stepped out. He grabbed Hal, yanked him off the bike, and shoved him into the carriage. By the time Hal righted himself, the steam car was chugging away at top speed.

"Good afternoon, Dr. Jekyll." Becher reclined against the black leather seat, a smug smile twisting his lips. "So good of you to join me."

"Go fuck yourself," Hal snapped.

Becher's expression didn't change. "My dear doctor, it's a shame to see you succumbing to such filthy habits. If only there was a movement you could join that preached wholesome and abstemious habits."

"I want no part of your nefarious schemes and poison drinks."

"Perhaps not, but you will assist me regardless."

Hal snorted. He folded his arms across his chest and leaned back in his seat, adopting a posture of indifference. If he timed it right, he could lunge for the door and leap out of the carriage. Foolish, perhaps; but if he waited until they slowed to turn a corner, he could minimize the danger.

"I have an upcoming presentation, you see," Becher continued. "My tonic water is poised to become the official drink of the temperance movement, and you are going to give it your approval as a respected member of the medical community."

Hal glowered. "Why don't you simply pay an unethical doctor like a competent criminal?"

Becher's pale face turned scarlet. "I *am* competent," he snarled, his voice so full of fury that Hal instinctively shrank back. "You are the flaw. You were so convenient. Such a do-gooder. The perfect candidate. And what did you do when I brought you into the fold? You embarrassed me! Denounced the cause in front of my most important backers. After I specifically recommended you!"

Hal regarded the other man in confusion. "What are you saying? Are you... Did *you* procure me that invitation to the Pike's dinner? And you've been targeting me because I didn't like your little club?"

Becher leaned forward, resting his elbows on his knees. His gaze shot daggers at Hal. "You failed me, Jekyll. But now you will atone for that mistake. I'd like your public endorsement of my tonic water."

"No."

Becher's voice lowered to an oily purr. "In exchange, I shall refrain from pointing the newspapers at the true culprit behind the recent lawlessness. Imagine my surprise when I traced the crimes to that house of vice you so enjoy frequenting."

Hal felt the blood drain from his face. His hands began to tremble.

Becher's anger subsided into a mocking sneer. "Such a pretty ladybird you have. It would be a shame to expose her foolish drunken antics to the world. I don't think prison would be kind to her."

"You fucking bastard."

Hal could hardly see through the anger. Not Callie. Not his Callie. He couldn't let anything happen to her. If he didn't cooperate, her library would be an impossibility. Even if she escaped arrest, she would be ruined. No one in "good society" would take the word of a courtesan over a well-known businessman. The rest of the women in the apartment building would suffer as well. Possibly the entire neighborhood. Her street was full of artists, eccentrics, and people who lived outside the rules. Hal couldn't let Becher and his spurious moral crusaders shatter their peaceful existence.

"I'll do it," Hal forced out through clenched teeth. "I'll give you your damned endorsement. You stay the hell away from my friends—forever—and I'll say whatever you want."

Becher relaxed and lit a cigarette. “I knew you would see reason.”

* * *

Callie hurried toward her apartment, the hard soles of her boots clopping against the wooden planks of the sidewalk. She checked her watch again. Five minutes to one. She had time.

Still, she moved quickly. She couldn’t be caught standing outside on the one day he happened to arrive a few minutes early. She wasn’t ready for that confrontation.

The doorman gave her a nod as she ducked inside, but said nothing. Nor did he look at the table where Callie’s mail always awaited her.

Callie looked. She couldn’t help herself. The stack had grown awkwardly large. Identical envelopes, addressed in an identical hand. Were the letters inside identical, too, or merely variations on a theme?

The one on top, delivered yesterday, appeared to be scrawled in haste. Perhaps he was growing anxious. A peek inside to gauge his state of mind might be reasonable.

She glanced away. It didn’t matter. He would be back again today with another letter that would surely look like all the others. Reading them was only asking for trouble.

A door creaked, and Betsy stepped out into the hall, freshly dressed and primped, ready to head out for the day.

“Waiting for your beau?” she asked, giving Callie a sly smile. “You gonna talk to him today?”

“No,” Callie replied. She checked her watch again. Hal came by the apartment every day, arriving by bicycle at precisely 1:07. Every day he politely requested to speak to Callie, and when informed she was not at home to callers, he left a letter. Exactly the same, every day, without fail.

Betsy made a little huffing noise. "You sure about that? He's awfully persistent. He must really want to see you. And you haven't asked Jackson to tell him to stop coming by, so..." She paused dramatically. "Seems to me maybe you *want* him to keep at it? Are you going to at least read your letters?"

"No."

"Want me to read them for you?"

"No!" Callie quickly composed herself. "I will read them myself once I feel comfortable doing so. Right now I'm focusing on other things."

Betsy shook her head. "Fine, fine. But I think he loves you, Callie. He must, to keep at it. And he's never angry or demanding, is he, Jackson?"

"Not at all, Miss Hill," the doorman replied. "Always quiet and polite. Never argues when I say Miss Finch is not at home. Just leaves his letters and always thanks me. The first few days, I think he was expecting me to tell him not to come back, but since you didn't ask for that..." Jackson shrugged. "I think he's content to wait for you, Miss Finch."

"Yes, well, maybe tomorrow I'll read the letters and see what he wants. Excuse me."

She dashed up the stairs and into her apartment. There was no chance she'd be reading those letters tomorrow. Not when her heart made wild leaps of hope at the mere thought he might love her and want to make amends. These moments were inevitably followed by the fear the letters were nothing but suggestions of prospective clients.

Callie walked to the window and drew back the curtain just enough to see out, without revealing her presence to anyone outside the building. Hal would be riding up any minute now.

The best thing to do was probably to tell him to go

away. Anything he wanted to say to her was irrelevant now. Since her current state of mind left her entirely unready to take on any new lovers, she'd declared herself officially retired as a courtesan. She'd chosen a new direction for her library project as well: seeking wealthy patronesses, fellow ladies of the demimonde who would applaud Callie's goals of providing women with knowledge, empowerment, and choice.

One of the women she'd contacted had already responded favorably. She'd suggested they offer classes to women working in or considering the sex trade on how to select safe and discreet clients and ways to protect against disease and conception. Callie loved the idea, and she'd already jotted down several ideas for similar lessons aimed at women of any occupation or circumstance.

Outside, a woman with a pink parasol sauntered past. A short time later a pair of men walked by, hand-in hand, taking advantage of the permissive neighborhood to show public affection. Then a nanny pushing a baby carriage—which was as likely to contain a spoiled dog as a baby.

No bicycles. No Hal.

Callie checked her watch, wondering if she'd arrived home earlier than she'd realized. 1:09. No. He was late.

She tugged the curtain back a bit more, peering down the street in the direction he would be coming from. No sign of him. A nervous tremor ran through her. Had something happened? A delay? An accident? She kept watching, telling herself she only wanted to be certain he hadn't come to any harm.

After ten minutes, Callie gave up. Some other business had detained him, probably. Or maybe he'd decided these daily visits weren't worth his time. Maybe he'd moved on with his life. The way she was doing with hers. She turned resolutely from the window and walked to her desk to write another letter to a possible sponsor.

Some time later, a knock at her door startled her from her work. She set her pen down and rose, frowning in puzzlement. Who would be coming by at this hour? Betsy was out, and likely the other women were too.

Callie opened the door to find Jackson standing on the opposite side, his mouth twisted in a look of uncertainty.

"There's a man here to see you, Miss Finch. Are you at home to callers?"

"A man?" She blinked. "Not Ha— Dr. Jekyll?"

"No, ma'am. Says he's a Mr. Valdez."

Callie's eyes went wide. "Marc? Here?" Valdez had never visited her here before, though she'd given him the address during their brief time together. Like most of her upper-class clients, he preferred his own residence. "I'll come down to see him. Thank you, Jackson."

He nodded and stepped aside to allow her to descend the stairs first.

She found Marc waiting outside, pacing in front of her building. He stopped when he saw her and tipped his hat.

"Miss Finch. Good day to you."

"Mr. Valdez," she replied, with a slight dip of her chin. "What can I do for you?"

"Answer a question, I hope. It's about Jekyll."

"Hal?" Callie blurted. Icy fear clawed at her insides. "What about him? Is something wrong?"

"I'm not certain. I thought perhaps you could enlighten me. I'd been trying to schedule a meeting with him, to discuss how his experiments might fit in with some of my plans for charitable works. I'd thought he'd been interested, but then he canceled abruptly with nothing but a brief note saying he was, quote, 'terminating his experimental endeavors.'"

Callie gasped. Ending his experiments? But why? Did he fear a repeat of the problem with the elixir? And what else had changed since she'd last spoken to him? She almost turned toward the house, struck with a sudden urge to grab the whole stack of his letters and tear them open.

Valdez made a noise of displeasure. "Judging by your reaction, I'd say you didn't expect that of him, either."

"No, not at all." Hal had devoted so much time and effort to his work. What could he mean to do if not that? "He'd had a problem with a particular experiment, but I didn't expect him to do anything so drastic."

"I was puzzled by it myself, but thought maybe he'd taken on a new project. Or perhaps that you and he were planning something together."

Callie felt her cheeks heat. "No," she replied.

"When I saw this morning's paper, however, I became concerned."

Callie's pulse quickened and her palms began to sweat. Something *was* wrong. Something bad enough that Hal had missed his usual visit. Any hope that she'd begun to get over him evaporated. She still loved him as much as ever, and the thought of him coming to harm made her sick with dread.

"I haven't read the papers today," she replied, calling on her best social manners to keep herself calm. "What did it say that worried you?"

Valdez pulled a newspaper clipping from his coat pocket. "You can read it for yourself. It's about Becher and his tonic water. He's doing a presentation tomorrow evening at a fundraiser for his temperance group. Promoting his beverage as part of a healthier, alternative lifestyle. He's providing enough for the entire crowd to toast with, instead of champagne. And then the article said the presentation is to include—"

Callie saw it before Valdez could tell her. "…A medical endorsement by local physician Dr. H. Jekyll."

"Exactly. Did you have any idea he was doing this? Or why? In all our previous conversations, Jekyll had been firm in his disagreement with the temperance movement. I can't imagine why he would agree to speak at one of their events. I hoped you could shed some light on this seeming reversal."

"I can't. Not directly." Callie's mind began to race. She needed to get back inside. She needed to read those letters, in case they contained any pertinent information. And most importantly of all, she needed to save Hal from whatever predicament he'd gotten into.

"What I can tell you is that he wouldn't be doing this if he thought he had a choice," she told Valdez. "Becher is pressuring him somehow." Damn. She should have known that bastard would try something. She should never have left Hal alone so long, with a known enemy operating unchecked.

"I need to get to that event." A vague idea began to swirl in her mind. "Can you procure invitations? Enough for four or five people?"

"Certainly."

"Excellent." Her wisp of an idea began to crystalize. "I have a plan."

Chapter 38
To Your Health

Hal slunk along the wall of the Grand Ballroom, wishing he could simply fade into the wallpaper. The Russell House Hotel was the place to be in Detroit, but right now he would have preferred to be anywhere else. The lush decor and fancy clothes were only so much gilding atop a steaming pile of manure. This was a swindler's game, a grab for money and power, and the smiling people with drinks in their hands were unwitting dupes.

Becher looked his way and Hal stilled. The beverage tycoon's eyes narrowed, his mouth twitching in the tiniest of smirks. A warning: Do as you're told.

Hal replied with the merest of nods. As if he could forget, when Callie's future hung in the balance. Once again, he had brought trouble to her doorstep. Literally, this time.

Hal resumed his slow walk, careful to avoid the humming drink dispensers at either end of the room. At first glance, the machines looked like square, metal tables with large glass kegs full of liquid on top. If you watched for a time, however, you could see sections of the table slide and shift like a great puzzle, maneuvering empty glasses beneath the spigot to fill them with Becher's tonic water, then depositing them onto a waiting tray for passers-by to grab. Hal wanted nothing to do with either the tonic water or the automated apparatus.

He might have been the only person in the room with such reservations. Everywhere he looked, ladies and gentlemen held tumblers of the foul drink. None of them knew the clear, fizzy liquid contained a cocktail of noxious drugs.

Dammit, he couldn't do this. He couldn't get up in front of all these people and testify to the health benefits of Becher's tonic water. He was a physician, trained and sworn to help, not harm.

Becher glanced at Hal again. Hal squirmed. What choice did he have? If it were only his reputation on the line, he would turn and walk out right now and never look back. But the bastard had learned Hal's biggest weakness.

The memory of Becher's taunts still echoed. *"Such a pretty ladybird you have. It would be a shame to expose her foolish drunken antics to the world."*

Hal's blood boiled. That son of a bitch! Blaming his own crimes on innocent women. Blackmailing Hal with threats against the woman he loved.

Damn him to the furthest reaches of hell!

"Good evening, Dr. Jekyll," murmured a familiar feminine voice.

Hal jumped and whirled around. His mouth opened in surprise, but he clamped it shut before he could greet her with her usual nickname.

"Miss Majhi." She'd dressed elegantly tonight in a gorgeous dark blue sari. Hal couldn't remember the last time he'd seen her in anything but trousers. "I wasn't expecting to see you tonight." The formal words were as close as he could get to, "What the devil are you doing here?"

"I wasn't expecting to be here," she replied, her words

clipped. "Until I discovered *you* would be here. Keeping secrets from your friends again, are you?"

"It couldn't be helped." He had no choice. He had to be here. He had to do *something.*

A flash of red caught his eye.

"Oh, sh—" Hal cut himself off before he could swear in public.

Across the room, Callie strode through the entrance in a dazzling scarlet dress. Blood-red roses adorned the curls pinned atop her head, and rubies glittered at her throat. Walking beside her, his arm threaded through hers, was Victor.

For an instant, Hal wondered if he'd fallen into an alternate reality where Callie had happily taken his suggestion and he would now have to step aside and stoically accept it.

His body had no interest in stoicism. His heart had begun pounding the moment he'd laid eyes on her. Just seeing her, even with someone else as her escort, made him wild with desire. He ached to run to her and beg her for a chance to apologize.

Another man stepped up to her opposite side. Hal gaped. Valdez? What on earth was going on? Why was she here? Hadn't she read his letters?

Maybe not. Or maybe she'd stopped after the first few. Most of them said more or less the same thing: he was sorry, he would like to apologize in person, he had no expectations, he would take no more than a few minutes of her time.

The last letter, though, was different. He'd agonized over it.

> *Becher has been following me. He's threatened to blame the "drunken antics" on you and your*

friends. I won't be coming back. I should never have come in the first place. I swear I will not let him do this to you. I'm so very sorry.

Surely if she'd read that letter she wouldn't...

Hal bit his lip so hard it hurt. Another error on his part. He ought to have disappeared without a word. This was Callie. Any inkling that he might need help and she'd come running. Because even if he'd broken her heart, he'd never crush her fighting spirit or her generous nature.

A hand gripped his arm. "Stay calm," Nemo whispered.

Startled, Hal rounded on his friend. "Calm? Are you in on this?" he hissed. "What's going on? What are you all plotting? Do you have any idea what you've done?"

If anything went wrong, Becher could blame Callie for his own misdeeds, right here. Even if her innocence was proven later, it wouldn't matter. The damage from the public spectacle would be irreversible.

"Good evening, ladies and gentlemen!" Becher's voice boomed from the voice transmitter. That was Hal's cue.

He was doing this. He would walk right up on that stage and endorse Becher's tonic water, and nothing was going to stop him. Later, he could pen letters to a number of respected doctors and scientists, telling them the truth and asking them to refute everything he'd said. It would utterly destroy his reputation. Better him than any of his friends.

He shrugged out of Nemo's grasp. "I have something important to do." He lowered his voice further and added, "Don't try to stop me."

"Hal." Nemo's tone was a warning.

Hal ignored his friend and strode for the stage. Running would draw too much attention, so he walked at a measured pace and tried to keep his face impassive. The swish of silk behind him announced he was being followed, and he turned, heaving a sigh.

"You must excuse me, Miss Majhi," he said in a conversational tone easily audible to anyone nearby. "I'm needed on stage."

She lifted one hand and waved frantically. Across the room, Victor and Callie separated, each headed in the opposite direction. Dammit, what were they doing? Hal hopped up onto the stage without waiting for an introduction.

Becher gave him a startled look, but then smiled. "I hope you all have had a chance to pick up a glass of my tonic water for our toast tonight," he said to the audience. "I'm extremely honored to have been asked to provide a healthy alternative to champagne." He lifted his own glass. Hal wondered if he actually drank the nasty stuff, or if his glass held only water.

Becher went on for a time, delivering a carefully written speech on temperance. None of it was new or interesting, and Hal wanted to scream at him to get on with it.

Instead, he took deep breaths to relax his muscles and watched the reactions around the room. Clusters of people smiled and nodded as they listened. Some were decent people like the Pikes, doing what they thought was right. Others, like the smirking gathering of the Detroit Ladies' Committee Against Vice, were eager to assert their superiority. Probably there were others like Becher in the crowd, using a social movement for personal gain.

Callie and Valdez stood by one wall, next to one of the tonic water dispensing machines, perhaps the only people not smiling. Callie's red dress made her impossible to miss. Becher must have noticed her. Hal couldn't risk even the slightest mistake.

His gaze darted in the opposite direction, looking for

Victor. His Mad Scientist friends were exactly the sort of people to try something unexpected. Perhaps cutting the electricity or bringing in a bizarre machine to create a distraction. If Victor had slipped away, he could be up to anything.

There. Hal let out a relieved breath. Victor stood beside the other drink machine, along with…

Hal did a double take. Mr. Robert from the apothecary shop was here, at a fancy temperance party, dressed in his ordinary working clothes.

Everything came together in sudden, perfect clarity. Hal swore under his breath. Callie's plan, as far as he could guess it, was brilliant. Bold. But not without danger. Becher would try to turn it on her. Valdez and Victor would vouch for her. But they didn't have the stage or a voice amplifier.

Hal did.

He'd come here determined to help Callie. She'd come here to help him. What they should have been doing—what they would be doing from now on, Hal hoped—was working together.

He looked at each of his friends in turn, staring until he caught their eye, then smiling to show he understood. *I know what you're doing. I won't mess it up.*

Nemo gave a tiny nod. Victor saluted. Callie smiled back.

Not her usual radiant smile, though it was hard to be certain from this distance. She was holding back. Worried, perhaps. Or still wanting nothing to do with him.

Hal was so busy implementing the new plan that he nearly missed his introduction.

"…For his generous offer to speak on the healthful properties of tonic water," Becher said. "Dr. Jekyll?" He stepped back from the voice transmitter and gestured for Hal to step up to the device.

"Thank you." Hal gave the crowd a nervous smile. Defying one's enemy and causing certain chaos in front of a large crowd was bound to set anyone on edge. Also, he had to use a machine. He prayed Becher would assume the anxiousness came from fear of stepping out of line.

Hal stepped in front of the transmitter. Little wires curled from the top and sides of the round, drum-like device. It had been mounted on a pole to put it at a comfortable level for speaking.

"Good evening." His voice sounded so loud he jumped. "Er, excuse me," he said more quietly. "I'm not good with machines."

A murmur of laughter ran through the crowd. Good. They were relaxed and he had their attention.

"For those of you who don't know me, I'm Dr. Henry Jekyll, a physician and experimental scientist. I have a medical degree from the University of Michigan, and I've been working for several years with medicinal formulae and their effects on the human body. I'd like to thank you all for having me here tonight in my capacity as a medical professional."

He paused to let them absorb his credentials. The more they trusted him, the better this would go.

"I am particularly pleased to be able to present to you—with the help of my esteemed colleagues—a scientific experiment to demonstrate the purity of Mr. Becher's tonic water. I'm sure you've all heard the rumors that certain beverages have been tainted with illegal narcotics to make them addictive." Hal struggled not to grin at the startled looks of the crowd, who had, of course, heard no such thing. He didn't dare glance at Becher, but quickly continued on before anyone could interrupt. “The formula we are using tonight has been carefully designed to react with dangerous substances such as cocaine and opium.”

Hal heard footsteps behind him and turned his body to block Becher from lunging at the voice transmitter. He raised his voice. “When used on a pure beverage, however, the formula will do nothing more than turn the healthful liquid a pleasant shade of pale blue. Miss Finch, if you would do the honors?”

A hand clamped down on Hal’s shoulder, spinning him to look into the furious eyes of Mr. Becher.

“Too late,” Hal whispered. The entire crowd had turned to stare at Callie, a shining jewel in her red gown, as she grinned broadly and dumped the contents of a small vial into the open top of the drink dispensing machine.

Chapter 39
Aftereffects

The entire assembly gasped when the tonic water in the dispenser turned a bright, almost glowing, red. A second later, cries of alarm went up as the liquid began to boil and steam. Callie skittered backward to avoid being splashed. The bubbling tonic water poured over the rim of the container, sluicing down the sides of the apparatus. Smoke billowed, and she fanned it away from her face. Near the opposite wall, Dr. Franklin leaned lazily against the wall next to a second bubbling vat of red tonic water while Mr. Robert motioned for people to step aside.

"Miss Finch! Miss Finch!" Hal's shouted words were painfully loud through the amplifier. "Are you all right?"

"You backstabbing scoundrel," Becher snarled. "What have you done?"

Hal faced him defiantly. Sweet, good-hearted Hal who had deciphered her plan and made it even better than she'd hoped. Callie took a step toward the stage. If Becher made any move to hurt Hal, she would pummel him with her bare fists.

Valdez grabbed her arm to stop her. "I'm here with her, Jekyll!" he called. "What's happening?"

Marc's words echoed those of the people around them. *What's happening? What's wrong?* Heads swung back and forth, looking between the boiling red liquid and the confrontation on the stage. Some guests stared down at the glasses in their hands, mouths agape in shock and horror. Miss Majhi walked calmly through the crowd, adding drops of the formula to the glasses of anyone who would permit it. Several partygoers dashed their drinks on the ground.

"What was in that drink?" Hal demanded, playing his part masterfully. "The red color is a reaction to cocaine. The boiling to laudanum. *What have you done?*"

"Sobridyne!" Mr. Robert shouted. "It must be Sobridyne!"

Another collective gasp went up. The temperance crowd had heard of the problematic drug.

"This is your fault!" Becher's face had turned almost as red as his drink. "You did this. *She* did this." He pointed an accusing finger in Callie's direction. "That woman is—"

Hal kicked the voice transmitter, sending the device flying off the stage, where it smashed against the floor with a crash so loud it left Callie's ears ringing.

Chaos erupted.

Half the crowd ran toward the stage, half toward the exit. Cries of anger and fear sounded from all directions, smothering the argument between Becher and Hal. A body jostled Callie from behind, knocking her from Marc's grasp. She seized the opportunity, hiking her skirts and racing for the stage.

"Hal! Hal!" He probably couldn't hear her, but he would see her coming. She hadn't chosen this dress solely to match the bright red, bubbling tonic water, after all.

Hal leapt down from the stage, deftly avoiding Becher's attempts to seize him and landing only a few yards from Callie's side. They pushed toward one another, reaching out, until at last their hands touched.

Hal's fingers entwined with hers. She tugged him toward the exit.

"Quickly. Before he recovers enough to send his minions after us."

Hal nodded, pressing close to her to keep from becoming separated. Shouts rose up all around them, and multiple pairs of hands grasped at his clothing.

Only a few of the cries were entirely clear, but they all seemed to follow the same theme.

"Doctor, help me!"

"Am I poisoned?"

"What can I do?

"Please! You must cure me!"

Hal squirmed away from the panicked people, his fingers tightening around Callie's. "You will all be fine," he said, his professional voice surprisingly even given that he was almost shouting. "Don't drink any more and you'll have nothing to worry about."

They pressed on, progress toward the door agonizingly slow as more people crowded them, begging for Hal's reassurance. Again and again he soothed and calmed, a single voice of reason in the melee.

You will be fine. No lingering effects.

Not from the tonic water, perhaps. But from him?

Heat seemed to radiate up Callie's arm from where their hands were joined. Despite the turmoil around her, the image in her mind was that of Hal on the stage, his gaze locked on hers, a smile of understanding on his lips. All the resistance she thought she'd built up during their weeks apart had crumbled in that instant.

The mob thinned out slightly once they finally made it through the ballroom doors, with most of the people scurrying toward the exit. When Callie had arrived, the square outside had been packed with autocabs and personal steam cars. With everyone leaving at once, traffic would be a snarled mess. Any attempt to flee the hotel would have to be done on foot.

She had a better idea. Holding tight to Hal, she whirled in the opposite direction.

Hal stumbled. "We're not leaving?"

Callie gave him a second to steady himself, then led him down the hall at a brisk pace. "We're hiding in plain sight." She steered him to the hotel's lavish restaurant, striding up to the maître d'hôtel with a smile on her face.

"Good evening. I'd like a table for two, please. Something quiet and secluded, if at all possible."

The headwaiter nodded. "Certainly, ma'am. We have a booth in the back that should suit you."

Moments later, they were tucked into the corner of the restaurant, menus in hand. Hal held his out at an awkward angle, shielding his face from any passersby.

"What if Becher comes barging in here?" he fretted.

"Why would he?"

Hal frowned, then set the menu down. He removed his spectacles and polished them with his napkin. "Good question. I don't think he would expect us to be here."

"I don't think so, either. And we're not visible from the entrance to the restaurant, so even if someone peeks in, they won't see us."

"Also, anyone coming in here trying to confront us will be seen as the troublemaker and thrown out," Hal reasoned. "We're likely as safe here as anywhere. I'm just worried for you."

"I know." Callie didn't need him to tell her that. He never would have come here at all if he hadn't been worried for her.

But speaking of it out loud appeared to ease his mind, so she responded in kind. "I'm worried about you, too."

"Thank you. I am both humbled and touched that you would come charging to my rescue."

"As if I would let you ruin yourself for that scum," Callie scoffed.

"It was all for you." Hal reached out, as if to take her hand, but stopped halfway, letting his hand drop to the table.

"I know." Callie did what he would not, covering his hand with her own. "But I couldn't let Becher hurt you any more than you could let him hurt me. Thank you for understanding my plan and reacting accordingly. You were magnificent."

Hal squirmed, his eyes dropping to where their hands were joined. "We made a marvelous team. I was a fool not to consult with you the moment he made his threat."

"I wasn't speaking to you, remember?"

Hal shrugged. "I should never have chased you away in the first place. I'm so sorry."

"I know." She was repeating herself—again—but Hal needed the verbal acknowledgement. She understood him better now, and the differences between them. People put on public faces too often for her to base judgments on anything but actions. Hal, though, was artless. He trusted the words of others, and processed with words of his own. "You made a mistake. It happens."

He gave a mirthless laugh. "Much more than one mistake, I'm afraid."

An approaching waiter interrupted the conversation. Hal withdrew his hand and straightened in his seat.

"A custard pie and a cup of coffee, please," Callie requested.

Hal ordered the same dessert with tea. The efficient restaurant staff had the food and drink to them in minutes.

Callie nibbled slowly. "By the time we're done here, the crowd should have dispersed enough that we can leave without trouble," she said. "Becher will be long gone. He won't want to be forced to answer questions."

Hal took a sip of his tea. "I agree. If any of his helpers are loyal, they could be left behind to watch for us, though. Your dress is quite noticeable." A shy smile touched his lips. "And gorgeous. Did you purposely dress as the tainted tonic water?"

"It did occur to me that I would match, yes."

"It was a perfect choice." His voice dropped lower. "You're full of energy, potentially dangerous, and definitely addictive. I can't seem to stop craving you, Calliope." He abandoned his food and drink, staring at her intently through the pale-green lenses of his spectacles. "Not only in bed, but this. Being with you. I've missed that."

Callie lowered her own cup. "So have I."

He sucked in a sharp breath. "I love you, Calliope Finch. I expect nothing from you because of that, but I owe you the truth. I only ever wanted the best for you. I wanted to give you the world. To see you achieve your dreams and have all the happiness you deserve. I'm sorry I bungled things. I'm sorry I assumed I knew what you wanted."

Callie's heart pounded in her chest. She clasped her hands in her lap, fighting the urge to lunge across the table and kiss him.

Tell him you love him too.

There would be no going back once she did. That alone gave her pause. When she said it, she needed to be certain she was doing the right thing, for the right reasons.

"And I'm sorry I didn't realize you needed things articulated more clearly," she replied instead.

Hal cringed and rubbed his temple. "Please, Callie, don't blame yourself for my failing. I should have asked you what you wanted. I should have asked you if you even wanted my help at all. I had no right to make decisions for you or to interfere in your life in any way. I've made error after error, and in the end I hurt you. I swear it was never my intent to do so, but I did and I deeply, deeply regret all the pain I have caused."

Callie carefully sipped her coffee. As far as she was concerned, he'd already atoned, first in the way he'd sacrificed himself to protect her from Becher, and then in the way he'd flung aside his plans in favor of hers. She wanted to skip ahead to the part where he said, "I love you," again and then kissed her.

But he needed to say his piece, and a part of her needed to hear it. Especially if they were to move on from here in the direction she hoped for.

"I do have something to offer you," Hal continued. "A way to fix the mess I made of your library plan. I don't want to make you take it or pressure you to do so. If you've found your own way forward already, you needn't use mine. But I do want to give you the choice, if you'll allow it."

Callie leaned forward, intrigued. This idea of his, whatever it was, wouldn't involve any suggestions of clients. He wouldn't make that mistake twice.

"Tell me."

He took a fortifying breath. "I've closed down my laboratory. Moved everything out of the house. I'd like you to have it. Or the option to have it. I believe the space is what you require. If it doesn't suit your purposes, feel free to offer it to someone else or sell it and use the money for your library or the charity of your choice. Whatever you decide, I'm done with it. I will, of course, have a new fence built to separate the two properties and remove the connecting passageway. I have no expectations—none—from you. You owe me nothing whatsoever. If you never wish to see me again, I entirely understand."

Hal reached into his pocket and removed a set of keys, placing them on the table in front of her. "You may take as long as you wish to decide and the house is at your disposal in the meantime. I can sign the deed over to you at any time, or you may return the keys to my residence. Or slap me across the face for my impertinence. Or tell me I'm being a fool yet again."

The laboratory.

Callie wanted to squeal with delight and clutch the keys to her chest. The house was perfect. In a nice enough neighborhood to attract the well-to-do patrons who would buy subscriptions. Accessible to the masses via the trolley tracks—important, since she intended to offer scholarship subscriptions to those of less means. An excellent size, with the first floor already renovated into the open space she needed.

Gingerly, she reached out and let her fingers graze the ridged metal of one key. No matter what her heart desired, her head had to rule here. No leaping to accept, no saying, "I love you." Not yet. Not until her path forward was entirely clear.

A knot tightened in her stomach—a dread that maybe her path would never be entirely clear. Then what?

Callie's hand closed around the keys and she picked them up and tucked them into her bodice, nestled between her breasts. Hal swallowed hard, but didn't comment.

“Thank you,” Callie said. “I will give the matter careful consideration and let you know what I decide.”

“Take as long as you need.”

Hal picked up his fork and stabbed it into his pie, but didn’t eat. His gaze was fixed on some point off in the distance, his mind occupied with an unknown thought or task.

“It’s going to be spectacular,” he said at last. “Your library, I mean. However you go about it. I can picture it in my head, how happy it will make people. You’ll do more for the world than I ever have.”

Callie could picture it too. But now that picture had a distinct sense of place. “You’re young. You have time.”

“Maybe I’ll go into academic research. Read books. Propose theories.” His unenthusiastic tone made Callie’s heart ache. He needed experiments of some kind. What was it costing him to give up his laboratory? “But enough about me. Tell me about your own plan. Have you purchased any interesting books recently?”

She couldn’t help but smile at that. “I ordered dozens of art books. Some about the study or art, some about learning to create it. I’m a terrible artist myself, but I’m excited to add this new section to the collection.”

That opening was all they needed. The conversation veered off, seemingly of its own accord, carrying them long past the time when their plates were cleared and their cups empty. Afterward, Hal paid for an autocab to drive her home, and she repaid the kindness by holding his hand the entire ride. Someday, perhaps, he’d be able to relax inside the vehicle.

“Thank you,” Callie said as Hal helped her down from the cab in front of her apartment. “For everything.”

“Thank *you*,” Hal replied. “You saved me from social

ruin, exposed a villain, and then gave me a beautiful end to the evening." He released her hand and stepped back. No goodnight kiss, apparently. It was probably for the best. Callie wasn't sure she'd be able to keep her wits about her if he kissed her.

"I hope this means we'll be speaking to one another again," Hal added. "At some point. If you like."

"I hope so too." Callie nodded goodnight and slipped into the building.

Hope. It swelled inside her like an inflating balloon. She tamped down the emotion as well as she could. She would do things the smart way. The rational way. Because this was one balloon she didn't want to burst.

Chapter 40
Terms and Conditions

Betsy settled herself on the stool beside Callie's dressing table. "You need to stop with all of the papers. It's not helping."

Callie sank heavily onto the edge of her bed. Three days of making lists and considering scenarios had gotten her nowhere. Businesslike and casual was so much easier than this mess of strong emotions. Some of her scenarios were so beautiful she'd let her imagination run wild and written down way too much. Others were so distasteful she'd hardly jotted a line.

"Yes. That's becoming increasingly clear. But I don't know what else to do. I want to make the right decision."

Betsy shrugged. "Okay. So make it."

"It is *not* that simple."

"It can be. Here." She picked up the penny that sat on the dressing table. "Heads, you confess your undying love; tails, you send him packing."

Callie nearly lunged from her seat to grab the coin. "Please be careful with that."

"It's a penny." Betsy gave Callie a questioning frown.

"It's special."

"From your sweetheart, is it?" Betsy twirled the penny

in her fingers. “Cute. Now. About him and this house he’s given you.”

“*Offered* me,” Callie corrected.

Betsy waved a hand. “Technicalities. The relevant question is, what are you going to do about it?”

“I don’t know.”

“Well, what do you *want*?”

A far easier question. Fantasies of the future played in Callie’s mind in detail more crisp than any kinetoscope film. A library bustling with smiling patrons. A cozy evening reading in the house next door. Hal, his black hair gone silver, telling Mad Scientist stories to the grandchild in his lap.

“Everything,” Callie replied.

“Well, there you are,” Betsy said matter-of-factly. “You want everything. Go and get it.” She dropped the penny back onto the table. “Ope! Tails. Send him packing. Sorry.”

“I’m not sending him packing. I want to be with him.” Maybe there was something to this method of talking things out. The words brought a sense of certainty. “But can I accept the house? I don’t want any more business between us. I don’t want to owe him anything and I don’t want him to owe me.”

Betsy nodded for Callie to continue.

“That makes me think I should turn down the house and continue on with the plan of looking for sponsors. But will that hurt Hal? Also I can’t stop thinking how wonderful it would be to have the library there. It’s a perfect location. Would it truly be wonderful, though, when it comes at the expense of Hal’s laboratory and career?”

“Hmm.”

Callie frowned at her friend. “What?”

“It sounds like you listed off everything you want. You

need to quit turning it all into questions. Instead, how about you stop fretting, walk over there, and tell him, 'Hi, it's Callie. Here's exactly what I want and exactly how I want it.' Easy."

Maybe not easy, but Betsy's words sparked an idea in the back of Callie's mind. *Exactly how I want it.* That was the key. She'd been looking at the picture from the wrong angle.

She rose abruptly. "I need pen and paper."

Betsy groaned. "Again?"

"This time it's different. No more agonizing over options that would give me some of what I want. I'm going to figure out how to *change* my options until I get all of it."

* * *

"You're in the papers again, Dr. Jekyll." Victor almost sang the words, waving the newspaper as he and Nemo sauntered into Hal's study.

Hal barely glanced up from his book. "I read it already. It was just a thank you from some retailer for allowing him to make an informed choice of beverages to stock. Says he's stocking some product called Coca-Cola from a pharmacist in Georgia instead."

"So I assume you saw the latest about Becher, then, as well?" Victor's shoulders slumped.

"I did."

On the heels of the "Sobridyne Water Incident," two of Becher's associates had admitted to disturbing the peace at his instigation to drum up support for the local temperance movement. Becher had fled town in disgrace and was unlikely to ever come back. Good riddance.

Hal closed his book and looked up at his friends. "If you wanted to break the news to me, maybe you should have come in the morning. You know, when the paper was new?"

"I only just read it," Victor admitted. "And then I swung by to get Nemo and come to check on you."

"I told him you didn't need anything, but he insisted," Nemo said, casting an annoyed glance at Victor. "I think he's anxious to learn the latest about you and Miss Finch. He's as bad as a gossipy old lady in a dime novel."

"Excuse me, I am a gothic villain," Victor huffed. "We are the *Mad Scientists*. Little old ladies don't do dangerous, revolutionary experiments."

Nemo raised one dark eyebrow. "Care to wager on that?"

Victor shrugged. "Fine. Maybe in your family they do."

Hal shook his head and opened his book, in no mood to banter. Reading was his only escape from the excruciating wait for Callie's response.

Nemo nudged Victor. "Let's leave him be. He'll just get more anxious if we pester him. He'll tell us if anything interesting develops. Right, Hal?"

"Interesting like someone in the house next door?" Victor challenged.

Hal's head snapped back up. "What?"

"Well, I can't say for certain." Victor gave another of his lazy shrugs. "But when we arrived there was a light on in your former laboratory."

Hal's pulse began to race. "Maybe I left it on."

"Days ago?" Victor sniffed. "And you haven't noticed?"

"I haven't gone out much." As the pile of books beside his chair could testify to.

"Ah."

"Come on." Nemo gestured toward the door. "Let's go get a drink. Hal, do you want to join us or would you rather I drag Victor's obnoxious behind far away from you?"

"Look, one of us has to be the pestering friend," Victor

protested. "You're too nice. And of course he's not coming. He's going to go next door and make love to his lady friend."

"I'm not coming," Hal agreed. But neither was he going next door. Even if Callie were there, which he doubted, he wasn't going to interrupt or interfere. He'd given his word and he meant to keep it. Besides, he'd locked the tunnel door on the laboratory side and no longer had the key. He turned resolutely back to his book. "Goodnight."

His friends made their adieus and departed, Victor grumbling that he hadn't learned anything. He really was a terrible gossip. But at least he cared.

Hal fidgeted for a time, reading the same few lines repeatedly while his mind drifted off to thoughts of Callie wandering the laboratory. *The library*, he corrected. It was hers now, and unless she invited him, he'd never set foot in there again.

By the time a quarter hour had passed, Hal's heart rate had slowed and his nerves had settled. She wasn't there. Or if she had been, she wasn't coming here. Victor could have lied about the light. Hal flipped a page and allowed the book to suck him in once more.

"Knock, knock."

Hal dropped the book and leapt from his seat so quickly that he tripped and nearly fell flat on his face. "Callie!"

"Careful."

She stepped through the doorway. The glass beads adorning her midnight-blue dress twinkled like stars under the electric lights, turning her into a celestial goddess. The affectionate smile she wore unbalanced Hal almost as much as her sudden appearance. He grabbed the arm of the chair to steady himself.

"I, uh, wasn't expecting you," he blurted.

"I was next door taking some measurements. The tunnel

was unlocked on your side. I thought I'd surprise you." Her mouth lifted slightly higher on one side, something that never happened with her polished social smiles. Hal's breath caught in his throat.

"You certainly did that."

Her expression grew serious. "How are you? No troubles? I heard about Becher leaving town."

Hal finally managed a smile of his own. "No troubles. Not much of anything. I've been waiting for you."

Callie strode toward him, her night-sky dress swirling around her. A touch of pink colored her cheeks. "I needed some time to think things over," she said, sounding unusually bashful. "I'm sorry it took so long, but I have it all sorted now."

Hal replied with a sober nod, his whole body tensing. "That's good."

It was. It had to be. She wouldn't be here if she meant to spurn him. Still, he trembled.

She stopped a few feet away from him and slipped a hand into a well-concealed pocket in her skirt.

"You were right," she said. "The house is exactly what I require. But I can't accept it for free."

Hal stuffed his own hands into his pockets, because the only other option seemed to be to curl them into fists. All around him the air seemed to crackle with tension, like in the middle of a lightning storm—or one of Victor's experiments.

"You said I owe you nothing," Callie continued. "But I would still *feel* as if I owed you something. Just as you will feel as if you owe me something if I don't take the house. And I can't have that. I won't have any more business between us. That's not the relationship I want with you."

"It's not what I want with you, either," Hal replied, his voice choked. He wanted nothing between them but love and affection and friendship. Nothing between their bodies. Nothing between their hearts. He shifted his weight from one foot to the other, fighting the urge to open his arms for an embrace. He couldn't. Not yet. He wasn't sure what Callie intended, and he wouldn't stand in the way of whatever she desired.

"Hold out your hand," Callie instructed.

Hal blinked in confusion, but did as she requested. Callie withdrew something from her pocket.

"Instead of taking the house from you, I will pay you for its use." She reached out and placed a penny in the center of his upturned palm.

He stared at it a moment, dumbfounded, before his eyes lifted to meet hers.

Our penny?

Her smile answered the unspoken question. "And I have a number of additional conditions."

Anything you wish.

"Such as?" he asked.

"It will not be my house. It will be *our* house. I will use the bulk of the space for my library, but a portion of my renovation funds will go toward a remodel of the old kitchen out back. It's not a large space, but I measured, and I think it will be just right to become your new laboratory. You are not giving up your career for mine. I don't want that. I want my dream *and* your dream. I want to see us thrive side-by-side. I want to walk through that tunnel at the end of the day and relax in this study with a drink and a book, or make love upstairs in our bedroom. So, yes, I will use the space you've offered me. But I'm going to do my part for you in return. We're going to share this. That's *my* offer."

"I accept." He closed the distance between them, tipping

his head until his mouth hovered only inches from hers. "But I have a question."

She tilted her chin up in invitation. "Yes?"

He held up the penny, rubbing it between his fingers. "If this deal is the end of all business between us, does that mean I can no longer trade this for a kiss?"

Callie's hand closed over his, her fingers stroking softly as she slipped the coin from his grasp. "I think maybe we can make a special exception." She raised up on her tiptoes and brushed her lips across his in a slow, gentle kiss. "I love you, Henry Jekyll."

Hal flung his arms around her, crushing her against his chest as his mouth came down on hers in a searing kiss. Weeks of pent-up lust burst free. He kissed her as if this kiss could tell her everything. His hunger. His need. His unending love. Maybe it could.

They broke apart, chests heaving, lips bruised and glistening.

"Calliope," he gasped.

Callie placed a hand against his chest, right over his thudding heart. "That deserved more than a penny." She tucked the coin into his vest pocket, then sealed her mouth to his once again.

They stumbled their way across the room, kissing wildly and tearing at each other's clothing. By the time Hal hoisted her up onto his big desk, the penny had been swapped back and forth so many times he'd forgotten who was giving it to whom. He pushed aside layers of sparkling skirt to fit himself between her thighs, kissing her neck and squeezing her breasts.

"Callie," he murmured. "God, Callie, I love you so much."

"I love you too." She dropped the penny on the desk,

where it clinked and spun to a stop. Deftly, she worked the buttons of his trousers, freeing his cock and guiding it inside her.

Hal moaned. "Christ, Callie, I'll never have enough of you. Never enough kisses. Not for all the pennies in the world."

"I know."

She rocked her hips against him, and he was lost. The world became nothing but her and the place they joined. Hal kissed her and thrust deep, pouring out all of his love, all of his being, until they trembled together in the throes of bliss.

"Fuck," he groaned.

Callie laughed, her arms squeezing him tight and her head falling against his shoulder. "Didn't we just do that?"

"I'm going to want to do it again," he admitted. "Once I catch my breath." He braced himself against the desk with both hands, his fingers finding the penny. "Penny for a kiss," he murmured, drawing back slightly to look into Callie's eyes, then bending to press his lips against her temple. "How much for forever?"

"Your whole heart," she replied without hesitation.

"It's already yours."

The coin slipped to the carpet as he kissed her again.

Chapter 41
Shadows

The ocelot purred, arching its back against the hand that stroked it.

"So," the deep voice rumbled. "Operative A has failed me."

"Yes, sir," the minion replied. "He has moved to San Francisco according to the latest reports. Shall I send someone to deal with him?"

Seconds stretched out. The hand moved back and forth over the cat's soft fur in an unwavering pattern.

"No. He is not worth the resources in money or manpower. I trust you have retrieved the reserve supply of the drug."

"Yes, sir."

"Good. Turn your focus to Operative B. I hope he will prove a more satisfactory ally than Mr. Becher has been."

"Very good, sir." The minion inclined his head and departed.

The hand continued its methodical movement, drawing another purr from the feline predator.

"You see, my pet? Humans are such sad, unreliable creatures. Unable to accomplish the simplest task without a hand to guide them. What are they but animals, after all? Kill or be killed, and let the strongest rise to the top. They need the leadership of the alpha wolf or the silver-backed ape. And, someday, they will thank me for always having their best interests at heart."

The man rose from his seat and the ocelot leapt to the ground, hissing its displeasure at losing its cozy perch.

"Yes, my pet. I, too, would rather remain as we were. But I must mail a package to a man in San Francisco."

Epilogue

One year later

The chattering crowd of happy women percolated down the staircase before flowing leisurely to the exit. Part of Callie wanted to hurry them out the door so she could close up for the night and spend some time with her husband. The other part wanted the event to linger so she could continue to bask in the glow of success.

Tonight's talk had been the most well-attended in the—admittedly short—history of her library. Delighted ladies were headed out with books tucked under their arms and wide smiles on their faces. A new patroness had donated a collection of five hundred books. Callie would be cataloguing for weeks. Even with circulation high, she would need to add a few more shelves upstairs and do some rearranging.

She grinned at the thought. Rearranging was one of her favorite library activities. Hal loved to help sort the books, so they always undertook the task together, chatting and laughing as they worked. More often than not they ended up pausing halfway through to rush off to their bedroom or slip upstairs to one of the third floor rooms Callie discreetly rented out to ladies in need of a safe space for a private tryst.

Maybe they'd pop upstairs tonight. Or maybe head back into their house. It had been a while since they'd made love in the study. Either way, Callie was in the mood for some celebratory fun.

"Mrs. Finch!" Mrs. Mary Clay, a young woman who visited the library every Thursday without fail and had yet to miss a single event, jogged over. She hugged a weighty science tome to her chest. "This was the best event yet! Miss Majhi's talk made the science of hydrodynamics accessible to anyone at all. I'm sure half the ladies in attendance now want to go sailing, while the other half want to study the rate of flow of Niagara Falls."

"Both would be fun, I'm sure," Callie replied.

"I'm going to take it into consideration as I study the difference between electrical impulses moving through air and through water," Mrs. Clay continued.

She launched into an enthusiastic explanation of her current project that quickly went far beyond Callie's understanding. Callie listened anyway, enjoying the woman's good cheer and watching the other visitors make their way out. Overhead, Eddie the library rat scurried through the maze of glass tubing Hal had installed near the ceiling, searching for the snack one of the library visitors had left him.

A door opened at the back of the room, and a moment later Hal stepped out from between the rows of shelves. He wore a stained apron over his suit, his glasses were smudged, and a faint burnt odor hung about him.

His eyebrows rose as he took in the handful of women still in the library. "I hope I'm not interrupting. I didn't realize your event would run so long."

"It's just clearing out," Callie answered. "I'll only be a few minutes."

"Your husband?" Mrs. Clay regarded Hal with curiosity. With his dirty clothes, tousled hair, and the smudge across his cheek that was probably soot, he looked every inch the Mad Scientist.

"Yes. Mrs. Clay, please allow me to introduce—"

"Oh!" The young woman clapped a hand to her mouth in shock before Callie could finish. "Oh, are you Dr. Finch? Of Dr. Finch's Headache Cordial?"

"I am," Hal replied. He'd adopted Callie's name when they'd married, deeming Jekyll "too notorious." Occasionally people who knew scoffed at the choice, but Hal had never shown a moment's regret.

"Thank you so much," Mrs. Clay gushed. "It's the only medicine that helps with my migraines without leaving me insensible. It's made such a difference. I can't thank you enough!"

Hal fidgeted with the strings on his apron. "You're welcome. I'm glad to hear it brings you relief."

"It does. And to think, I never connected Mrs. Finch from the library with Dr. Finch from the medicine. Sometimes even the big city can be such a small world. I'll leave you two to your evening. Thank you again, to both of you." Mrs. Clay inclined her head and rushed out.

"Look at you, changing the world," Callie teased.

"Little by little," Hal agreed. "Just like you're doing."

She looked him over. "My way involves less fire. What did you burn up this time in your pursuit of the next great patent medicine?"

"I only singed a few things," he protested. "And I neither tasted nor inhaled anything."

Callie slipped an arm around him. She appreciated the way he still articulated his resolve never to test anything on himself again. They would always have some lingering fear, but the regular reminders kept it to a minimum.

She gave him a squeeze. "At least you didn't explode anything this time. I like you in one piece."

Hal edged closer and lowered his voice. "I believe I promised you I'd only ever go to pieces in your arms."

Suddenly, the library couldn't clear out fast enough for Callie. She began dousing lights to hurry the stragglers along, and she and Hal made a hasty goodbye to Nisha, who gave them a knowing smirk as she departed.

Callie only managed to make it through the door to the tunnel before she hauled Hal into her arms and kissed him soundly.

"Your event was that good, eh?" he asked when they paused for air.

"The best so far."

"Well." His fingers began to unfasten the buttons along the back of her dress. "Since success appears to make you amorous, I wish you much, much more of it."

"You would wish me success even if it didn't."

"True." Hal kissed along her neck. "But this way is more fun." He eased the dress off her shoulders, tugging it down to expose her breasts to his sight and his touch.

"Do you intend to ravish me right here in the tunnel?" she wondered.

Hal's lips began to follow his hands on a decidedly downward path. "Of course. You know me, love. You always bring out my wicked side."

The End

About the Author

Award-winning author Catherine Stein believes that everyone deserves love and that Happily Ever After has the power to help, to heal, and to comfort. She writes sassy, sexy romance set during the Victorian and Edwardian eras. Her stories are full of action, adventure, magic, and fantastic technologies.

Catherine lives in Michigan with her husband and three rambunctious kids. She loves steampunk and Oxford commas, and can often be found dressed in Renaissance festival clothing, drinking copious amounts of tea.

Visit Catherine online at
www.catsteinbooks.com
Join her VIP mailing list for a free short story.

Twitter
@catsteinbooks

Facebook
@catsteinbooks

Also by
Catherine Stein

Potions and Passions

The Earl on the Train - Book 0.5

How to Seduce a Spy - Book 1

Mishaps & Mistletoe -
A Holiday Novella -Book 1.5

Not a Mourning Person - Book 2

Once a Rake, Always a Rogue - Book 3

Love at Second Sight - Book 4

Sass and Steam

Love is in the Airship - Book 0.5

A Shot to the Heart - Book 0.75

Eden's Voice - Book 1

What Are You Doing New Year's Eve? -
A Holiday Novella - Book 1.5

Sass and Steam (cont.)

Priceless - Book 2

Dead Dukes Tell No Tales - Book 3

Beyond Repair - Book 4

Arcane Tales

The Scoundrel's New Con - Book 1

The Spinster's Swindle - Book 2

Other Books

Mating Habits - Book 1

Idle Nature - Book 2

My Heiress 'Tis of Thee

Thank you so much for reading!

If you enjoyed the book and are so inclined,
I would love for you to leave a review.
Happy readers make an author's day!

I love hearing from readers, so feel free
to contact me on social media, or email:

catherine@catsteinbooks.com

CPSIA information can be obtained
at www.ICGtesting.com
Printed in the USA
BVHW040948150822
644609BV00003B/110